POWER PLAY

Energy fumed inside her head, clawing to come out. She let it surface, unable to fight the intense force anymore. Unwilling to fight it.

Harper summoned the hatred, the need for vengeance, and the grief for her brother, harnessing all of it with her psyche into a resounding dynamo. She then spread her arms and willed the raging force out of her mind.

Her flesh seared, as though every fiber underneath was pulling away from the bone. Molten heat swept through her, like she'd been turned inside out under a volcano as the power flowed from her mind, down her arms and to her hands.

She let herself go, giving in to the furious rapture. A deafening hum rippled through her ears, and her body lurched backward as powerful energy shot from her open palms. The near invisible wave flowed toward the dazed men standing before her, stirring the air and space between them. The energy engulfed her enemies.

A heartbeat later, the raging heat was gone. Harper felt light-headed. Sheer destruction lay before her. Dead. They were all dead. And she'd killed them.

"What's happening to me?" she managed to howl before she passed out.

FALLEN ROGUE

Amy Rench

LEISURE BOOKS NEW YORK CITY

A LEISURE BOOK®

December 2009

Dorchester Publishing Co., Inc.
200 Madison Avenue
New York, NY 10016

ISBN 10: 0-505-52812-6
ISBN 13: 978-0-505-52812-4
E-ISBN: 978-1-4285-0779-1

Visit us online at www.dorchesterpub.com.

ACKNOWLEDGMENTS

I am forever grateful to my editor, Leah Hultenschmidt, for making this book a reality and the best it could be.

Thank you to my sister, Laura Rench, and my mom, Susan, for their unwavering support. They've put up with a lot.

Thanks to the Divas critique group: Laura, Kate Dandel, and Kendra Uhler, for their guidance, fun, and for not bringing food.

Lastly, thanks to Pooka and Anya for just being there.

FALLEN
ROGUE

CHAPTER ONE

The blur of greens and browns filtered into the shapes of countless pines and firs spanning the highway as far as the eye could see. The constant whir of the engine for the past 650 miles became gruff chugs as the bus prepared for the stop ahead. Harper Kane sat up and stretched in the worn faux leather seat in an attempt to ease her cramped muscles.

She'd fallen asleep almost immediately after leaving the San Francisco terminal, but had an abrupt awakening when the bus suffered a thunderous tire blowout and lurched to the side of the road just before the Oregon border. Since then, she had just dozed, with that prickly feeling of being not quite asleep or awake.

Harper admired the infinite shades of color in the surrounding autumn foliage. She loved living in northern California, but Oregon would always have a fond place in her heart. Especially because her elder brother, Bobby, still lived here.

She hadn't seen him in six months, a long time for them to be apart. But with the Olympic trials nearing, her training had been rigorous. She needed all the time in the water she could get.

But she needed this time away from the pool even more. Her focus had been waning a little lately. Besides, her racing times were better than they'd ever been.

The bus finally slumped to a halt, assaulting her senses with exhaust. She took a few sips from her twenty-four-ounce water bottle to wash the filmy taste from her mouth, and then tucked it in the worn backpack resting on the adjacent seat.

"Hood River." The driver's monotone voice sounded tinny over the microphone.

They were actually stopping way outside the town limits. Given that she was the only passenger on the bus, the driver had grudgingly agreed to stop close to Bobby's remote home in the woods. Which meant the side of the road rather than the station in Hood River itself.

As she descended the broad steps of the bus, she searched for her brother's baby blue clunker of a pickup truck. The heap was barely legal, but Bobby loved it. Two hours ago she'd left him a message that she was being dropped off close by, but neither the truck nor her brother were visible through the light misty rain.

Grumbling at his absence, she began slogging through the mushy gravel on the shoulder of the road. The bus was inconvenient, but her Jeep wouldn't make the long trip up. The old vehicle barely made it to the pool where she trained. And lately it hadn't even done that. She'd had to hoof the five miles from her apartment for the last month, pleasing her coach to no end.

About a half mile down the road was an obscure turn-off for the bumpy dirt road that led to Bobby's house. The hazy sprinkle soon shifted to a steady downpour.

Harper pulled her jacket collar taut around her neck to keep from getting absolutely soaked, but she knew it was futile. Rain seeped through her jeans and flooded her sneakers. Being wet was a way of life for her, but a warm, comfortable pool was a far cry from the chilly Oregon rains. She just hoped that the clothes in her backpack were staying somewhat dry.

The smell of wet vegetation and cool air caused her to sniff a little and expel a moist cloud of breath. It was colder than normal for late October. Maybe Bobby was busy building a nice welcoming fire for her in the woodstove. Hopeful, she squished forward through the puddles and pine needles.

About a hundred yards from Bobby's road, she heard the familiar rumbling of his truck's archaic motor. Seconds later the blue cab poked its nose out from the trees, gravel spewing everywhere from the sudden braking.

Bobby glanced at her through the open driver-side window. Rain pounded his face, which held a look of obvious delight; the look quickly changed to one of alarm.

The truck door flew open and Bobby started to slide out, giving her a terse wave. She raised her hand in response.

A crack of gunfire sounded. Harper stopped cold.

Another shot rang out. Then another. Confusion paralyzed her in the whipping rain, and a pained roar came from her throat.

Her brother slumped and fell backward into the truck cab. A vise of horror seized her body, and the truth hit her like a gale wind: Bobby had been shot.

Time froze. Harper saw her body move toward the truck as though watching a movie somehow outside herself. Her brother needed her.

She made it to the truck door and impatiently shrugged off her backpack, barely hearing the splash of it hitting the sopping ground over the pounding of her heartbeat.

Blood pumped out of the three holes in Bobby's chest. Harper ripped his shirt away from his body and tried to press it against the wounds. The white material stained red but was unable to hold the blood at bay. There was just too much pouring out. Too fast.

"Harper." Bobby's voice was a strained whisper.

"Bobby! What the heck is going on? What—"

"No time," Bobby interrupted. "Remember the Barracks?" He wheezed and coughed.

"What?" Harper grabbed his shaking hand. It was freezing. She frantically searched through trees, but could see nothing through the rain. "Just hold on. I'm getting my phone. I'll get help." She gave his hand a squeeze and turned to reach for her drenched pack on the ground. Bobby's iron grip on her forearm stopped her motion and forced her to face him.

"No time," he repeated softly. She could barely hear him. "G-get to the Barracks. I left something." He coughed again, fainter this time. "For you. Left something for you."

"I don't understand." Harper couldn't believe what was happening. "Bobby, don't leave me." Her brother was going to die. And there was nothing she could do about it. "I need you."

"Please, Harper," Bobby pleaded, his breath coming in small gasps. "Do this. For me."

"Anything for you, Bobby," she vowed, and held his chilled hands. "Anything." She still didn't understand what he was talking about, but she'd do whatever he asked. She owed him that. He'd always been there for her. She would do the same for him. Tears streaked down her face, mingling with the rain, then dropped onto the blood-spattered pile of clothing draped over his chest.

"Thanks, Harpie." He smiled weakly. And closed his eyes. "Didn't know w-what else to do."

"Bobby, what's going on?" she asked again.

"I'm s-sorry. You'll know . . . what to do" was all he said in response, the words slurred and hushed. "Love you, sis." He said it so quietly that she wasn't even sure he'd spoken.

"Love you, big bro," she choked out. She leaned over him and reached behind his shoulders, pulling his weak body to hers in a tight hug, desperately trying to give him comfort. Hoping for some miracle to save his life.

"Be careful. . . ."

After a slight shudder and a doting smile, he closed his eyes for the last time, and his body went still in her arms.

Harper crushed Bobby's lifeless body against her. Shock poured through her every fiber, chilling and bitter. The driving rain continued in heavy sheets and pounded against her while she just held him with disbelieving ferocity.

Her mind raced with questions she feared would never be answered and words she knew would never be spoken. Why? Why had her brother been shot? What had he done to deserve having his life taken away in such a grisly and abrupt way? Who would have done this? And what in the world did he leave for her that had cost him his life?

Time meant nothing. How long had she sat there, clutching the cold shell of her brother? Wasn't it just minutes ago that she was annoyed with him for not picking her up and for making her walk in the drizzle?

And now? Now, he'd never pick her up again. Never hear her tease him about being late. Never . . . anything.

Red splotches drenched her clothing. Bobby's blood. Harper couldn't help releasing a guttural cry, a primal sound among the tall trees and rain. Painful and bleak.

An ominous flock of black crows suddenly scattered across the desolate sky. Their raucous calls of outrage mingled with the rolling thunder. She watched them disappear into the sinister black clouds.

The trees seemed to shroud and suffocate her. Shock turned to despair. She was truly alone.

A crack pierced the air, quickly followed by a fracturing split and a *thump* punching through her thick veil of anguish. Ducking next to the cab, she saw a bullet had shattered the pickup's windshield and embedded itself into the seat only inches away from where she'd been. The cheap upholstery had a little round tear where stuffing spewed out.

She zeroed in on the area where she'd heard the unmistakable sound of gunfire. Thunder roared and lightning spidered across the sky, illuminating the dark rain-glazed trees. Squinting, she saw a sliver of metallic sheen.

Danger flooded her mind. She knew any sane person should be hightailing it out of there, but the impulse to run was beaten down by a ravaging anger that grabbed ahold of her gut, twisting and snaking a white-hot rage through her blood, savagely replacing the utter coldness in her core. Someone had shot her brother. Deliberately. She narrowed her eyes toward the trees where she'd seen the out-of-place glint.

Harper warily rose to gently rest Bobby's body on the bench seat. She had started to back away when something dropped from his rigid hand and thudded to the squishy floor mat, just under the brake pedal.

A key. Attached to an otherwise bare key ring. In a daze, she picked it up to get a better look. No inscription. No markings whatsoever.

Another gunshot was followed by a slow hiss. The vehicle leaned to the left as the front tire lost its air. And then another shot, blowing the other tire, which tilted the truck forward as it rested on the flats.

Harper shoved the key into the front pocket of her jeans. She slid out of the cab, but slipped in the loose mud. Relentless torrents of rain pummeled her raw body and soul as she lay on the ground, confusion warring with anger at what was happening.

She flinched when a metallic bang hit the bed of the truck. A grenade bounced to a clanking halt against the tire. Another one followed, landing near the first.

Harper came out of her daze and started to run—away from the guns, away from the impending blast.

The explosion tossed her body through the driving rain and dropped her in the brush like a cannonball. Her bones rattled on impact. Pain. There was so much pain. Harper drifted on the fringe of consciousness while she fought the blackness trying to take hold of her. She dared to breathe in the damp air and opened her eyes to the greens of rich moss and dripping ferns. Facedown in the brush, she tasted moist earth on her lips and blood in her mouth. She ran her tongue along her lower lip, confirming the source of the copper tang.

Sickening smoke began to fill her nostrils, drowning out the lush smell of the woods. Awareness flooded her mind. Fire. The truck. Bobby.

Harper pushed herself up, ignoring the sharp agony prickling through every nerve. She stood, trying to steady herself against the stinging rain and destruction.

Her brother's beloved truck was nothing more than a fiery metallic skeleton. Burning chunks of debris littered the surrounding area. The hammering rain kept the flames from igniting the foliage. A small harbor of light in the sea of gloom.

Sheer anguish seized her, grasping her heart and squeezing relentlessly with a crushing fist.

Harper fell to her knees, hands on her head.

Her brother was truly gone.

She hopelessly watched the rain splash into brown puddles and drain down to the muddy soil in little rivers. The heavy droplets became fierce and loud. She suddenly realized it wasn't the rain, but bullets splattering the mud.

They'd seen her, and they weren't going to let her get away alive.

CHAPTER TWO

She dove onto her side and rolled into the dense brush. Peeking out between the thick branches and wet leaves, Harper saw four bulky figures emerge from the tree line beyond her brother's smoldering truck. Dressed in dark green camouflage, they materialized one by one through the whirling smoke like every sinister ghost-infested nightmare she'd ever had. Each had a rifle drawn and ready.

She had to make a decision. Fast. Hide or run? Instinct refused to let her just lie there.

So she ran. She ran as fast as she could. Into the endless forest of trees. Into the middle of nowhere.

Gunfire rang in her ears as she sped through the woods, weaving and dodging, eating up the wet landscape. Rough branches ripped at her coat and lashed at her legs, stinging her skin through the wet denim. The rich pine air assaulted her throat with every breath she took. Her evil personal trainer had made sure she had immeasurable endurance. She was used to running miles upon miles of grueling terrain.

But her pursuers were relentless as well. She spared a quick backward glance to check on their progress. Through the speckled green branches, it was difficult to locate all four of them. Another bullet whizzed past. The men were definitely still there.

She had to lose them, but where would she go? She knew this area well enough, but in her shock and haste, she hadn't paid much attention to her direction. She glanced up to the sky. No help there. Just treetops disappearing into the low mist of murky clouds.

Then she heard it. Rushing water. Not just showering from the sky, but the roar of water dashing over rocks, cutting its way through the forest. The river. Harper thought fast. The speed of the current could carry her farther than anyone could run. She could escape there. If the rapids didn't kill her first.

Harper burst through the tree line to find herself at the edge of a small cliff. She slid to a halt in the mud just a few feet from the overhang. Peering over the ledge, she saw the river about thirty feet below. Racing and powerful in its chilling glory. The daunting rapids mocked her, daring her to challenge them. And she was ready for it. No one had ever bested her in the water but herself.

A last glance over her shoulder showed the four lethal figures just coming out of the trees. Before they could get a bead on her, Harper took a deep breath and jumped.

She smacked the water and immediately sank, her sodden clothes dragging her down. The cold seeped into her bones as the water swallowed her. Breathless, she fought to orient her body and find air.

Harper kicked forcefully and broke the surface. She gasped in a lungful of bitter air and whirled toward the cliff she'd jumped from just as her brother's killers peppered the choppy water with bullets. But the swift current quickly carried her out of range. Shouldering their rifles, the four killers stood still for an eerie moment, just watching the river carry her away. Then they retreated, disappearing into the woods like phantoms.

She turned forward again and put her mastery of water to its full use. As she hit a set of rapids, swelling whitecaps and mist enveloped her, tossing her around and pulling her under. Holding her breath, Harper calmly rode with the rough, untamed waves, grateful for her lifetime of swimming experience.

Moments later she was suddenly airborne. Her fall lasted mere seconds before she made a big splash when she plunged into the water on her back. She gasped at the stab of pain and gulped down some of the freezing water. The waves felt sluggish as she used powerful strokes to break the surface. Coughing and spitting, she floated, quickly gazing at the surrounding area. More trees. But the river had widened a tad and the rushing waters had slowed considerably following the waterfall she'd just tumbled over.

Taking a deep breath, she swam toward the mossy riverbank, cutting through the lazy ripples with smooth, graceful movements.

Reaching the water's edge, she heaved her battered body out of the icy water to stretch out on the squishy bank. Breathing deeply, she gazed up at infinite treetops. Twilight was hovering among the storm-darkened clouds. She listened carefully for the sound of booted footsteps, but thankfully all she could hear was the dripping of rain against the foliage and the odd birdcalls as creatures began to settle in for the night.

Harper felt dizzy, as if the world were spinning beneath her. She squeezed her eyes shut and pressed her hands hard against her hammering skull, trying to relieve the sickening pressure. Hoping against hope the events of the last hour were all just a horrible dream.

She slowly opened her eyes. She still saw the suffocating woods. Still saw the terrifying flash of fresh memories.

A harsh rustling caught her attention as two squirrels

chased each other up a rough tree trunk. The scratching of their tiny claws sounded curiously loud in the settling forest. She rose to a sitting position and scooted over to lean her back against the coarse base of the tree. Above her, the squirrels chittered in annoyance. It reminded her of how she and Bobby would bicker as kids.

Bobby.

He was dead. His body consumed by the fire. She had nothing left of her brother.

Grief pummeled her body. It was too much. Harper had no idea how much time had passed when she finally felt as though she'd cried herself out. For now. She gazed into the pitch-dark woods, shivering and spent, not even wanting to look at her watch.

Rubbing her stiff hands along her upper arms, she was immediately aware of the icy clamminess of her clothes. Knowing her body's high threshold for cold, she left most of her wet clothes on, but decided to remove her T-shirt.

The rain had stopped and the stormy clouds had twisted away. She draped her T-shirt over a low branch and huddled back into her North Face coat. Having left her backpack near the burning truck, she realized all she had were these clothes and her wallet with her driver's license, debit card, and insurance card. She stuffed her hand into her coat pocket, pulling out a wrinkly five-dollar bill.

Letting out a deep sigh, she settled under a veil of trees and the surrounding undergrowth—which sheltered her from the fall weather—and rested her hands on her thighs. She was bone-deep cold. She ran her hands along the hard muscles of her legs in an attempt to get her chilled blood circulating. Her shaking hand brushed over a tiny lump in her hip pocket. Bobby's key.

She fished it out, closed her hand around it, and raised

her fist to her heart. This meant something to Bobby. So it meant everything to her.

Her brother wanted her to have this. What had he said? The Barracks? It was their favorite childhood hangout, where they'd played all day and talked about everything and nothing. Though he was seven years older, they were as close as twins. They were best friends. Were. And now he was gone.

What could he have left there for her? What did that key go to? What was so important? Important enough to use up some of his last breaths? Whatever it was, she had promised. Promised him that she'd do anything for him. So she'd find whatever was there. He'd said she'd know what to do. And whatever it was, she'd do it. He'd been her world and now she'd be his.

Adrenaline pulsed through her blood, warming her from the inside. The cold seeped away, replaced by a fierce determination that stirred and slowly burned within her, flowing through every nerve, simmering in her blood. The pain disappeared, replaced by a feral hunger. And rage.

Harper gazed at the key one last time.

She was used to competition. Used to the battle. Used to winning.

Whoever had ripped Bobby away from her would regret it.

Harper walked through waist-high ferns, paralleling the set of old train tracks zigzagging through the moss-draped trees. Having grown up in the area and having visited Bobby fairly regularly, she was familiar with the forests. There were some trails, but mostly she made her way from memory. Using the digital compass on her watch, she had been able to orient herself. She'd been hiking since dawn and as she looked up to the sky, she realized dusk was approaching through the lazy fall sunshine. Though on the move all day, she had no desire to stop.

Sleep had somehow come to her last night. In fact, Harper was surprised to find she had slept for almost twelve hours in deep exhaustion. Hazy rays had wakened her from a heavy slumber. At first she'd been startled to wake in the woods. Had it all been just a really bad dream?

No, it hadn't. Stinging scratches and damp blood-stained clothes were an ugly reminder of the hell her life had become. And the sole purpose she now had.

Now the waning sun cast shadows on the uneven ground. The air held a chill, but the sun added the illusion of warmth, which had tempted her to tie her coat around her waist.

The familiar hike was as beautiful as she remembered, but it was impossible to enjoy. A sad smile crossed her face as she recalled the last time she'd wandered down this trail. She'd been so excited. The Olympic trials. She was one meet from making the team. She and Bobby had raced each other up here to the Barracks to celebrate. Just the two of them. It had been their exclusive place to share everything. Bobby's getting into graduate school. Their parents' deaths. Earning her swimming scholarship to Stanford. And countless times in between.

Now, for the first time, it was a solitary trip. And it would be forever.

She reached the clearing. Abandoned train cars dotted the rows of corroded railroad tracks. Stowed up here for decades, the cars hadn't been in use for more than the twenty-four years she'd been alive. She and Bobby had found the place on one of their hikes and claimed it as their own, dubbing it "the Barracks." They knew every inch and crevice of the old railroad junkyard.

Raking her fingers through her blonde hair, she weaved in between the old trains, balancing on weed-draped rails. Reaching the center of the deserted lot, she searched for car number 61. Bobby's lucky number.

Harper spotted it two tracks down and walked to the side door, rusted open for eternity. Grabbing the corroded handle, she easily hauled herself up. She paced around inside, her steps echoing starkly in the dim compartment.

She ran her fingers along the simple drawings and crazy phrases she and Bobby had carved into the crusty metal over the years, smiling at the memories they stirred. Then she retreated to the rear of the car, moving in and out of the sunlight lancing through the slits in the decaying walls. In the back was a small concealed compartment built into the floor. A smugglers' hold. As kids, they had pretended to be relic hunters, hiding their treasures like those generations before them had in the secret hidey-hole.

This had to be where Bobby would have stashed the "something" he'd left for her.

Harper bent down on one knee and patted the filthy flooring. Finding the recessed latch, she brushed away the freshly disturbed dirt and pulled upward. The brittle hatch resisted, but gave way after a few more tugs. Reaching in the darkness, her fingers grazed a small metal box. She fit her hand around the container and pulled it out. The box was the size of a recipe-card holder, but heavy like a chunk of pure lead. She saw no markings or decorations.

She ran her index finger over the smooth surface, searching for a way to open it. It took several passes, but she finally found an obscured keyhole flush with the solid exterior.

Reaching into her front pocket, Harper pulled out Bobby's key and stuck it in the hole. With a clockwise turn, the top of the box snicked open. It was hard to see in the shadows of the train car, so she moved closer to the door.

In the fading sunlight she noticed the sides of the box were close to an inch thick and lined in velvet. She reached in to remove a thick cloth, and then sat down on the open door's ledge, dangling her legs over the side.

After setting the box on the floor next to her, she unfolded the cloth to reveal a tiny computer flash drive and a full syringe.

"Great," she grumbled. "Just great."

Whatever these were, Bobby was murdered for them. So that made these two objects the most important objects in the world. If Bobby had faith in her to know what to do with them, then by golly, she'd figure it out.

Harper smiled. Maybe Bobby did know what he was doing. Although she trained as much as possible, swimming didn't pay the bills. But programming part-time at a video-game company did. She knew computers inside and out. If this drive had as many convoluted layers of coding as she suspected Bobby had dumped in there, she'd probably be the only one in the world able to read this thing. Maybe he was counting on that. Maybe it held the answers. It had to.

She picked up the syringe in her other hand, watching the syrupy amber liquid glisten in the clear tube.

What did it do? Bobby was a scientific genius, having graduated at the top of his molecular biology class. He had landed a coveted government research job right away. Harper knew he worked on highly confidential projects, but she really had no idea exactly what he did. They never actually talked much about it. Now they never would.

Shaking off that haunting thought, she focused on the syringe. She had a job to do. She had to find answers and strike back.

"Freeze," a cold voice said, startling her.

Harper's gaze shot up to see ten burly men, covered head to toe in jungle camouflage, standing in a semicircle about thirty feet away from the train car. Carrying massive guns. All pointed at her. They looked just like the guys who'd chased her. And the ones who'd killed Bobby. Her blood boiled as she sat rigid.

"Hands up," the brute ordered. "Slowly," he added.

No way. There was absolutely no way she was doing anything these guys told her. She kept her hands closed in her lap and her mouth shut.

The guy fired a shot right past her head. It clanged off the back wall of the car. Though it made her flinch, she still wasn't going to give in to them.

"Do it now," came the command. "We just want to talk."

Right. Talk. That's why they tracked her down and brought so many guns.

But maybe they did just want to talk. Maybe that's why they hadn't shot her on sight. They thought she knew something.

She couldn't get justice for Bobby if she was dead, so she made a choice. "Okay," Harper answered steadily.

"Open your hands flat." Another stern order.

Her fingers closed tight around the small flash drive and snapped it apart. "Here you go," she said with a cool smile and threw the broken pieces at them. The plastic bits scattered in the dirt and rubble that covered the ground.

"That was a big mistake." The leader sneered. "Now open your other hand," he demanded tersely.

Harper did as he said, revealing the syringe in her palm. She watched their faces intently as she did so. Several of them, including Mr. Bossy, gasped in surprise and then quickly tried to hide it. So the syringe was completely unexpected and extremely important.

"Drop the needle." The demand was spoken deliberately and carefully.

"Let's just shoot her," the thug to his left piped in.

O-kay. Really, he was right. They could just kill her and take it.

But she couldn't let them have it.

The men took a few menacing steps forward. She stood and held up her free palm in a nonthreatening gesture, clutching the syringe warily in the other as her brain whirled to come up with some kind of solution.

More steps closer. And then they lunged, tackling her.

She hit the floor hard and tried to squirm away from their grabbing hands. But they were all over her. At least three, maybe four of the men clutched at her hand, trying to pry the needle away. She grasped the syringe as tightly as she could, her knuckles white with the strain. Using her powerful swimmer's legs, she began kicking at any surface she could manage. Grunts were her only reward.

As strong as she was, the brawny men were wearing her down. One of her fingers loosened. Then another. One more tug and she'd probably lose the syringe. Back and forth she waved her arm, but her attackers were relentless.

Harper pulled against the firm grip on her arm, twisting her body away as a bigger body pounced onto her shoulder. Momentum jerked her left arm across her body, forcing her grip on the syringe to waver, jabbing the needle into her right forearm. The plunger depressed in reflex, hard and fast, emptying every drop of the tawny liquid into her bloodstream.

The attack halted. The men gawked at her in stunned silence and backed away warily. She stared back.

What the heck had been in that vial?

Her body jerked involuntarily. She twisted her forearm around to look at the spot where the syringe had stabbed her. The mark was rosy red. Her arm began to prickle as though a hundred needles were piercing the tender flesh.

Harper cried out. As quickly as the sensation came, it left. Only to be replaced by a freezing rush through her entire being, like jagged ice fighting to escape her unyielding skin.

An uncontrollable shudder overtook her body. Terror seized her mind. What was happening to her?

The cold disappeared in an instant. She gasped and hunched over, crossing her arms over her abdomen as if her insides were being violently ripped apart and then pasted back together. The pain was so severe, she was sure she'd pass out. She wheezed in a deep breath.

And then it started again. But this round was a brutal heat, searing every fiber and sparking every ounce of blood she had like fireworks.

Facing her brother's killers, she felt hate simmer deep inside her gut, melding with the heat that was already roiling and blazing white-hot. Her mind seized the wild emotion with an iron fist, bonding it with the roaring inner flames.

Energy fumed inside her head, clawing to come out. She let it surface, unable to fight the intense force anymore. Unwilling to fight it.

Harper summoned the hatred, the need for vengeance, and the grief for her brother, harnessing all of it with her psyche into a resounding dynamo. She then spread her arms and willed the raging force out of her mind.

Her flesh seared as though every fiber underneath were pulling away from the bone. Molten heat swept through her, as if she'd been turned inside out under a volcano. The power flowed from her mind, down her arms, and into her hands.

She let herself go, giving in to the furious rapture. A deafening hum rippled through her ears, and her body lurched backward as powerful energy shot from her open palms. The near-invisible wave flowed toward the dazed men standing before her, stirring the air and space between them. The energy engulfed her enemies and ravaged their bodies like a tidal wave.

A heartbeat later, the raging heat was gone. Harper blinked to settle her shimmering vision. She felt light-headed, as if she'd just swum a nonstop relay. After a moment, her gaze cleared to an unthinkable scene. Sheer destruction lay before her. The bodies of the men looked as though a whirlwind had swept them up and spit them out. Mere rag dolls in a gale-force wind. Dead. They were all dead. And she'd killed them.

"What's happening to me?" she managed to howl before she passed out.

CHAPTER THREE

"We have a situation," a stiff voice informed him the instant he stepped into the dreary room.

Rome Lucian hated that word. *Situation.* Either there was a problem or there wasn't. But if there wasn't, he wouldn't be here. He'd be at home finishing off his homemade sausage pizza and a cold beer in front of a late-night movie.

He rubbed his eyes and sat on the cushy leather chair facing Jeff Donovan, his expressionless boss. The seat was as soft as butter. Rome waited for him to continue, vaguely noticing that the man always wore the same damn thing. Crisp pale blue shirt with a navy striped tie. Rome would kill himself before he'd sit behind a desk wearing a tie.

"The Five Watch," Jeff said in monotone. "Their lab was destroyed."

Great. The Five Watch. A secret government group, so hush-hush that most agents even doubted its existence. But Rome knew better. It was his job to know better. From what he'd heard of them, which was very little, he thought they were a little shifty. Weren't they messing around with plants or something?

"You need to find this woman," Jeff demanded, sliding a nondescript manila envelope across the smooth desk.

Rome pulled out a glossy photo of a man and a woman standing arm in arm in front of a clear blue swimming pool. The man was slightly taller than the woman and sported a beaming, proud smile.

The woman's spiky blonde hair was slightly wet, and she was wearing a black warm-up suit. Sea green eyes stared back at him, complemented by a slightly upturned nose and a lush, cheerful mouth. Not what you'd call beautiful, but it all seemed to work. She held up three gold medals with obvious delight. Rome, prompted by her infectious grin, couldn't stop the faint smile from creeping onto his face.

"You're kidding, right?" Rome asked skeptically, turning the photo around toward Jeff. Experience had cruelly taught him to not judge a book by its cover, but come on. This woman hardly looked like a dangerous threat.

Jeff held his gaze, not even looking at the picture. "Find her and bring her in," his boss directed coldly.

Rome waited for more. Nothing. The whole tone of the order seemed wrong. Jeff was always a stone-cold son of a bitch, but something lurked behind the man's eyes. Something was off. Rome just couldn't put his finger on it.

"She do it?" Rome questioned, twisting the photo back around to take another look. It was his job to hunt people down, no questions asked. But something about this woman made him want to know a little more before he did his grim job. An instinct.

He flipped it over to see a few words written in blue pen. *Me and Harpie/Nationals*, with the date scrawled below.

"Bring her in," Jeff repeated, ignoring Rome's question. "Dead or alive."

That was that. He had his orders. Dead or alive. As far as Jeff was concerned, that's all Rome needed to know. And really, it was enough. He stood up and ambled out the door, closing it tightly behind him.

Rome took one last glance at the smiling woman in the photo before stuffing the picture into the inside pocket of his black leather jacket. "Just another job," he mumbled, as if trying to convince himself.

The lab. He'd start there.

The cool darkness of the concrete hallway soothed her colossal headache. Harper ran her hands along the solid walls, finding comfort in their sturdiness. She felt completely drained, sapped of her strength and wits.

She'd come out of her blackout facedown and drooling on the grimy floor of the train car. Night had fallen and the dead bodies were still there. Their flesh was withered and seared from whatever she'd done.

Horrified couldn't even come close to what she'd felt, knowing that they were dead because of her. How could she even be capable of something like that? But then she remembered the sheer hatred she had felt for those men and the rush of heat and power that had accompanied it. At that moment, she had wanted them dead.

With no idea what to do about the devastation she'd created, she had gotten up on wobbly legs and walked over to one of the fallen men. It had been tough not to throw up from the rubbery feel of his damaged body as she fished a cell phone from his coat pocket. She dialed 911 and left the connection open without speaking, hoping the location of the signal could be traced.

She also probed around in the dirt for the broken flash drive. She shoved the pieces into her jeans pocket, desperately hoping the data could be recovered.

Then she ran. Shocked and frightened to her very core.

Harper's first idea was to return to Bobby's house, but she thought better of it. By now someone would have noticed the charred wreckage. She couldn't face any of that yet.

Besides, the people who killed him had probably torn the place apart. Maybe they were even still there, waiting. Whatever extreme power had been accidentally injected into her body was beyond valuable. No wonder someone would kill for it. She wholly wished she'd just given it to them.

Now she wandered down the hidden underground passage to the lab where her brother worked. He'd shown her the secret entrance the last time she was up for a visit, wanting her to fix a finicky bug in his computer, but not wanting to have to waste time clearing her through the overbearing security.

The lab was the only place she could think of that might be of any help. Maybe Bobby had some sort of antidote for the serum, or something that could rid her body of it. Actually, rid her head of it. The raging energy felt as though it stemmed directly from her mind.

Harper reached the last turn and patted the wall, searching for the recessed light switch she knew was there. Finding it, she pressed the control. A single clear bulb cast a shadowed light in the narrow hallway, bouncing weakly off the dull gray concrete.

Walking the remaining span of the passage, her nose tingled with the tang of damp smoke. The tunnel was underground and nearly airtight, so the only place it could be coming from was the lab. Not a good sign.

She flattened her palms against the lab door. The metal was cool to the touch.

She unlocked and spun the latch, reminded of a heavy vault door at a bank. Easing it slightly open, she peered through the crack. The room was filled with shadows caused by the peculiar muted lights set in a square area in the back of the lab. The space looked dingy and chaotic, but at least no one was there.

Harper eased her lithe frame through the door, shutting it soundly behind her. The stench of doused fire and chemicals was strong enough to make her gag. She slumped back against the door to catch her breath and survey the area.

Now torn apart, the lab was the polar opposite of the immaculate order from the last time she'd been there, six months before.

Solid glass walls had graced the back of the lab, which housed Bobby's flourishing test plants and his specially designed lights that simulated genuine sunlight. The clear natural glow from the bulbs was the only light still on in the room, illuminating the area where vibrant greens and poignant fragrances previously filled the senses.

But now broken glass was everywhere and various supplies were strewn about haphazardly. It looked as though a pack of wolves had run through, greedily tearing everything apart. Upturned file drawers littered the tiled floor and research materials lay scattered over the once-pristine worktables.

A huge pile of burnt gunk sat in the middle of the lab. Scorch marks snaked from the mound like ugly black tentacles. Sooty spots dotted the ceiling around the disengaged smoke alarm.

Harper walked over to take a closer look at the remains. But whatever it had been was now damaged beyond recognition. The acrid smell of burned vegetation and chemicals burned her throat once again as she nudged the charred and gooey heap with the toe of her shoe.

She moved to the desk, hoping to find something salvageable. Like everything else, this formerly neat and orderly section of the lab had been trashed. Chunks of small electronics and plastic that were clearly the remnants of a laptop littered the floor by the desk. But the hard drive was missing. Probably the melted square among the burned pile.

A rectangular chrome frame lay facedown on the desk. She brushed off some debris and picked it up, turning it around to take a look.

It was a double picture frame. One of the pictures was missing, but the other photo was unmistakable. She and her brother at the beach. A five-year-old Harper was frozen in time with a huge toothy grin, sitting in the middle of the sand castle Bobby had just finished building. But instead of being mad at her for flattening his masterpiece, she remembered he'd laughed even harder than she had.

The picture frame dropped from her fingers and crashed to the desk. Harper's shaking hands shot up to her head as grief and fury pounded her mind.

"Oh crap." Harper gasped and doubled over. It was happening again.

She took a deep breath, struggling to calm her frenzied mind. Tried not to think she was standing where her brother used to stand daily, bathed in the natural light he'd created for his precious plants.

Harper was breathless now, as if someone had kicked her hard in the gut and smashed a board across the back of her skull. Aching sorrow blasted behind her eyes. She fell to her knees.

Icy shards sliced through her veins, only to be replaced once again by a scalding heat—so hot, she saw a red inferno glow behind her tightly closed eyelids. Pain swarmed within her rushing blood. Energy vibrated inside her brain, thrashing around to get out of its cage.

Harper howled in agony and shuddered as she felt the ravenous wave of power surge from her mind. The wild force hammered everything around her with barely perceptible currents emanating from her body, sending Bobby's desk slamming into the wall just as someone burst through the door.

A tortured wail from inside the lab pierced the air. Done with decoding the lock on the lab's secure door, Rome reached under his coat and withdrew his gun from its holster. Holding the gun downward and ready, he gripped the door handle and shoved it open.

Rome instantly dove to the floor, barely missing the flying desk coming straight at him. It crashed hard against the concrete wall right above his position, raining thick splinters on top of him. He bit back a moan and struggled to clear the broken parts away enough to get into a crouch.

He stilled, listening. It was quiet save for some creaking and settling of scattered tables and other debris. What the hell just happened? An explosion?

Then he heard it. Heavy breathing. Panting. The suffering wail he'd heard outside had an owner. He clutched his gun and started to glide along the wall like a ghost.

A stumbling noise made him freeze. Peeking around the corner of an upturned lab table, he spied the source of the sound and aimed his weapon. The dim lighting, mixed with the lab's destruction, cast irregular shadows, bathing the hunched figure in an ethereal glow.

"Don't move," Rome ordered with quiet intensity.

Edging closer to his target, he now had a clear view. The person was on hands and knees, gasping for breath, back arching and bowing with each labored gulp of air. Rome's sharp gaze tracked from the dirty running shoes, along the jeans, to the tight rear end. Mussed blonde hair was evident just above the folded hood of a raincoat. The shape of the body told him this could very well be his quarry, returned to the scene of the crime. That'd be nice. He'd be able to have his pizza and beer after all.

He pulled out a firm cord from his leather jacket, meant for binding his prey. He stowed the gun in his holster and silently unraveled the line, creeping even closer, ready to spring.

Rome pounced, but hit solid ground with a thud. Instantly he rolled to a squat. His target had slid out of the way and now mirrored his crouch mere inches away.

They faced off. Hunter and hunted. Wild and savage. Though still cloaked in shadows, he could see that it was indeed the woman from the picture. Much scruffier than she'd been in the happy photo.

Her frightened eyes glinted in the low light. Good, she should be scared. He was the best. And he loved a good chase. He didn't want this to be too easy. Blood raced through his body, readying it for a strike. Excitement and anticipation surged in his muscles.

He shot her a feral smile. Her eyes widened, then narrowed.

Without warning, she threw a hard jab to his nose. His head snapped back. Well, the girl had some guts. He liked a little fire.

Rome snatched her arm, pulling her close, then forced her down onto her back. He pushed her arm into her chest, holding her in place. He lifted his leg to straddle her. Tears and sparks blurred his vision when her knee solidly connected with his groin.

Okay. Enough playing around. Still holding her arm, he tucked his pain away and sat on her hips, kicking his legs out to pin her lower body and lie on top of her. To her credit, she didn't scream.

Rome held strong while she tried to squirm away, but his bulk encased her slimmer frame. He was surprised by her solid strength. Every place his body touched hers was firm and coiled and hot.

The woman kept struggling, her breathing coming in huffs, warming his stubbled cheeks. She thrashed around like a trapped animal.

The photo had done very little justice to the woman. Hair the color of moonlit straw framed a face that wasn't striking but fit well together. The green eyes held fathoms of depth that could never be captured on paper. And in stark contrast to the cheery picture, absolute terror and sorrow etched her features. This wasn't the face of a villain. He'd seen enough of them to know.

Her stamina was impressive. She didn't seem to be wearing down. But he was getting impatient.

"Stop," he growled, and pulled out his gun to show her he meant business. "I'm taking you in one way or another." He'd hate to have to shoot her. But he would.

"Why?" the woman rasped. Her husky voice and bleak tone shocked him. Shouldn't she be belligerent rather than surprised? She sounded downright confused. "I don't understand. Why are you doing this to us?"

Us? He took a quick look around. No, they were alone. What was she talking about? She was a wanted woman.

"You did this," he countered. Was she playing him?

The woman finally stopped floundering and gave him an aching stare that shot straight to his soul.

"You killed my brother," she whispered brokenly, cold pain behind each word. She closed her eyes tight and cringed. Then she passed out.

Rome cautiously released his hold, and her body sank to the floor, totally limp, her breathing shallow.

Leaning on his haunches, he gazed at her. She'd thrown him for a loop. His duty commanded that he take her in. That was his directive. But something in her shattered voice touched him. And her eyes, wounded and searching. They tugged at the frayed edges of his heart.

For the first time in his life, he doubted his orders. His instincts told him to help her. And usually his instincts were right on target. She was a firecracker for sure, but a dangerous threat? Of that he wasn't so sure.

His targets almost always fought back, but not in self-defense. The guilty never asked why. But she had.

Rome made a decision. He needed to find out more.

He stuffed his gun into its holster and slid his arms under her amazingly broad shoulders and solid thighs. He stood, hefting her sinewy weight, and tossed her over his shoulder.

He'd get his answers—one way or another.

CHAPTER FOUR

Sunlight blasted through the window, blinding Harper as she stirred. She tried to raise her hand to block out the bright beams. Only her hand didn't budge. She tried to move her other hand, but met the same result.

Alarm flared through her body. She lay on her back with several layers of rope around each wrist. Making tight fists, she flexed her arm muscles and struggled against the secure bindings, but the more she fought, the tighter they became.

Relaxing for a moment, she sat up a little farther only to find that she couldn't move her feet. She strained her neck to see similar rope trussed around each ankle. Harper also noted that she was lying on a brown and orange plaid couch. The rope tied to her right arm disappeared over the seat back and the left arm's bindings trailed underneath the sofa.

Experimenting, she pulled her left hand toward her right. As she moved, her right hand shifted farther up the back of the couch. She then pulled her feet upward and found that motion caused her arms to be dragged downward. Her arms must have been tied to her feet.

Panic flooded her. She closed her eyes and wrestled it down. She had to keep her cool or suffer another vicious bout of whatever was happening to her.

Besides, it couldn't be too bad. Though she was tied up, she was bound to a really comfortable couch. So she couldn't be in too much trouble. The rushing anxiety drained away as she fought for control and flopped back down into the plump cushions, feeling the tickling strain on her abdomen fade.

Harper looked carefully at her prison. Unfamiliar. Nothing sparked recognition. A solid, hearty wood coffee table sat between the couch and a huge flat-screen television, nested above matching wooden shelves stocked with sophisticated black entertainment components. Sparing an appreciative glance for the sleek technology, she then peered at the rest of the area.

The decor was simple, yet the pieces there were of good quality. The space was wide-open and airy, especially with sunlight gracing every corner. The walls were adorned with snowy mountain landscapes encased in heavy wood frames. Dark blues and rich greens, which mingled with the plentiful natural light from the wall of windows that commandeered half the room, were the only colors present.

She hated to pigeonhole the place, especially given her own spartan dwelling back in San Francisco, but the place hinted at a man's touch.

Man's touch. Harper shot forward, wincing at the tight bindings. She flopped back into the plush confines of the couch.

Flashes of memories showered over her, crackling inside her head like sparks. The last thing she remembered was wrestling with a shadowy figure just before he'd pinned her to the cold concrete floor of Bobby's ruined lab. She'd had a second episode of the mind thing and events had been pretty hazy until all of a sudden he was there, facing her.

Her recollections were spotty, but she recalled the man had quicksilver moves. Thankfully, her body's fighting instincts had kicked in. Hadn't she gotten in a solid jab? She flexed the fingers on her right hand. A slight prickling of pain radiated from her knuckles. A smile broke out despite the circumstances.

He'd held her down under his hard-as-granite body, clasping his feet around her legs like an unbreakable vise and pinning her arms hard to her chest. She remembered her futile attempt to squirm out of his unyielding confinement. Then she'd finally asked him why. Why was he doing this? He'd seemed strangely confused at her question. Almost as confused as she was. And then she'd passed out.

Was this his place? Was he keeping her hostage? Had he done something to her? The man seemed to have known her. Been looking for her. Why? As if things could get more convoluted.

Shaking her head to clear it, Harper decided she'd better try to escape before finding the answers to any of those questions. Regardless of the cozy setting—not including the rope—she had no idea where she was or whether she was safe. Maybe there was no safe place for her anymore.

Raising her head, she searched her immediate area for anything she could use to cut through the thick rope. The four electronic remotes scattered on the table wouldn't do the trick. Neither would the rolled-up, half-empty bag of potato chips.

But that glass might. Though a little crusty from recent use, it looked like the edges of the hefty pint glass would be thick enough to slice the twine as long as she could break the glass itself. It was resting on a coaster. Coaster?

If she could only get to it. About a foot from the edge of the table, it would be a challenge. If she could just jar the table enough, the glass would roll off and shatter against the hardwood floor. Or better yet, break against the solid table itself.

Harper squirmed on the couch in an attempt to twist close enough to bump the table. Wriggling like a worm, she knocked her knee against the wood table. Sucking in a wince from the clumsy bonk on her kneecap, she watched as the glass wobbled across the tabletop, moving closer to the middle instead of the edge.

Taking a deep breath, she pulled her bindings taut and shimmied again. She banged her knee harder against the table, ignoring the same painful jolt. The glass fell over and rolled away from her, off the far side of the table. It dropped to the hardwood floor with a clatter. But it didn't break. Sighing in dismay, she closed her eyes and sank into the couch.

Her eyes snapped open at the deep snickering coming from the room's large open entryway. Straining her neck to see the source, her breath caught when she gazed into the laughing, clear blue eyes of her nemesis from the lab. The shadows there had masked him well, but here in the bright daylight, she was absolutely sure this was the man who had gotten the best of her last night.

He lounged against the wall, holding a bowl in one hand and a spoon in the other. She guessed he was easily half a foot over her five feet ten. She could see the evidence of rock-solid muscles under his tight black T-shirt. Snug blue jeans barely concealed the similarly evident muscles in his legs. Memories of that firm strength against her own body washed over her.

He was staring at her, the slight quirk of his alluring mouth indicating his patience with her appreciative perusal.

Cropped dark hair framed a rugged face. Stubble shadowed his jaw, maybe a day or two of it. Harper couldn't stop the grin from creeping onto her face as she saw the beginnings of a hearty bruise covering the upper part of his nose just below his left eye. She'd done that. Good. She hoped he had a rhino-sized headache.

"Yes, it hurts," his deep rumble confirmed. Long fingers from a large hand gripped the spoon tighter and dipped it into the bowl. He scooped some cereal into his mouth without breaking his piercing blue gaze.

Harper didn't know what to do. Should she demand that he free her? Should she ask nicely? Should she act crazy and make threats? Having never been tied up before—well, she'd been tied up for naked fun and games, but never by a stranger with a gun—she really had no frame of reference for this kind of thing.

The man took another spoonful and moved to the oversized green chair to the left of the couch. He eased down and propped his booted feet up on the table, then stared while he chewed.

Her stomach shuddered with an involuntary growl. Watching him chomp away, Harper suddenly couldn't remember the last time she'd eaten. Was it yesterday? Two days ago?

"Hungry?" the man asked, the muscles in his square jaw flexing with another crunchy bite of cereal.

The truth? "Yes." Harper sighed, plopping her head back down onto the couch, keeping her gaze steady under his. She was actually starving.

"Honesty," he stated with a hint of surprise and a twitch of his lips. "Good. That'll make things easier."

"What things?" She couldn't stop herself before the apprehensive question escaped. She mentally slapped herself. In movies, hostages were cool and calm, right?

"I'll make you a deal." He leaned forward and set

down the bowl. His muscled forearms rippled as he rested his elbows on his denim-covered thighs. "You tell me why you're wanted, and I might give you something to eat."

Meeting his ice blue gaze with her own, Harper suddenly felt tired. His eyes were like clear glacial pools, compelling her to jump in and spill everything. She relished the thought. Her life had been a complete nightmare since she stepped off the bus. She was truly alone now. So it would be nice to tell someone about it. She craved someone to talk to. Maybe doing so would help her begin to deal with it.

But she wasn't sure she was even ready to deal with it. Especially while tied to a couch. Albeit the supercushy couch of a supersexy man.

Wait. He'd said she was wanted. Fear fizzled in her stomach. He must be a cop or something. They must have found the bodies up in the Barracks and somehow tracked them to her. Oh, goodness. What was he going to do to her? She was probably going to prison. Forever. A sickening flush crawled across her skin.

"Look, lady." He sighed heavily, rubbing his hand over his dark hair. "Either you talk to me or I take you in. Right now. Your choice."

"Take me in where?" Harper asked, a little shakier than she had intended. She couldn't help it. She hadn't meant to do anything to those guys. Holy cow. "Jail?"

"I'm not a cop," the man said. She closed her eyes in relief. "I'm a government agent." Her eyes snapped open in sharp panic. Holy herd of cows. The government was after her.

He raised a hand, his palm facing her in a calming gesture, as he obviously saw the alarm written all over her face. "Honey, just tell me the truth. Why was I sent to find you?"

She tried to calm down. It was hard to do under his intense scrutiny, but she had to; otherwise she might have another episode. They seemed to come when she got upset. She'd hate to rip him apart like she'd done to those other men. One, it would be an incredible waste of very nice man flesh. Two, he'd actually been okay with her, other than keeping her tied up and hungry. And three, he seemed to really want to hear her story.

Curious. Why bring her here, and not just turn her in to whomever in the government wanted her? Very curious. Maybe she should just come clean. It wasn't as though she had many options. It could get a lot worse from here; that was for sure.

Meeting his gaze, she decided to give in and talk. "I don't know." Harper shook her head, the weight of her recent past lying heavily upon her. "I don't know why any of this is happening."

"Any of what?" he asked, leaning forward. Serious interest sparked in his eyes.

"I don't know," she countered hastily. He slumped back; a look of skepticism and disappointment washed over his rugged features. "Honestly, sir, I don't understand what's happening. That's the truth."

He raised a dark eyebrow and frowned, pulling out a stiff piece of paper from his back pocket. He turned it toward her.

Harper's breath caught. In his hand was a photograph of her brother with his arm around her at the National Collegiate Swimming Championships three years ago. She'd won gold in every one of her events.

"Who is this man?" His deep voice broke her out of the proud memory. "And which one of you is Harpie?"

She almost choked at the nickname her brother had used for her since she was three. "That's my brother,

Bobby," she managed in a shaky tone. "I'm Harper. Harpie is—was—his name for me."

"Your brother," he repeated immediately, demandingly. "The one you said was killed." Did she say that? When had she blurted that out? Oh, right. When this man was forcefully restraining her. Before she passed out. "What did he do?"

"Nothing" was all she could say. She closed her eyes and shook her head sadly. "He was just a scientist."

"Why was he killed?" the man asked levelly. But she couldn't speak. She was too busy trying to control her misery and rage from the relentless questions. "Harper?" Her name rumbled off his lips, with a slight growly tone that tickled her tummy, strangely calming the simmering emotions within her.

She opened her eyes to look at him again, trying to emanate resolve. "I don't know why my brother was killed," Harper answered quietly, "but I'm going to find out." A startled flicker passed through his blue eyes, then was gone. "And when I do, I'm going to make the people who killed him pay for it."

His gaze remained locked with hers and she could see the wavering belief there. It was apparent that something was warring inside of him, as though he sincerely wanted to trust her. Why, she had no idea.

"You're not lying to me, are you, Harper?" There it was again. Some kind of Midwest accent. The rolling way he said her name was too compelling, too dangerous.

"I'm telling you the truth," she replied.

He stared for a long moment, then hoisted his long body from the chair and moved behind the sofa, out of her line of vision. Shadows flickered through the rays of sun shining into the room as she listened to him pace behind her.

Frustration threatened to surface, but she soon realized that the man was thinking. She remembered her father would pace—no, stalk, actually—back and forth at the top of the stairs while she and Bobby sat on the steps, waiting for him to come up with a punishment for whatever outrageous stunt they had pulled.

"Okay, Harper." He suddenly appeared in front of her.

"Okay, what?" she answered, aware that she hadn't heard him move. She'd have to be more cognizant of that. If she got the chance.

"I'll help you," he said, flopping down in his chair once again, his gaze burning into hers, making her blink. "I'll help you find out why your brother was killed."

"No way." Even flatly refusing his offer, Harper's smoky voice sent a thrill of excitement straight to his groin. The fact the woman was tied up on his couch didn't help. "No thank you. No."

"So, tell me how you really feel." Rome shot her a sardonic half grin. He watched her expressive face closely, looking for clues to unlock the mystery and conflict she'd unwittingly brought into his life.

Harper was obviously keeping something from him, something big. But he was convinced that what she had revealed was the truth. He'd spent a lot of time deciphering people and cracking their personal codes, figuring out what they were hiding. His job, his very survival, demanded it.

So he more than trusted his well-honed instincts. And he was honest enough with himself to admit that she tapped something in him. Maybe it was how her resilient strength mixed with her naked candor. Or her terrified gaze mixed with her steely resolve.

"Why help me?" she asked simply, her emerald eyes imploring.

Why, indeed? She'd shocked him with her steadfast

vow to find her brother's killer. And find out why he was killed. Really, that was what bothered him the most. This woman, Harper, honestly had no idea why her scientist brother would end up a murder victim. Combine that with her frank confusion about what she had to do with it all. Plus, her apprehension about his being a government agent was also puzzling. He wanted answers that she apparently didn't have or wouldn't disclose.

Only once had he ever questioned a job before, and that one time had ended in tragedy. But Harper's bleak fear was real. So was her fierce courage and strength. He needed to know why this beguiling woman was forcing him to doubt his duty.

"Why not help you?" His elusive answer caused her eyes to narrow.

"Before, you said you were taking me in."

She twisted her hands nervously against the binding, the rope coiling and twisting. Maybe he should remove those now that he'd inexplicably decided to help her.

"Now you want to help me out. I don't get it."

"Neither do I, but I have an instinct about you," Rome said, gritting his teeth. He knew it didn't make sense, but he had a gut feeling about her. And his sharp instincts had never failed him. Even if he hadn't always listened to them. That was a mistake he would never make again. But that was in the past. The simple fact was something just wasn't right with this situation. And that hint of a doubt made the decision for him. "Look, Harper, I will help you find your answers. Whether or not you believe it, you do need my help."

"I don't need anyone's help," she argued in what was practically a growl. A positively sexy growl. He watched her ball her fists, her knuckles white, her wrists straining against the rope.

Obviously she didn't know half of the danger she was in, given that he'd been the one called out to bring her in dead or alive. Rome's reputation was that he always brought in his quarry. By any means. He was called upon for only the most dangerous and critical jobs. Jeff really wanted her for some reason, which was never a good thing.

"Honey, you don't even know what you're up against." Rome shook his head. "Hell, I don't even know what you're up against. But I'm ready to find out."

"How do I know you won't just take me in later?"

"You don't." He shrugged and decided to level with Harper to make her understand that the fact he was sent to apprehend her meant bad things for her. "If I wanted to bring you in, you'd be there by now. I haven't done that, so you know you can trust me. Believe me, I'm the lesser of two evils."

She looked as though she was thinking about it, staring at him. Trying to figure out his angle. Clearly she didn't trust easily. Then again, he couldn't blame her; he did have her tied up to his sofa.

"Harper." Rome leaned forward, speaking low. He liked the way her name tasted. "You can trust me." She looked away. He moved in for the kill. He covered her bound hands with his own, noticing the long powerful fingers flex beneath his. A surprising little shiver crawled up his arm from where their skin touched. Her gaze shot to their hands, as if she felt it, too, then rose to look directly at him. Eyes that swirled like the stormy ocean bore into his soul, wanting to believe, sending a quiver down his spine. "You can trust me." And he realized that he meant it.

"I don't want anyone else to get hurt," she whispered. Scared. Her hands twisted to grasp his. She was scared. "I need to do this alone. I can't trust or risk anyone else."

She took a deep breath and let it out slowly. "And I'll do whatever I have to do."

Rome wasn't sure what she meant by risking anyone, but he could take care of himself. He wanted to find out what was going on as much as she did. Why a scientist was murdered and this enigmatic woman was being hunted. And he played by his own rules, too.

"You want revenge," he whispered back. She confirmed this with a slight nod of her dirty, ruffled blonde head. "I want answers. Let's find both together." He could barely believe what he was saying. What was making him commit to this woman he knew nothing about and was tasked to bring in as an enemy of the government? Whatever it was, he had a feeling it hinged on her working with him to uncover the truth. Finding himself mesmerized by her powerful green gaze, he nodded back at her, willing her to believe in him. At least enough to find out the truth.

"You won't take me in?" Her breathless question drew him closer, only an inch or two from her warm, prone body. Rome remembered her firm curves sliding against his body from when they had wrestled in the lab last night.

Removing one of his hands from hers, he reached into his back pocket, pulling out his knife. It opened with a crisp *snick*, making her jump. Lifting her hands, he brought the sharp blade around to slice easily through the rope like the finest silk.

"No strings attached." Rome winked at her startled expression. Smiling, he stood, mentally shaking off the intensity he felt crackling between them. He couldn't deny the intoxicating pull of her determination and inner strength. "Let me get you something to eat." He retreated toward the kitchen, listening as she began to untangle his expertly tied rope prison.

"Who are you?" Harper's husky voice drifted to him just as he reached the edge of the room. Pausing to lean against the wall, he was captivated by the sunlight playing over her body.

"Rome," he answered, after briefly toying with the idea to give her one of his countless aliases. But for some reason he couldn't fathom, he didn't. "Rome Lucian."

"I'm Harper Kane," she offered cordially, finally escaping the couch to stand up stiffly. She rubbed her bare arms and then her thighs, presumably to get her circulation going. His certainly was.

She was taller than he'd thought. In the stark sunlight, he could see her athletic form was built from years of vigorous training, not just occasional gym visits to look sporty. That physique was solid and efficient, not a hollow shell.

It was going to be interesting getting to know this woman. Getting to know what it was about her that spoke to him. And finding out why she was wanted dead or alive.

"Harper Kane," Rome repeated, and turned toward the kitchen. Throwing her a glance over his shoulder, he tilted his head for her to follow. "Do you like Cocoa Puffs?"

Harper sat quietly in the passenger seat of Rome's black Land Rover. The tinted glass cast a dreary sepia tone to the countless trees they passed on the drive to Bobby's secluded home. She absently tapped her foot to the song on the radio. "Dancing Queen" was among her favorites.

After two full bowls of Cocoa Puffs, Harper had blissfully relaxed in a long hot shower. The double jetting heads had surged their soothing spray over her battered body, while she'd generously lathered on Rome's spicy soap and shampoo. She knew she smelled a bit like his scent now. It was a curiously intimate feeling, but at least she was clean and refreshed.

Before she'd undressed for the shower, she had taken a look around Rome's place, admiring his high-tech computer system. She'd even toyed with one of his flash drives. Unbelievably, the tiny memory chip from Bobby's drive had remained undiscovered in the folds of her jeans pocket. She thought for sure Rome would have confiscated it, but he hadn't. So she'd cracked open one of his drives, removed the existing memory chip, and replaced it with her own.

Harper had then found Rome in his bedroom, picking out some clothes for her from his own wardrobe. He had even taken care of washing and drying her soiled clothes while she'd showered.

Returning her attention to the present, she glanced at Rome's rugged reflection in her window and wondered again why he was helping her. Generally, Harper took things at face value and never bothered to look for ulterior motives. Not anymore.

Rome was helping her for his own reasons; she was sure of it. What those reasons were, she had no idea, but while she didn't trust him, she didn't have much choice at this point. And she knew he didn't trust her, either. He knew she was hiding something. Her new power wasn't something she reckoned she could share with him.

But no matter what she told herself, she could use the help. Especially the help of someone as competent as Rome Lucian, who was also on the inside of the government, which was now after her. She was alone in this world and had little choice but to use him for whatever he offered.

After a brief rundown of what she chose to tell him about her last few days, Rome had decided that they should start at Bobby's house to look for clues. The thought of going back to Bobby's place so soon made her sick to her stomach. Anguish and foreboding danced under her skin and prickled through her nerves. Tension wired her body, but it was of utmost importance that she kept her emotions under tight control until she figured out Rome's motives and found out what happened with Bobby. And then she would let loose.

"What's that smile for?" Rome's rich voice broke into her thoughts. She wasn't even aware she was smiling, but she knew she couldn't admit why.

"Just glad to be clean and dry," she answered instead, which wasn't a lie.

"Look"—he reached over and gently covered her hand on her lap with his own warm one—"after this, we'll get you some things. Okay?" His fingers squeezed hers with gentle reassurance.

"That's fine." She tried not to notice how nice his touch felt against her skin and thigh. Shifting in the heated leather seat, she gazed at his profile. He had a strong nose that looked like it had been broken at the bridge several times but somehow maintained a solid shape. Though he'd shaved that morning, his rugged cheeks were darkened by a perpetual shadow. His corded neck disappeared into the collar of a black T-shirt under a black leather jacket.

"We're close?" he asked, not turning to face her even though she knew he could tell she was checking him out by the ticking muscle in his jaw. She moved her inspection from the attractive view inside to the abundant landscape outside.

"The next turn, actually," she answered, recognizing the familiar sights. "Just about two more miles, then make another right."

And they'd be back to where it all began.

Quiet reigned until they reached the turn.

Bitter, aching memories flooded over her as the car maneuvered onto the isolated roadway. Approaching the hidden turn to Bobby's house, Rome slowed the vehicle. Her breathing caught as she saw the charred pavement where Bobby's truck had burned. With Bobby inside. Nothing remained but a disturbing sooty stain on the road.

Harper raised a palm to her forehead, desperately trying not to let her emotions swirl out of control. Her pulsing mind began to spiral, and she closed her eyes, taking a few deep, calming breaths.

A firm squeeze of her other hand caught her attention. She snapped her eyes open.

"Harper." The tone of his deep voice rolled over her name, soothing her churning insides. She looked into his clear blue eyes. "It's going to be okay." Squeezing her hand once more, he said, "You can do this."

"How can you say that?" she whispered, wanting desperately to believe him. "You don't even know me."

"I know all I need to know." His confidence in her was reassuring. She let it settle around her like a cozy blanket, warm and secure. "You're strong. Inside and out. You can do this."

Nodding, she covered their entwined hands with her other one. He gave her a quick nod back and put the car in motion down the isolated bumpy road. Clearing the last of the heavy trees, Bobby's inviting home came into view.

The two-bedroom house was more like a log cabin, built of rich wood and surrounded by various small firs and cedars. And the dogwoods whose leaves added vibrant color when they adorned the now-bare branches. Acres and acres of forest enveloped the property, which was how Bobby loved it. It was his private haven of timberland. Serene and alive. But now it seemed still and lifeless.

Gravel crunched under the Land Rover's chunky tires as they rolled to a stop near the back door. She'd told Rome to park in the back when he'd asked her earlier about cover. There was no garage, just a cleared space out front, enough for two, maybe three cars, and the one-car spot here in the back. He turned off the powerful engine with a twist of his wrist and jiggled the keys.

"Let's go around front," he said, opening the door and hopping out of the driver's side.

She unlocked her door and slid out of the seat, hitting the gravel with a thud. Shutting the door, she saw Rome come to her side and pocket his keys. He gave her a soft, encouraging smile and nodded toward the house.

They moved around the side and approached the entryway, the aging floorboards creaking with their footsteps. Rome pulled out his gun and held it ready.

Harper gave him an inquiring look at the aggressive motion. He quirked a half smile at her. Should she be worried about something? Stepping ahead of her, Rome grabbed the doorknob and turned it. The door opened easily when he slowly pushed inward. Pressing a finger to his lips in a shushing movement, he gripped his gun tightly and eased low through the door and disappeared. Harper remained silent outside on the porch.

A long moment later, Rome opened the door wide and gestured for her to go inside.

"It's clear, but it's been run through," he said, expelling a breath and holstering his gun.

Gazing around the familiar confines in miserable shock, she saw what he meant. It did look like it had been run through. By a herd of wild animals.

Everything was wrecked. Everything. Furniture was

upended. Books and papers littered the hardwood floor. The minimal knickknacks that Bobby had were either broken or discarded haphazardly. The inviting dark wood walls that made the home comfy and charming were bare. All the woodland paintings and mountain photographs were on the floor, with broken glass and bent frames.

Harper took a slow, deep breath and blinked away heavy tears. Somehow she'd known this was coming. After the vicious scene in the lab, she'd known this was a possibility.

But to be slapped in the face with this stung and was harder than she'd imagined. Seeing Bobby's personal things treated like they were worthless and tossed around like yesterday's trash was utterly devastating.

A strong hand on her back made her jump forward, knocking her shin hard against the solid leg of the upside-down coffee table.

"Yow!" Harper exclaimed, bending over to run her hand across the quick-forming knot on her leg. "Don't do that again. Please."

"Sorry." Rome rubbed her back with warm strokes. He could do that all he wanted. She was eternally grateful not to have to face this alone. "Let's take a look around. We're looking for anything they might have left behind. Anything that seems like it was gone through."

"Everything looks like it was gone through," she murmured, straightening.

Harper nimbly maneuvered through the debris toward the heavy brick fireplace that monopolized half the far wall. In the corner was a thick wooden shelving unit. Most of the shelves were missing, thrown about the room, except the middle one. The one that had held the carefully maintained glass cases of her swimming medals. The cases that were now shattered on the floor at her feet.

Bobby had asked to keep some of her medals here so that he could share her triumphs with her, even if they weren't together.

She carefully picked up one of the fallen golden discs. It felt enormously heavy as she peered at it, the memories flooding her vision while she scanned the words.

U.S. Champion, 400-meter Individual Medley. Her best race. She'd set a record. And won this medal. The first of three golds at the Olympic team trials.

Running her thumb over the raised etchings, she remembered how proud Bobby had been. How proud she'd been. She'd won other competitions, but that was her first big one. Her first national gold. The one that set her on the path to reaching her dream to compete at the Olympics. And put her among the elite in the nation.

Harper gripped the medal tightly, realizing that she may never earn another one of these ever again.

"Is there an office or something?" Rome asked as he moved to her side, running his hand along the smooth wood of the empty shelf. His other hand rested on her shoulder, warm and encouraging. "Maybe he was working on a project of interest."

"Yes," Harper answered quietly, gently setting the medal next to his hand on the shelf. She turned away and moved toward the small hallway. "There're only five rooms. This one, a bathroom, the kitchen, an office, and the bedroom." She stopped outside the rectangular room that was Bobby's office, looking over her shoulder to see Rome just behind her. "I usually slept on that couch." She pointed to the sofa bed tucked in the corner. Its cushions were on the floor on top of some open file folders.

"I'll go through this stuff." Rome squeezed by her to enter the office, brushing his hard body against hers and giving her a reassuring pat. "Why don't you check the bedroom?"

She watched him bend to one knee and start sifting through the papers on the floor, scanning each before he stacked them neatly to the side. The motion tightened his jeans against his taut rear. Though she was struggling mightily to hold her emotions in check, she let herself indulge in the ordinary act of appreciating the fine male specimen before her eyes.

Shaking her head, Harper paced down the hall to Bobby's bedroom. Again, ugly destruction greeted her. She stood in the doorway and surveyed the morbid scene. In a daze, she walked in.

Picking up a rumpled T-shirt from the floor, she stared at the faded symbol of the Green Lantern. Bobby loved comic book heroes as much as she did. They had competitions of who could find the coolest vintage shirts of their favorites.

She carefully folded the shirt and held it in one hand as she reached with the other to pick up an upside-down wooden picture frame on the floor. Turning it over, she saw her own image next to Bobby's through the cracked glass. They were facing the camera, each with an arm around the other's shoulder in front of a glorious mountain backdrop.

Ah yes, their summer trip to Whistler a few years back. They'd ridden up the open chairlift to the summit of Whistler Mountain. Smiling, Harper remembered being absolutely petrified to ride the lift high above the craggy, rocky mountainside. Bobby had laughed at her anxiety, but had also held on to her arm with doting support and talked to her the whole way, both up and down, to keep her too distracted to freak out.

Her eyes misted over. She stood, then leaned back to sit on the disheveled bed. Bringing the shirt up to her face, she could faintly smell the fresh, cool scent of Bobby's cologne.

The picture frame slid from her unsteady grasp, but she barely heard the *thump* as it hit the floor. Instead, she buried her face in Bobby's well-worn T-shirt and finally let loose her crushing anguish.

It was just too much. Surrounded by Bobby's things, knowing he'd never see them again was just too much. The silent tears just kept coming. And she didn't even care to stop them.

She had no idea how long she'd been crying when she heard faint footsteps and felt the bed sink next to her. Strong arms circled her trembling shoulders and pulled her into a solid embrace. Leaning into the warm body, she heard Rome's strong and comforting heartbeat while his hand made soothing patterns on her back.

Rome tightened his grip, startling her. She sniffled and raised her head to look at him. Head slightly tilted, he was clearly listening for something. He released her and stood silently, pulling his gun just seconds before she heard the front door crash open.

CHAPTER FIVE

Rome heard the footsteps trying not to crunch on the gravel outside just seconds before the front door was bashed open. He silently cursed for allowing himself to get caught up in Harper's naked grief. She was undeniably distracting. He'd known coming here would be hard for her, but he'd also known she was strong and could handle it well enough.

And she had done better than he'd expected. Really, he couldn't blame her for falling apart at seeing her brother's place in shambles, and it also justified his belief that she truly was shocked that Bobby was dead. No, he didn't know her well at all, but what he did know from all the cruelty he'd seen in the field was that depth of sorrow couldn't be faked.

"Get behind me, fast," he hissed.

Harper quickly got up and stood still at his back. He could feel the warmth of her taut body just a breath away from his as he listened. It was impossible for whoever was out there to keep quiet with the amount of debris littered over the floor. Someone stumbled and grunted. Idiots.

It was difficult to tell how many people had entered the house, not to mention how many might be wandering around outside. Rome was glad he'd parked in the back, obscured by some dense and drooping trees. It came to him while he was digging through the clutter in Bobby's office that Jeff would have expected him back by now—with Harper in tow, dead or alive.

Well, the woman most certainly was alive. And he'd inexplicably committed himself to help her. So it was somewhat possible Jeff was looking for him as well. But he was pretty damn sure whoever was bumbling around out there was after the enigmatic woman standing right behind him with her hand resting lightly on his shoulder blade.

He turned toward her. *Is there a way to the back?* he mouthed. Damn, she was close. Close enough that he dropped his gaze to her full lips. He nearly moaned when the tip of her tongue poked out to wet them. Sheer willpower forced his attention back to her eyes. She shook her head no.

Tearing his gaze back to the hallway, he noticed shadows milling around near their position. Could Harper and he get through the window and to the Land Rover without causing alarm? It was likely that the intruders didn't know they were even here.

Deciding their best tactical option was to run, he turned to look at Harper, then immediately pulled her to the floor in a tangled crouch. Outside the window he caught a glimpse of motion. Damn it all to hell. Whoever was out there was going to find his car.

He and Harper had to do something fast before they were completely trapped.

"There's a window in the office." Harper's breathy voice in his ear gave him a jolt. *Shake it off, boy.*

He nodded, trying to clear his mind, which was tough considering the snug contact of their bodies. He peeked around the corner. All clear. If they moved fast, they might beat the intruders to the car via the office window. "Let's go." He readied his gun, barrel down, wrist steady, and grabbed her hand, hauling her up with him.

Leading her cautiously down the hallway, he hugged the wall, briefly smiling when he noticed her doing the same. As they reached the doorway, he pulled her with him inside the room.

"Stop!" boomed a loud voice. *Crack!* A bullet splintered the doorframe directly above Harper's head.

Too damn close. They needed a new plan. Rome was smart enough to know when to give in. But he never gave up.

"Get out here now," the man commanded. "With your hands on your head." Maybe they didn't know he was there. Maybe he could catch them off guard. But that left Harper alone to face them.

Yes, she was tough, but against the hostile firepower that was probably out there? She was wanted dead or alive. Which, to most agents, meant dead. If they had been sent by Jeff, there wasn't much that would stop them from pulling their triggers.

"All right," Rome answered loudly enough for anyone in the house to hear. "We're coming out." He nodded to Harper and gave her a look he hoped was reassuring. She narrowed her eyes and tightened her lips, but nodded back. "It's going to be okay," he told her in a low voice, and gave her arm a comforting squeeze.

Moving ahead of her, he holstered his gun and put his hands on his head, motioning her to mimic him. He was thankful she did, though she seemed a bit more passive than the woman he knew—albeit briefly.

As soon as he stepped out into the hallway, two men roughly grabbed his upraised arms and dragged him into the trashed living room. Gritting his teeth, he watched as they did the same to Harper. His captors abruptly stopped and Harper stumbled as she was shoved to a halt next to him. The men moved around to face the two of them.

"Are you Harper Kane?" one asked in a blunt tone.

Rome wasn't sure whether she would answer. He kept staring straight ahead, not wanting to tip them off in case she didn't.

"Are you Harper Kane?" the man repeated curtly, and raised his rifle to settle it against her chest, as if she had a bull's-eye over her heart.

Rome held back a twitch and looked sideways at her face, trying to gauge her reaction. Would she cave in? Maybe, maybe not. He was guessing not, but he wasn't so sure this guy was bluffing.

He was about to tell her to answer when she tilted her head to meet his gaze.

"Get behind me," she said in a chilled and calm tone. What? What the hell was she doing?

More men bounded through the open doorway, probably the shadowy guys from outside.

"Last chance, bitch," the man with the pointed gun said impatiently, tapping the barrel against her. He wasn't bluffing at all. "Are you Harper Kane?"

"Rome, trust me." Her cool gaze never wavered from his face. He had no idea what to do. This guy was going to shoot her. These were Jeff's guys. He knew it. They may or may not know who he was; they'd given no indication either way. Regardless, they suspected who she was and would no doubt finish the job that he hadn't.

He'd asked her to trust him. Maybe he should do the same for her. Decision made, he gave her a tight smile and ducked behind her.

The man cocked his rifle and repositioned his aim on

her chest. Rome watched from his position slightly be-hind her as she tipped back her head and spread her arms. What on earth was she doing?

Harper bowed her head forward and her body began to tremble. Lightly at first, and then she started to shud-der, rippling into a controlled convulsion. Worried, Rome put a hand on her shoulder. Her body was white-hot. He instantly removed his hand, his palm stinging as though he'd grabbed a burning log. Everyone in the room was still focused on her.

All at once, Harper's head snapped back, she cried out, and her arms spread wide, palms facing out. A barely perceptible pulsing wave shot out from her body, displacing the air and pounding against everything in its wake. It was as though a surge emanated from her be-ing.

Rome witnessed the utter devastation originating from Harper with horror. The charged air flared from her hands toward their enemies. The clear shimmery wave coiled around them and rushed into their bodies. The men standing before her crumpled, their faces fro-zen in fright, and fell to the ground motionless. Life-less.

The front windows shattered from the residual en-ergy throbbing through the room, the glass shattering outward with a roar. The upturned furniture slammed against the far wall, and the debris that had littered the floor whirled around the room like a mini tornado. De-struction ravaged everything in the area in front of him.

Finally, it stopped.

Whatever she had done had seized the life out of the men and torn apart what was left of Bobby's living room.

Rome remained completely still, shock rushing through every fiber, stirring his blood. Tearing his gaze away from the sickening annihilation, Rome glared at Harper. She was standing, shaking, with her hands clutching her head. Then she fell to her knees, heaving in every breath. Like the first time he'd seen her in the lab.

He just stood there. Staring.

She looked up at him, her eyes wild, stark pain and dread written all over her flushed features.

"I'm so sorry." The broken whisper came from her trembling lips just before she slumped to the hard floor in an unconscious heap.

Stunned, Rome squatted down next to her and mechanically felt her neck for a pulse. He found it racing faster than he ever thought possible.

He then got up and began to maneuver around the debris to reach the fallen men. There wasn't much that made him queasy, but looking at the shape these guys were in made him sick to his stomach.

The pulsating shock wave that had radiated from Harper looked like it had ripped through their bodies, inside and out, like a harsh wind viciously gusting through a dense forest, whipping and tearing away matter.

He bent to check on the closest to see whether any life remained. The skin at the man's neck felt like old parchment, roughly withered by time and the elements. There was no pulse.

Rome walked silently to the front of the room, leaning against the wide-open entryway. The door lay scattered in thick shards over the porch and threshold, though he didn't know whether it was from the forced entry of the men or Harper's attack.

Sucking in several breaths of the fresh woodsy air, he surveyed the ugly scene with a troubled gaze. Uncontrolled weapon explosions; cruel, torturous behavior; monstrous strikes of natural weather. He had seen all of that and more.

But this? This was something different. Harper was something different. Never before had he seen such an act of power. A terrifying, inhuman act of power. How had she done this?

Walking back over to her slumped form, Rome was forced to admit that she scared him. She absolutely frightened him. Just minutes before, he was cursing himself for wanting her. Now he was cursing himself for trusting her.

Damn it all. He'd known she'd been hiding something. Information, maybe, but not the fact that she was some sort of supernatural freak.

Jeff had been right. Harper Kane was most certainly dangerous. She was a walking lethal weapon, for crying out loud. So much for his razor-sharp instincts. This was a doozy. Mentally slapping himself for forsaking his duty for a gorgeous woman, he retreated out the back to his rig for some rope.

Promise or no, he had to take her in.

CHAPTER SIX

Pain. Darkness. The two had been her constant companions since she'd been here. Wherever here was.

Every breath she sucked in made her ache. Harper had no idea how long she'd been in this awful place, but judging from the sporadic food trays she'd been brought, it seemed like two, maybe three days had passed. The most recent meal had been shoved through the door just a few minutes before. She hadn't even gone searching for it in the darkness, preferring to stay seated in the farthest corner from the entrance.

The last thing she remembered was seeing the stark fear on Rome's shocked face after she'd tried to use her new power to help them escape the ambush at Bobby's house. Then she'd passed out.

And awakened to an experience beyond her worst nightmare. Alone.

She'd opened her eyes to inky blackness and immobilization, her body secured and bound upright to the wall. She couldn't see a thing. Panicked and confused, she'd attempted to focus on the special force in her mind, knowing full well she had no real control over it. But it wouldn't work. Somehow she'd been able to summon the power at Bobby's house, but she couldn't do it here in the totally dark room.

After a while, they'd come for her—burly men dressed all in black and carrying guns and thick clubs. They'd already yanked her out of her dark prison and dragged her to a small, badly lit room with twisted contraptions and threatening devices.

Cruel medical tools and wicked-looking equipment had gleamed ominously on chrome tables, complete with rough, padded restraints straight out of the nastiest horror movies ever made. Again she'd tried to beckon her mind to do its thing, but nothing happened.

Though she'd struggled with all her might, her larger captors had forced her onto one of the platforms and latched the restraints onto her. A shot like a dart had pricked her arm and after that, her vision blurred and she'd felt nothing but pain. Sheer unadulterated pain. Then someone in a harsh white lab coat began to go to work on her.

They'd asked her countless questions for which she had no answers. That hadn't made the person in the lab coat happy. She couldn't remember even saying anything, which had made them even more furious.

Harper had alternately been drugged with who knows what, and they'd drawn what seemed like gallons of blood. Again, she'd been questioned beyond reason. And still she hadn't been able to give them what they wanted.

Then the brutes had lugged her back to this dark room and left her here for hours. Food had come, but she didn't eat it. She couldn't eat it. Even if she had been able to see it in the complete darkness, she didn't think her groggy and battered body could stomach it. The water bottles they threw in were all she dared to handle.

After that they had come for her again, and it had started all over. She'd lost count of how many cycles of the same treatment she'd endured.

Between the interminable bouts of interrogation, she had nothing but barren time to think. Think about everything.

Just a few days ago, she was finishing up her last spirited swimming practice in Palo Alto. Drying off from a great workout. Two hours in the pool and she'd broken some of her personal-best times. Her coach had been ecstatic, and pleaded with her to keep going. But she'd said no. Though her times were better than they'd ever been, she'd needed a break. Mentally she had become exhausted thinking about what the Olympic trials would mean to her. Her coach had wanted her to stay sharp, but she needed to step back before the sharpness nicked her. Time with Bobby would have unwound her tight thoughts and kept her focus on track with her impressive output in the pool.

How quickly things had derailed. Now she had some kind of mysterious mind power from a serum Bobby had created. Her brother had been killed for trying to make sure it didn't fall into the hands of the very people keeping her captive, testing her like some interminable lab experiment and treating her like she was the world's worst enemy.

And she was alone.

Rubbing her arms, then instantly regretting it as her skin prickled from the drugs she had been given, Harper thought about Rome. Had he been subdued after she passed out? Or had he brought her into this hideous hole? She desperately preferred to believe the former, but knew deep in her exhausted gut it had to be the latter. The fright on his face had been obvious. Rome believed she was a threat. Which was precisely the reason he was sent to detain her and bring her here in the first place.

He'd promised he wouldn't, but that all had changed

when she used her strange power to save them. It had been difficult, and she hadn't even been sure she'd be able to do it, but she didn't see any other way out of Bobby's house. So she'd done it. And it worked. The only problem was, it had turned Rome against her.

She'd deliberately kept her power from him, hoping she'd be able to somehow explain it once they'd learned more about what was going on. She'd put her faith in him, having no one else to trust, and he'd betrayed her. One moment, the man had held her close while her grief overflowed, and the next, he'd pushed her back into her worst nightmare.

Could she really blame him? Honestly, she herself was frightened by the power surging through her mind and body. But he'd asked her to trust him. She had, and look where it had gotten her.

Never again. She would do this on her own. Just as she'd vowed that night in the forest. She was truly alone.

Sitting in the cold darkness now, Harper realized that it didn't matter. For whatever reason, they were keeping her alive. Only taking her to the edge of her limits, allowing her to look over the cliff, see the valley of death, but never plummeting into the merciful void.

They needed her. Whatever this serum was that Bobby had been working on, they wanted it. That meant Bobby didn't want them to have it. That he wasn't involved in all of this trouble.

That would keep her going. Keep her believing that she would somehow survive this and get the revenge she was beginning to crave. The only thing she wanted now was to make everyone involved pay for it.

It wasn't just for Bobby anymore. It was for what they were doing to her. For Rome bringing her here. For being accidentally injected with that serum and having a destructive energy surging through her mind. She didn't ask for this, never expected it. But she would finish it. Find her answers and find vengeance.

A clank and a grinding noise diverted her attention. They were here again. A bright artificial light cut through the pitch-black, shining directly in her eyes, blinding her as she squinted against the sudden beams. She raised her hand to shade the light until she could adjust her vision.

Footsteps clomped grimly against the solid concrete floor. Two sets of arms grabbed her on each side and secured her hands with cold metal clamps, then dragged her upright and out into the cool, dimly lit hallway. Harper's sight cleared and she noticed the usual four-man posse had been joined by six more black-clad goons. These guys looked a little unusual somehow, but it was hard to say what was different about them. The normal four passed her off to the big six.

Leading her roughly down the corridor, they surprisingly turned right instead of the dreaded left that had become her customary routine. Was that good or bad? Of course, bad was relative. How much worse could it get?

After climbing countless flights of uneven stairs, they reached a level area and turned down yet another eerie hallway. At the far end, a sliver of natural light poked through the bottom of a thick metal door.

Harper was a touch curious. Was she not coming back this time? Fine with her. Again, how much worse could it get? Unless they were taking her away to kill her. That could definitely be worse. She hazily hoped she was wrong and they were just going outside. One modest breath of fresh air would sure make her day. Although there wasn't much that wouldn't make her day right now.

The closer they came to the door, the more it looked like they were going outside. Her mind faintly rejoiced. Sunlight at last.

"What are you doing here?" Jeff Donovan's distracted question hit Rome the second he walked in his boss's office. Jeff hadn't even looked at Rome, his attention on the papers in his hand.

What indeed? Rome had asked himself the same question nearly every second since he'd arrived at the isolated government facility. Located just outside of downtown Portland, only those who needed to know were aware the site existed. Underground and hidden from the unassuming world. Though not many up on the surface would want to know what went on down there. Lucky bastards.

Which was the real reason he couldn't stop himself from coming. Rome didn't sit down, instead leaning against the unadorned wall just inside the door. "Just checking in," he answered with cool but fake nonchalance. Since the moment he dropped off the unconscious Harper Kane three days ago, he'd been restless. Edgy and unable to sleep, he couldn't stop thinking about her. About the cold despair in her fascinating green eyes and the barren tone of her husky voice as she rasped an apology for the horrific act she'd committed.

"Checking on what?" Jeff asked curtly, resting a page facedown on his desk, continuing on to peruse the next. Jeff's abruptness had that same anxious tone he'd tasted when the man had given him the job.

Most of the time, Rome highly appreciated Jeff's no-nonsense brusqueness. And even more of the time, he didn't much care what happened past the completion of the job.

But not this time.

"Just curious." Rome tried to inject an appropriate amount of casualness in his attitude. "What happened to the woman?"

"We're taking care of her," Jeff answered in his normal cold monotone as he read.

Not good. Not good at all. Rome knew exactly how they took care of people where there were no prying eyes of official intelligence and even less accountability. Down here you did what you had to do to get what you needed from your captives and your methods were your own.

It was what he'd been afraid of since an hour after he'd left her here three days ago. And really, what had he expected? He'd washed his hands of her once he saw what she was capable of. As confident in his skills as he was, Rome knew he couldn't handle anything with that kind of power. He'd watched her kill eight men with it. He knew in that intense moment why Jeff had wanted her dead or alive. She was dangerous.

But she was also a vulnerable and broken woman. And alone. He could not forget how the doubtful look on her lovely face changed into hesitant belief at his condo. Belief in him. He'd asked her to trust him and she had. In return, he'd brought her to this hellacious place. He'd had to once he'd seen what she could do. Even if his instincts screamed otherwise.

It was the worst damn no-win situation he'd ever been in. There was no good choice for him. No lesser of two evils because both choices were equally nasty in their own hideous ways.

Yet he couldn't stay away for another minute. He needed to see her. To be sure he'd done the right thing.

"Can I observe?" Rome added a detached note of interest to his voice.

That got Jeff's attention. His boss didn't look up, but he stopped reading. Rome knew it was unusual that he was even here, let alone wanting to take a peek, but he had to make sure Harper was okay. She brought out his protective instinct. She touched something deep inside him and he needed to find out what it was and why.

"No." Jeff's reply was definite. No room for negotiation. But that had never stopped Rome before.

"C'mon, Jeff." Rome chuckled, adding a smirk for good measure. "It's been a while." True. He hadn't been down there for some time, with the exception of the order to find Harper a few days ago.

"We're taking care of her," Jeff repeated with a stern and direct stare, leaning back in his chair, his full concentration on Rome now. Finally.

"Fine." Rome returned the chilled stare with one of his own, treading carefully, not wanting to give Jeff any reason to be suspicious. He wasn't sure at all that Jeff was being straight with him, either. Something in the way he was responding was prickling Rome's instincts. And not in a good way. "Any more jobs?"

"No," Jeff replied, giving Rome a narrowed look and straightening his navy striped tie before turning his attention back to his all-important papers, ending their brief discussion.

Brief but informative. Jeff fully believed in letting you know only what he thought you needed to know. Working with him over the years had taught Rome a great deal about learning to figure out what wasn't being said by what little was said.

The repeated "we're taking care of her" meant she was still in the facility. The adamant refusal to let him observe meant they were still working on her. And the firm disinclination to even discuss it with Rome meant Jeff was having a hard time getting what he wanted from her.

So Harper was out-toughing Jeff. Rome had to fight to keep a smile off his face, thinking about her gumption and strength. He could count on one hand the number of people who were able to outlast Jeff's "care." Being aware of Jeff's methods, Rome knew that was an extraordinarily impressive feat. And the same knowledge also made him cringe deep down.

But now he could do something about it. Now, through Jeff's noninformation, Rome knew the level of security he'd have to go through to get to her.

And he *would* get to her. Otherwise he'd go crazy. Well, crazier than he'd been without her.

"Later, boss," Rome said with a wave, halfway out the door. Jeff grunted without looking up from his reading. Yes, the man was definitely on edge. Rome shook his head and ambled down the hallway that looked like every other drab hallway in the place.

His destination was the bottom floor, which housed the idiotically dubbed "romper rooms." Also known as the rooms decorated wall to wall with torture and experimental equipment. Rome quickened his steps at the thought of Harper down there.

And he'd put her there.

The cool halls were empty, as were the rough stairwells. There were no elevators and very little electronics. Basically it was a cross between a crude basement and a rustic cave. No surveillance, either. No one could get in or out of the facility unless you knew how, so once inside you were trapped. Besides, they didn't want any superfluous accounts of what went on inside.

Finally reaching the last step, Rome took a right turn and faced a solid gray door. He stuck his master key in the dead bolt, turned the knob, and walked in. The lighting was very sparse and very synthetic. He couldn't understand the handful of folks who worked here every day and night. He'd go crazy without fresh air and sunlight, even if it was watery northwest sunlight.

After a few long steps down the corridor, he stopped at a good-sized room. The light was brighter here, and he easily found the person he needed peering at the screen attached to a bulky machine. The display cast a bluish tint to Dr. Andy's face.

Dr. Andy—a doctor of what, Rome wasn't sure—managed everything in the romper room. Read all the data that was extracted. Processed any samples taken. Administered who knew what. Made decisions about methods. Jeff was the boss and directed everything that happened. But down there, Dr. Andy saw that the orders were carried out.

"Hey, Doc." Rome's voice boomed across the open space, and he held back a smile when the startled Dr. Andy jolted forward face-first into the monitor.

"Agent Lucian," she murmured, pushing up the thick-rimmed glasses that had fallen down her diminutive nose. Dr. Andrea "Andy" O'Brien pulled herself to her full height, which was still a good foot shorter than his, as he sidled up next to her, trying to look at anything that would clue him in about Harper. "What can I do for you?"

"Just checking in." Rome glanced around, but didn't see anything except Dr. Andy's myriad of scattered Diet Dr Pepper cans and a bag of Oreos, half of which were gone, the crumbs left everywhere. "How's my favorite gal?"

Blushing and mumbling something, she swung away from him and grabbed one of the aluminum cans. She took a long swallow, refusing to meet his eyes. She was always a little nervous around him, which surprised him, considering her chilling job. He rarely visited and even more rarely stopped to chat with the doctor when he did. Truth be told, she creeped him out a little, but he'd never let on.

"So, what's with the woman I brought in the other day?" He turned on the charm, but knew not to underestimate her. Dr. Andy appeared as a shy mouse, but underneath she was a cunning predator. Her intelligence was limitless and she knew how to get what Jeff wanted, one way or another, no matter how long it took.

She gave him an inquiring look, raising her reddish eyebrows. He knew it was unlike him to ask, but not unheard of. He had followed up a time or two.

"She has something inside her," Dr. Andy answered vaguely. "Something giving her an unusual power."

He already knew that. He also knew that she wasn't telling him the whole story. "Really." Rome feigned casualness. "Any idea what it is or how she got it?"

"Not yet," she answered, and stacked some papers mechanically. Then she smiled that eerie smile she got when she encountered a particularly difficult challenge. One she loved to conquer. "But soon."

"Well, you mind if I take a peek?" He gestured to the row of small flat-screen monitors that showed video of each holding cell for observation.

"Go ahead." She waved her hand and then brushed it through her short red curls, bouncing them around like a nine-year-old.

"Thanks, doll." Rome winked and gave her a sexy grin as he sauntered over to the monitor bank. He watched her return to the big machine she'd been viewing when he'd first walked in, her face reddening even more.

The screens were on, yet all completely dark. No shadows or anything. Adjusting them to infrared, the pictures revealed two ethereal red-hued figures. Two captives today.

"She's in B, monitor two," Dr. Andy supplied from across the room. Giving her a sideways glance, he saw she wasn't even looking at him. Creepy.

Rome peered at monitor two, disregarding the larger figure on monitor six who was lying flat on the floor. The specter of Harper was hunched, unmoving, in the far right corner of the square room. She couldn't have looked more alone. He tweaked the monitor controls a tad, morphing the shimmering infrared visual to a sharper night-vision display. Ghostly green and gray instead of red, but now he was able to focus in on her closely.

He gritted his teeth in anger at seeing the raw anguish in every short breath Harper took. Still wearing her jeans and T-shirt, she had undoubtedly been subjected to some of Dr. Andy's most creative "treatments." Seldom was the damage visible on the flesh, but the signs were in the tentative angle in which Harper held her arms as they hugged her body close, and the slight, intermittent twitching of her body. She probably didn't even know she was doing it.

Balling his fists, knuckles white, he suppressed his rage and resentment. He'd done this. He'd brought her here. But he thought he'd been doing the right thing.

She was dangerous; that was a hard fact. But what happened to make her that way? What was she caught up in? She'd purposefully killed those men, but then she'd apologized for it as though she couldn't help herself. Remorseful, as if she really was a victim. Rome wanted to kick his own ass. He cursed himself every way and sideways for bringing her in. Even if it was his damned duty.

"She's a toughie." Dr. Andy's impassive voice floated from across the room. He looked over his shoulder to see her fiddling with some glass tubes of blood from a little wooden rack. Yuck. He'd spilled more than his share of blood, but to see it sitting there like a thin glass of runny tomato juice . . . yuck.

"Yeah, I bet." He forced his voice to sound controlled, when all he wanted to do was tear apart the office. He had to see Harper. To tell her . . . what?

What exactly would he say? *Sorry I brought you in to be tortured and experimented on even though I promised I wouldn't. But hey, you freaked me out.*

Damn it all. He had to get her out of there.

"When's her next session?" He almost choked on the word, but kept his tone light.

"One hour and thirty-three minutes," the doc replied after consulting her giant analog watch.

"Taking her to the rumble seat?" he asked. The torture chair was usually only for the most reticent of their captives.

"No, off-site today," she answered with a spine-chilling smile, pulling out some clean test tubes and a couple of long syringes.

Off-site? That could mean only one thing: Harper was being given one last chance to come clean and produce the results Jeff expected. Off-site could be anywhere, but the subjects never came back.

Rome decided he'd nab her then. He'd be at the door when the transport occurred and somehow break her out. Otherwise, she was dead.

"Great." Rome drew the word out and gave Dr. Andy

a big toothy grin. She matched it with one of her own. Creepy. "Later." He gave her a pat on her skinny shoulder and walked to the door. Waving back to her as he stepped out into the dim hallway, he started to plan how he'd save Harper and where to take her.

He could swipe Harper—of that he had no doubt. But then what? If he did this, he would really be at war with Jeff. Somehow, his boss would find out Rome was responsible. He always did. Was Harper really worth going against Jeff? Going against his job? His duty?

Rome was no closer to finding out what her story was. In fact, it was even more convoluted than when he'd asked her to trust him. Double damn. He was going crazy. Over a damn woman he knew next to nothing about.

But that wasn't completely true. He knew Harper was full of courage and incredibly loyal. Smart and resilient with unwavering conviction. She also possessed a natural athletic strength and an innate confidence that he found amazingly attractive for some reason he couldn't fathom.

And her eyes. The emerald color of the greenest sea he'd ever seen complemented that sun-kissed hair.

He had to get her out. To help her figure out what was happening to her. What had happened to her brother. And how this all related to Jeff.

Because he couldn't shake the thought that his boss was up to no good. Even if Harper never trusted him again, she could help him get to the bottom of this.

His job was to fight evil. To protect those who couldn't help themselves. It was his duty to do the right thing for the greater good. He just needed to figure out exactly what that was. And at the moment, he felt a deep and inexplicable pull toward Harper.

He'd told her he had an instinct about her, and that was the truth. An instinct that told him she needed his help. Two years ago, he hadn't listened to his gut, and people had died because of it. He'd sworn never to let that happen again.

And yet, he'd once again gone against his instincts. This time, with Harper. He'd been afraid of what he saw and brought her here, maybe at the cost of her life.

No, he would not pay that price. Not again. Not with Harper. She was worth it. He knew it. He felt it deep down in his soul.

Glancing at his watch, Rome reached the door that led to the safe outside. He had a little over an hour to figure out how to snatch Harper during transport and remain anonymous in the process.

No problem. He'd been in tighter positions before. He'd find a way to get it done. He'd find a way to make it right with Harper. And this time he would help her find answers. No matter what.

The thick, solid door opened, momentarily blinding Harper as she was pulled through it. Her instinct was to shield her eyes, but she was unable to move her bound hands in their cold clamps.

Squeezing her eyes shut against the bright sunlight, she couldn't hold back the smile that broke across her face at the wash of natural light bathing her weary body.

Opening her eyes a fraction, Harper glanced at the open area they were walking across. The wide blacktop space was surrounded by tall gray concrete walls with high girders slicing through the sky. The sun beat through the concrete beams, creating a natural stripe of welcome rays.

The huge rectangular parking lot was nearly empty. At the far end was a black vehicle, similar to a UPS delivery truck. Only she was sure no promising packages waited inside. She took several deep breaths of the cleansing air.

Just a minute before, when climbing the stairs to the outside, each step she'd taken radiated agony through every corner of her body. But now each pass through the sunshine rejuvenated her, like a dormant flower tasting the first kiss of spring. Wherever the sun traced her skin, her body tingled as if her blood was awakening. Stirring to life again. Rousing her mind.

The pain receded when they moved into the full sunlight. Her mind reveled in the glorious feeling of the natural radiance. A surge of electrifying energy pulsed through her veins, leaving invigorating trails in every fiber.

Approaching the truck, Harper tested her hunger for the power she'd missed the last few days while confined in the cold darkness.

She concentrated on her bindings, closed her eyes, and in her mind saw the clamps break apart. Her head whirled with the rush of ice and heat. A shiver of burning energy passed from her brain through her shoulders, and then shot down her arms to her wrists. She looked down and saw the clamps fracture and fall to the ground with a heavy clank.

Harper raised her hands, full of awe and surprise at her success. She'd controlled it. She had actually controlled it. And she hadn't passed out.

All six of the huge guys stared at her. Though not with the terrified shock everyone had before. Curiosity with a hint of challenge colored their expressions. She wasn't sure what that meant, but she wasn't about to stay and find out.

This was her chance to bolt. Her power, or whatever it was, seemed to be working again. She wasn't about to waste time questioning that or the lack of horror in these guys.

Summoning the energy force again, Harper spread her arms and focused on driving her captors back so she could escape. Prickles of power sparked under her skin as she called upon the energy force flowing eagerly through her body.

A cold rush, then a hot charge blazed within her and she forced a clear wave of energy to surge forward toward the waiting men, seeing the air ripple from the pulse. She watched, mesmerized as the two men in the forefront raised their hands and somehow halted her surge with a filmy current of their own.

Just like her.

A whoosh of displaced air rushed over them as their forces canceled each other out.

Well, that was a new one. The hulky men looked as stunned as she felt. They all stared at the empty space between them as if it would provide the answer.

Now a little drained, Harper caught their eyes and smiled at them with a shrug. And then ran as fast as she could.

She saw a gate just beyond the front of the truck and headed straight for it. Footsteps thundered. A tackle from behind knocked the air from her lungs just as she reached the gate. The momentum carried her and the men on top of her through the wired gateway.

Tumbling onto the ground, she kicked and punched wildly. She heard grunts and thuds as she was able to connect on some of the blows. A clinking noise caught her attention. They were trying to wrestle her into another pair of clamps.

Twisting in their grasp, Harper ended up facedown on the hard ground. Raising her head, she peeked at the surrounding area, checking it out. An alley. Squirming and striking, her darting gaze fell on an unforgettable face tucked behind a rusted green Dumpster.

Rome.

Fury consumed her. It was his fault she was here. She'd killed those men at Bobby's to protect him, and he'd betrayed her.

Harper grasped on to her rage with her mind. Focused on it. Thirsted for it. Her body vibrated as power pulsed through every fiber. With a wail, she bucked with power and once again hurled a crushing wave from her mind. The heavy bodies pitched away from her through the air and she was free.

Harper's vision blurred, and she felt a prickly detachment as she began to fade from consciousness. No. She was going to pass out again.

The Dumpster where she thought she'd spied Rome had been hurled against the graffiti-stained brick wall. Warped and creaking. Could she have crushed him? Her mind reeled.

Fiercely fighting the roiling of her mind and her heart, she struggled to scrape her exhausted body from the hard pavement. The sunlight beat down on her, seeping into her skin, charging her blood.

Feeling a boost of strength, she dragged herself up and staggered forward, shooting a look over her shoulder at the prone men. They were stunned, but beginning to get back up.

She hadn't killed them? No, all six were standing now. They weren't dead. And they had a power similar to hers. What the heck was going on here? Though, where her stronger power surges were clear and barely perceptible, theirs were tinged with a filmy coating, like pure water versus soapy water.

Stumbling away from them, Harper's head began to swim. All she was finding were more and more questions instead of answers.

But right now, she was losing it. Not much longer and she'd pass out again. Fear encompassed her, blurring her sight. She didn't know whether she could handle captivity again. She didn't want to find out.

Shaking her head, she began to run, but stopped as a black streak filled her vision, accompanied by the screech of tires.

"Get in!" a deep voice commanded from the open passenger-side window.

She paused.

"Harper. Get in. Now!" Rome? He was alive? "Trust me."

Hesitation. He was alive. Thank the stars. But he'd betrayed her and now he was here to help? Again? She glanced over her shoulder. Her tunneling vision showed fuzzy, bulky figures racing toward her. She swung back around to face Rome, both hands braced against the vehicle.

"Harper, please." It was indeed Rome. That much she could tell.

At this point, she wasn't above accepting his help without trusting him. So she hauled herself in the vehicle and clumsily pulled the door shut as the car sped away, tires squealing. Gunshots rang out, but sounded hollow and far away to her ears.

She tried to focus on the rugged profile of the man she'd trusted. The man who had let her down. The man who now reached over and grasped her clammy hand in his strong one. And she'd almost killed him.

"Don't worry, Harper," he was saying, but he sounded far off. "It'll be all right."

Would it? Would anything ever be all right? She sincerely doubted it. But it was nice anyway, given those were the last words she heard before embracing the darkness of an unconscious oblivion.

CHAPTER SEVEN

Jeff reread Dr. Andy's report again. He simply could not reconcile the words and charts that covered the pages with the woman they depicted.

Harper Kane. She was one tough bitch.

When he'd first heard about the incident at the train yards, a rare excitement had overtaken him. Though he'd lost some good men, the sheer power unleashed upon them was immeasurable.

And that power was exactly what he'd been striving for.

Somehow, Ms. Kane had gotten her hands on the pure serum and used it. The pure serum that had evaded him. Her damned scientist brother must have given it to her before he destroyed his own lab and all remnants of his research. The details were still a tad sketchy, but the fact was the pure formula pumped through her much-too-healthy body.

The pure formula that was proving very difficult to replicate. Jeff had yet to be successful in reproducing the serum Dr. Kane had used on his precious plants.

Something was missing. Something that Harper Kane possessed. Something she'd refused to give him.

She was damn tough. Everything he'd had Dr. Andy expose her to had failed to produce acceptable results.

Every extraction of blood had given him nothing. Plus she refused to utter a single word and barely screamed when subjected to his most inventive interrogation drugs. Drugs that had made experienced and trained men twice her impressive size break like dried twigs. It was as though Harper Kane were impenetrable.

And according to Dr. Andy's reports, she was.

A loud smack vibrated through the quiet of his office as he slammed the papers on the top of his desk. Resting a fist against his mouth, Jeff thought hard about the decision he'd made just before Rome's impromptu and unusual visit. To move Harper was risky. He wasn't sure what to expect from her. But he had to take the chance. He wanted more intensive and invasive experiments. The larger lab facility was better equipped for the comprehensive trials and dissections he intended for her.

Jeff needed to find the serum inside her and wring out the elusive formula. His project depended on it. And this project meant everything. Not just to him, but to the future. Dr. Robert Kane hadn't understood that. So the brilliant doctor had been taken care of.

But now the doctor's sister was in the way. And, in time, she'd be taken care of, too.

A harsh knock on his door brought him out of his thoughts.

"Yes," Jeff called out, picking up the reports to read over once more.

"Sir." One of his brawny subjects stepped through the doorway. Jeff narrowed his eyes at the man's dingy appearance. He looked as though he'd been in a tussle. "She got away."

Jeff shot to his feet and threw his papers against the wall. He stalked toward the man and grabbed his shirt.

"Find her," Jeff growled, less than an inch from the

man's face, and then shoved him out the door. The brute lumbered down the cold hallway, barking out orders into his shoulder mike.

How in the hell did she escape? Had her powers returned? Even once outside, they shouldn't have worked so quickly.

Did she have help? Jeff thought hard. No, everyone in this facility was more than loyal. He'd made sure of that long ago. But then, there had been someone else here, not that long ago.

Rome Lucian.

No. Rome was bound by duty. Jeff knew too well what horror the agent had gone through with his team several years ago. The man was dutiful to a fault.

Yet Rome had just been here. Asking about Ms. Kane. Could the agent have had a hand in her escape? Jeff didn't want to believe it. Rome could complicate his plans for the serum, especially if he was helping the bitch.

Jeff shook his head and rubbed a hand over his face. He had a hard time thinking of Rome as a rogue agent, but this project was bigger than one agent. And one challenging woman.

He'd have to be wary of Agent Rome Lucian from now on. Just in case.

She heard a gurgling rumble as consciousness returned. The rolling and sputtering forced her eyes open, and she blinked, then took in her surroundings. She was in a car. A very loud car. The jumbling ride reminded her of the old red Volkswagen Bug Bobby had when he was in high school. The curved, dotted ceiling and the rounded rear window confirmed it. She was indeed in a Bug.

Flexing her arms, Harper pushed her weary body up

to take a peek out the elliptical side window. Dusk appeared to be approaching. They were driving through a quiet suburban area. Wait. They?

Disorientation flushed through her. Hadn't Rome come to her rescue in his Land Rover?

"Stay down," Rome's familiar deep voice filtered from the driver's seat directly in front of her. "We're almost there."

"Where's there?" she asked hesitantly, her voice scratchy from inactivity. Did it really matter? He could be taking her anywhere. Maybe to an even more ghastly place than before. But right now, this minute, she had a reprieve.

"I have a place just outside of town," Rome answered, rounding a corner. She slid a little on the slippery vinyl of the backseat. "A safe house of mine."

Safe. That sounded absolutely blissful. And highly unlikely. But what choice did she have? She had gotten in the car with him, after all. She'd have to trust him for now. Darn it.

"You passed out," he offered quietly. "I switched cars, just in case." She appreciated his keeping her in the loop.

Another ten minutes and they were just on the outskirts of Portland when Rome turned the car into an unfamiliar private warehouse area. Harper peeked out the back side window as soon as they slowed down to wait for the gate to glide open. Rome weaved the Bug around several of the buildings to one in the back that bordered a wooded area. The metal door of the midsized structure slid aside just enough to allow him to maneuver inside. She watched out the oval back window as the door skated shut with a loud, ringing *clank*.

Rome slipped out the driver's side and walked over to

a panel on the wall and punched some of the buttons. Lights illuminated the area, and a red light flickered on the little plate.

He came around to the passenger-side door and opened it. He reached down to pull the seat lever and moved the seat forward, gesturing with the sweep of his hand for her to get out.

Harper unfolded her long frame from the cramped backseat of the Bug. Stiff and achy, she stumbled a little as she crawled out. She felt Rome's sure grip on her arm steadying her.

Murmuring her gratitude, she stretched out a little, hearing several pops and cracks. Grimacing, she glanced at Rome and saw a gentle smile crease his rugged face. She gave him a small smile in return, and then turned away to study her newest confinement. Goodness gracious. How many resources did an agent have?

"C'mon, Harper." He placed a large warm hand on her shoulder. "Let's get you cleaned up." He tugged on her slightly.

She stared pointedly at the hand on her shoulder and he immediately removed it. Harper saw a pained look of remorse cross his face, quickly replaced by a reassuring one. Good. He should feel guilty about locking her away like some psychotic freak. She knew she had big problems and had done some terrible things, but she hadn't needed him to dupe her into trusting him and then treating her like enemy number one.

"Harper, you're safe here. Trust me," Rome implored.

"Trust you?" She couldn't stop the burst of laughter, but she wished she had when she started to cough a little. "You turned me in."

He nodded as his hand started to rub soothing circles

on her back. Harper wanted to punch him and sink into his comfort all at once, but held herself in check. Until she knew what he wanted and what he was going to do to her now, she had to be on her guard.

"Look, I know you hate my guts right now." Rome met her eyes. "I know you think you can't trust me. Hell, I wouldn't trust me." He removed his hand from her back to swipe it across his face, frustrated. She missed his touch. "But, Harper, give me a chance to explain. To convince you I'm on your side."

She looked away, but turned her gaze back when his fingers brushed her jaw with a touch so light, she might have thought she'd dreamed it.

"Please?" he asked quietly. Goodness, he was intoxicating.

"I guess I owe you for the ride," Harper whispered, wishing she'd made a different decision back at Bobby's house and not used her power.

"You don't owe me anything." His voice rang with self-disgust. "Please, Harper."

Well, it couldn't hurt.

"All right." She allowed him to take her hand and lead her deeper into the square building. She didn't have much choice, and realized she didn't want one. So much had happened recently, she didn't want to think about much of anything right now.

There were many things worth noticing as she followed Rome. Though crude, the one-floor warehouse had several rooms and cavernous ceilings. Some were finished, but most were just encased by bare two-by-fours, making it feel as if she were walking through a wooden jungle.

One half-completed room they passed sported a flat-screen television with a PlayStation 3 hooked up to it. A video-game nerd herself, she decided she wanted to poke around in there later.

Spying the modest stack of video games prompted her to realize that she was supposed to be returning home to California to resume her training and getting back to her job soon. Her coach, and maybe even her boss, would call when she didn't show up. And she had no idea where her cell phone or her backpack were. Probably in the hands of the jerks who tortured her.

But there was no way she could go back to her normal life now. At least not until this was all over. If it ever would be. A cold wash of loss rained over her. She really had nothing.

With great effort, she shook the morose thoughts from her mind and resumed her attention to her surroundings.

Moving down the rough hallway, the next space had a humongous bed that looked cheerfully lumpy with goose-down quilts. A little farther in, the area opened wide like a great room with a kitchen and another big flat-screen television in front of three huge rust-colored beanbag chairs. A tacky yellow and red striped couch was at an angle to the television behind a low, chunky wooden table. The place looked to be a work in progress. It wasn't musty or dingy, just unused and unfinished.

"There's a bathroom through there." Rome pointed to a smaller area just to the side of the kitchen. The only room with a door. "I'll get some towels." She watched him move toward a far closet as she headed to the idyllic room with a shower.

And what a shower it was. It was at least as big as her whole bathroom in her little studio apartment in San Francisco. A double-headed shower in a waist-high tiled rectangle. She sighed out loud in enchanted anticipation.

She pushed the door shut, leaving it open just a crack. She peeled off her grungy T-shirt and bra and tossed them aside, then reached in to twist the spigots on each side to steamy-hot.

A knock sounded before the door opened wide. Looking over her shoulder, she saw Rome standing there with his arms full of fluffy foam green towels, his mouth agape. His blue eyes darkened to the color of midnight as they swept down her naked torso.

"Harper." Her name was spoken with a raspy breath of regret and desire. "I am so, so sorry." He set down the towels and a new box of bar soap on the freestanding wooden towel rack and moved to stand within a breath of her. A whisper of a touch caressed her skin as his fingertips glided gently down her back. Peering over her shoulder, she followed the trail of his hand.

She knew she shouldn't be shocked to see the angry red marks there; after all, she'd experienced every single one. But to see them in the bright light of the gleaming white bathroom was daunting. Also a little scary that they weren't as bad as she would have thought.

She watched him while he continued to run his fingers softly over her back. His face was a kaleidoscope of emotion. Sorrow. Shame. Compassion. Fury. And, finally, determination. Then his face cleared and his gaze snapped to hers.

"Take as long as you need," he said quietly, turning away. He picked up the box of soap, opened it, and set the fresh bar on top of the pile of towels. "I'll fix us something to eat." He shut the door gently as he left.

Hot steam clouded the room while Harper removed the rest of her grubby clothes. She briefly wondered whether Rome knew just how expressive his face could be. Probably not. He was a supersecret government agent or something. They weren't supposed to have facial expressions, right?

Stepping around the shower's tiled wall, she was enveloped by the cascading hot spray from both showerheads. She was a tad surprised at his affinity for double-headed showers. It was a luxury she definitely wasn't used to. But she sure wasn't complaining.

It was absolute ecstasy.

The lavish fall of water seeped warmth into every inch of her skin, soothing and healing the plentiful aches she knew were there and some she hadn't known existed. The pain of the last few days slowly ebbed away under the restorative tide, spiraling down the drain.

She brought the bar of soap to her nose. Spicy and clean. Just like Rome. She was surprised when a low growl came from her throat at the thought of his scent.

Shaking it aside, Harper lathered a generous froth over her entire body. The thorough cleansing stung in a few places, but it was a small price to pay for the fresh feeling it created. Invigorating, really. She ran the bar through her hair several times, watching the soapy bubble rinse down the drain, relishing the feeling of grime sliding out of the blonde mop.

After she'd scrubbed herself off, she simply let the water flow over her, enjoying the clean and tranquil sensation, trying to stamp it into her memory just in case it was a while before she'd feel it again.

Harper reluctantly turned the water off on one side, then the other. The thick steam embraced her, caressing her dripping skin as she picked up the downy towel Rome had left for her. Drying herself thoroughly, she wrapped the thick fabric around her body and opened the door.

She spied Rome standing at the stove. Moving into

the kitchen, the inviting aroma of eggs invaded her senses. A small smile broke out as she moved closer, spotting a heaping pile of shredded cheddar cheese and an open package of Canadian bacon on the counter, chopped into little chunks. He was making an omelet. And it smelled like paradise. The spatula looked odd in his large hand, but he capably flipped around the pan's steaming and crackling contents.

"That smells wonderful," Harper purred, leaning her toweled hip against the white tiled counter.

Rome swung his head to stare at her. His intense gaze raked across her bare shoulders, then down the towel to her thighs and back up. The swirling blue gaze virtually stripped the towel right off her freshly scrubbed body. The air between them sizzled with desire. She knew the feeling. There was something inexplicably hot about a manly man cooking.

"Uh, um . . ." He blinked and cleared his throat. "This'll be ready in a minute." He shook his head and turned his attention back to the steaming pan. "I set out some clothes for you in the bedroom. We can throw yours in the washer later." He gave her a rueful sideways glance. "Again."

Rapping her knuckles on the counter, she nodded with a smile and walked toward the room with the big bed. Spread out on top of the comforter were a pair of well-worn gray sweatpants and a soft cotton T-shirt. The black T sported a faded green and gold Minnesota North Stars emblem on the chest that just screamed Rome. She hardly knew him, but somehow, it was right. She tossed the towel on the floor and pulled on the clothes—his clothes. The fit was large, but comfy from wear.

Harper bent to pick up the towel and saw a pair of

thick, gray wool socks on the bed as well. Donning them, she relished the cozy, cushy feel as she padded to the bathroom to spread the towel on the wooden rack. She then returned to the kitchen to see Rome setting full plates on the wooden table in front of the television. He then brought out two frosty bottles of water, setting them on coasters.

Smiling at the strange thought of a man using coasters, she sank into the nearest beanbag chair and grabbed one of the steaming plates, along with one of the nearby forks. The cheesy omelet tasted even better than it looked and smelled as she took the first scrumptious bite. It simply melted in her mouth.

"Mmm." Harper couldn't help the moan that escaped. "Good." She shoved another forkful into her watering mouth.

"Cooking's kind of a hobby of mine," Rome said through his own mouthful. "But don't tell anyone." He lowered his voice and gave her a mock severe look. And added a killer wink.

"My lips are sealed." She brought her fingers up to her mouth, mimicking the turning of a lock and key. Then she frowned. "Well, they're sealed after I finish eating." She gave him a playful wink back and smiled at his reactive grin.

So, he cooked. Something she was admittedly lousy at. Most everyone had a hobby. She thought his would be fixing motorbikes or snowboarding. Something rough and tough. But it was also somehow fitting that a strong, confident man like him would cook. Actual food, no less, not just reheated premade stuff. His joking about keeping it a secret was for show. He had a confidence in everything he did. And he did eggs very well.

Harper finished her omelet in silence and then studied Rome while she crunched on a piece of cinnamon-sugar toast. His muscles were tensed, as if he was upset and wanted nothing but to spring away from there. He was wearing jeans and a black T-shirt, which she was beginning to think was his usual garb. The shirt hugged his chest and shoulders like a second skin. Corded muscles flexed along his forearms as he consumed his meal. His jaw sported dark stubble and his close-cropped hair looked a tad mussed. Rugged and sexy. Like her own personal model for the annual firemen's calendar. Being able to look at him was the one bright spot in this whole thing right now.

As if sensing her gaze, he took a deep breath, but kept his eyes on his own plate.

"I didn't know they'd hurt you," he said quietly. "I mean, I did. I know exactly what they do there, but I . . ." His voice trailed off and he took another bite. His jaw was hard with tension as he chomped hard. She watched him swallow and sigh heavily through his nose. "I didn't know what to do, Harper. Your power—or whatever it is—it's like nothing I'd ever seen. It scared me." He took another deep breath and unleashed his blue gaze upon her. "I'm so very sorry."

Sitting there, enraptured by him, Harper had no idea what to say. *It's okay?* No, it wasn't. He'd betrayed her. He'd just admitted it. As alone as she was now, that wasn't something she could just forget. She took the last bite of her toast and set her plate down on the wooden table with a slight thud.

"You said to trust you," she said softly, squinting with the aching thought. "Then you turned on me." She watched him wince ever so slightly.

"You should have told me," he countered.

"It shouldn't have mattered," she shot back. He

whipped his glance away from her. Trust was trust. Wasn't it?

"You still should have told me," Rome persisted, turning back to her. A puzzled look crossed his face. "How can you do . . . that?" He wiggled his hand around, obviously referring to her power.

"I don't really know," Harper answered, leaning back into the chair. Its tiny foam balls wrapped around her nicely, as if she were sitting in a cloud. "Bobby left me a syringe of something. Some kind of serum." She could practically hear her brother's last words. "The men who killed Bobby tracked me down. We fought and the serum was injected into my arm by accident." She could practically feel the intense fire racing in her head to consume her mind. See the fierce energy surge through the air toward the men. Killing them in less than an instant. "Right after that, I felt this power run through my body. It made my mind burn. And I killed them. Just like you saw at Bobby's house."

She kept her weary gaze on him, hoping he didn't see her as some monster. She still hated that he'd betrayed her trust, but she didn't hate him. In fact, she rather liked him. More than she knew she should. But she wasn't sure she could ever trust him again.

"I never believed you were dangerous," Rome finally said after a moment of soaking in her words. He clenched his jaw, a sign of tension she was coming to recognize. "Then I saw what you could do. You tore up that room. Killed those men. With some kind of semi-invisible force that came from your body." He shook his head slowly and faced her once more. "That's dangerous."

Tightening her lips, she vividly recalled the scene in Bobby's house. The bright sunlight filtering in. The guns pointed at her and Rome. The thought of being captured. She hadn't meant to kill anyone. It made her sick to her stomach. She'd never even thought she was capable of something like that. Heck, every fish she'd ever caught, she'd set free.

But in that moment, just like at the Barracks, she'd come to know what was truly meant by "life or death." It was them or the bad guys.

She'd chosen them.

And he'd chosen the bad guys.

Harper suddenly realized she shouldn't be there. With him. The little respite he'd given her was now over.

"You're right." She shook her head sadly. "I am dangerous." She looked around the room, searching for answers. This afternoon, she was able to control the power somewhat. That was good, right? She wouldn't need his help now. But somehow that made her feel more alone than she ever had in the cold, dark cell. More than his betrayal had. She swung her gaze to meet his unreadable one. "I guess I'd better go. Thank you for helping me escape." She began to wiggle out of the low chair.

"Harper, wait." Rome rested his warm hand on her wrist, halting her antsy movement. "I can't change what I did. I was just doing my job. My duty. You need to understand that." He lifted his hand away from her and shook his head. "But you also need to understand this: There's something about you. Something . . . I don't know. I just know that I want to help you. Help you get your answers." His imploring look captured her completely. He genuinely seemed out of his element. Well, they were on even ground there. "I know I said that before, but you weren't telling me everything. Now I know what you were hiding. And I want to help you. Now more than ever."

"Why?" she asked. "Why do you care so much?" And he did care. The fact that he'd helped her escape and coddled her since were all the evidence she needed. But could she trust him again?

He was right. She hadn't told him everything. A girl had to have some secrets. And she still had one more. One she needed to keep to herself for now, just in case.

"I told you I had an instinct about you." He sighed, rubbing his hand over his head. She remembered him saying that when she was tied up on his couch. "I need to trust that." His gaze became a little unfocused and uneasy. "A couple of years ago, I worked with a team. Three other people. We were supposed to go into a warehouse and steal some contraband weapons. That's all."

She watched him reach to take a sip from his bottled water before he continued, obviously upset, but trying hard to hide it.

"Once we got in," he continued, "we got the weapons, but we also saw the leaders of the smugglers' ring in a meeting. My gut told me to wait and call for backup. Our orders were to only take the weapons. I'd never gone against my instincts, but I did this time because I thought it was too good of an opportunity. So I ordered the attack and my team was killed. I was the only one who survived. My mistake killed them. Since then, I've worked alone, strictly following orders. And I've never doubted my instincts again. Until I turned you in."

"So what does your gut tell you now?" Harper asked, fascinated that he'd open up like that. And at the same time, his honesty touched the part of her that wanted to believe in him again. Believe they could figure this all out together. Yet his betrayal pricked at her like a bee sting.

"It tells me something isn't right." His voice was

troubled. "What's inside of you. What you can do. There's something else going on here."

"What do you mean?" She frowned.

"Those guys at the facility," he started. "I saw you face off against them." She remembered. Her power had been met head-on with theirs. Maybe he was right.

"They were like me," Harper said, watching his face closely. It had surprised her when those men had negated her power with ease and without fear as though they possessed it, too. Maybe she wasn't unique in this mess after all.

"They were like you," he confirmed. "Only different somehow."

"Different?" She was confused now. What exactly did he mean by that?

"I know it sounds crazy, but they just didn't seem, I don't know, as pure as you." Rome smiled and held up his hands in a puzzled gesture. "Their powers were foggy, not clear like yours. It was like looking at dishwater."

She shot him a skeptical look mixed with a smile. What kind of man said "dishwater"?

"Harper, my job is to fight evil. You're not evil. But something out there is, and you're somehow a part of it. I will help you find out why all this is happening to you. Why your brother was killed. I will help you get to the bottom of this. That's my duty."

Harper had to admire his personal code of honor. His loyalty to his duty. Those principles meant something to her. Rome Lucian was just doing what he felt was right. Though she had ended up in a worse than crappy hole for a few days, this man was the real deal. A real live hero. He may have betrayed her, but at least now she could understand why. He believed this was bigger than she was. And after facing those guys today, she believed it, too. Maybe she should consider trusting him again. She really, really wanted to.

"I have something for you," he said, leaning forward and reaching behind him to pull something out of his back pocket.

Her medal. The one that had meant the most to her. The one she'd found tossed aside at Bobby's. Really, the only tangible thing she had from Bobby. Rome must have picked it up and kept it safe.

Rome held it out to her and dropped it in her open palm. A tingle passed through her arm from the thin solid disc, warmed from his body heat. The thoughtful gesture reached deep inside her, tugging at her soul and gently sheathing it with compassion.

It was more than a token act; this was Rome's way of attempting to bridge the chasm of trust between them. Something she imagined he didn't often do.

Closing her fingers around the medal, she thought hard. Could she survive another betrayal from Rome? The only person in the world who claimed to be on her side? The choice was to go this alone in cold solitude or believe in a broken trust.

Harper shook her head slightly. Whereas she cherished his sincere expression of concern, she knew in her heart that she couldn't afford to put her complete trust in him this time. But she also knew she could seriously use his experienced help.

And that was a good enough reason to give this alliance another chance, albeit a cautious one.

"An offer I can't refuse." She gave him a crooked smile, hoping she wouldn't be made sorry yet again. "Thank you."

"No, thank you, Harper." Rome expressed his gratitude with a tender hand squeeze that sent pleasant little tremors through her arm. Then his whole demeanor changed in an instant. The tension filtered away and purpose streamed in. "First of all, I think we have a few days. No one knows about this place. It's my own private safe house. The Bug, too. So we've got some time."

"You won't get in trouble for helping me?" She had to ask. She didn't know much about his world, and what she did know was incredibly cruel. But, as much as she wanted his help, she didn't want his life to follow hers down the pooper.

"They won't know for a little while yet." Rome didn't seem worried. He held up a hand, obviously understanding her concern . "Besides, they won't know it's me with the getaway car. Like I said, the Bug is safe and I know how to cover a trail." She wasn't sure she believed that, but he would know better than her for sure. "And this is what I have to do. It's the right thing to do. If it costs me my job, so be it." His smile was unwavering.

"All right," she conceded, her body releasing a tension she hadn't even known had a hold on her. Now that she had an ally again, she realized she really had no idea what to do. "Where do we start?"

"Let's get comfortable." He gave her a big grin, grabbing their plates and walking toward the kitchen. "Stay put. I'll be right back with dessert."

She watched his retreating rear end, thinking dessert sounded fantastic.

After a gentle shake from Rome, Harper realized she'd dozed off. How long had she been out? A playful pat on the shoulder and a saucy smile later, he'd returned all fresh and showered with a huge bowl of chocolate chip cookie dough. How did he know cookies, raw or cooked, were her weakness? One of the few sweets she allowed herself while training.

Rome set down the bowl, then brought out two tall glasses of unsweetened iced tea. As he flopped down on the other beanbag next to her, he divulged that he'd made both himself. From scratch. And put her clothes and towels in the wash. He was quickly climbing close to perfect on her scale.

"The Five Watch is the group that's after you," Rome said after they'd shared a few spoonfuls from the bowl. "I think."

"You're not sure?" she asked around her own mouthful of gooey rapture.

"It's a small unclassified section of the government that keeps very quiet." He shrugged and ran a hand over his damp hair. The short dark locks were curled from the wetness of his shower. "So quiet, most doubt its existence, but they're around. Everything they do is top secret, unofficial, and unsupervised. From what I know, they do a lot of—how should I put it?—ambiguous research." She watched him watch her carefully, his eyes intense. "Ever heard of them?"

"No, never." Harper licked the spoon clean and delved into the bowl for another tasty chunk. "If it's so secretive, why would I know about it?"

"Your brother's lab was a Five Watch facility," he answered.

"My brother was a good and decent scientist, not some shady cloak-and-dagger operative." She heard her voice turn cold and narrowed her eyes. How dare he accuse her brother of crooked deeds? She felt like dumping the bowl of cookie dough on his head. "He wouldn't, couldn't hurt anyone."

"Whoa, easy. Harper, I'm not saying he was a bad

guy." He held up a hand in a calming motion. "I'm asking if he ever said anything to you about what he did. Or if you ever saw anything."

"I'm sorry, it's just . . ." She backed down a little, consciously trying to relax. Her brother's death was still very raw and the questions surrounding it even more cutting. She cleared her throat. "Bobby rarely talked shop. All I really know is that he experimented with plants. I think." She had to own up to her ignorance.

Honestly, she and Bobby hadn't talked much about his work. All she knew was that he did research for the government and was a genius when it came to vegetation and biology. Maybe she should have been more interested in her brother's career. He had always been involved with her swimming and was at almost every meet. Sadness filled her, knowing that she should have shown more interest in his work.

But right now, his work was all that interested her.

She tried to clear away the sorrow. She knew she needed to buck up and talk this out with Rome.

"Okay." Rome seemed to sense her misery and covered her knee with a comforting hand. "It's okay, Harper. We just need to pool our information. We'll figure this out." He gave her a reassuring smile. Oh, how she wanted to believe him.

"The place I was just at." Harper watched him flinch at her words. "Was that a Five Watch place?"

"No." He shook his head and sucked another bite off his spoon. "It's just a local government branch. My boss is located there."

"That's where you work?" she asked, wanting to know more about what he did.

"I don't have an office," he said wryly. "I just go there to get my orders sometimes." She watched his face as curiosity passed over it. "What do you do for a living?"

"I'm a swimmer." She was thankful to be talking about something normal for a change. "I'm in the middle of training for the Olympic trials. I was just up here for a break."

"Olympics? So you must be really good." Rome seemed genuinely fascinated and impressed, which charmed her to no end.

"I am good," she said with confidence, but knew she was blushing under his admiration. When was the last time she'd done that? It usually took a lot more than a compliment to make her self-conscious. "But to pay the bills, I'm a programmer for a small video-game company."

"Really? Video games?" Rome's face lit up like a Christmas tree. "Cool. Maybe I'll have to take you on in the other room." He wiggled his eyebrows suggestively. Her blush deepened. For crying out loud, she felt like an idiot. He meant the PlayStation. She reached a hand up to try to rub the heat from her cheeks.

With a leer, Rome reached forward and picked up the bowl. He used his spoon to scrape the last bits of raw dough. A big hunk clung to the utensil. They both stared at it. She caught him looking at her inquiringly.

"Split it?" he asked in a friendly tone. Thank goodness he offered. She could eat another bowl by herself.

"Absolutely." She smiled back and held out her spoon for a scrape.

Harper just about moaned when he put the spoonful in his mouth and sucked off half of the dough. He then passed the spoon to her, picked up his iced tea, and leaned back, just watching her, spinning the ice around in his glass.

Keeping her gaze on him, she licked the last of the dough off the spoon, imagining the taste of him as she swallowed.

Holy cow. With that one innocently simple, yet un-expectedly provocative act, the festering aches in her body gently drifted away, like a riptide brushing the shore, gently pulling her grief along for the ride.

She was certainly no stranger to the art of flirting. She'd had her share of men. More than her share, Bobby used to say. But never a serious relationship. They were way too messy. Nonetheless, she hadn't ever lacked for companionship. In her experience, guys loved no-strings-attached girls, and she took willful advantage of that.

But Rome was a different kind of guy altogether. He was a man in every sense of the word. Hard and intense. And the way he purred the r's in her name made her want to crawl into his lap. Made her want to get to know him. To find out things about him, such as why this tougher-than-nails government agent liked to cook.

The inclination was a first for her and one she was surprised to find she wanted to pursue despite the gloomy circumstances. It just figured that her timing would be so bad. As much as she didn't trust him, she sure was fascinated by the man.

"More tea?" Rome's rumbling voice drew her out of her musings.

"Sure, thank you," she answered. After her recent thoughts, she was feeling a little parched.

A wide smile creased his strong face and he stood, taking the bowl and their empty glasses with him. She couldn't help watching him saunter to the kitchen. His worn jeans hugged his hard body close enough for her to easily see the muscles in his thighs shifting underneath the fabric. And his taut rear practically called to her just before it slipped behind the open refrigerator door.

Harper decided she needed to move around. Maybe

she should indulge herself with a battle in the PlayStation room. Something as normal as a video game might take her mind off of her unreal situation and her budding attraction to Rome. She was with him for his tactical expertise, not his sexy tushie.

"I think I will take you on in the other room," she said to him as she walked into the kitchen, clasping her hands together and stretching her arms behind her head, drawing the cotton fabric of the T-shirt snugly across her breasts.

The Tupperware pitcher dropped from his hand and bounced on the hard floor, coming to rest on its side as tea gushed out the open top. She shifted her gaze from the spill to his face. Liquid blue eyes stared at her with an intensity that burned a trail from her raised arms down her shoulders to her stretched-out chest and then to her face, which reddened under his blatant appreciative scrutiny. Dropping her arms, she crossed them tightly and turned her attention back to the floor.

"Do you have a towel or something?" she asked, hearing a huskiness in her voice as she nodded toward the floor. His gaze must have also burned her throat.

"Um, yeah, um." Rome's tone was low and gravelly as well. "Um, no. Go ahead and pick out one of the games." He raked his hand across his head, ruffling his damp hair. "I'll clean this up and meet you in there."

Good idea. She nodded slowly and headed toward the other room, away from the heated kitchen.

Harper stepped into the room with the PlayStation 3 and perused the stack of games piled on the table against the semifinished wall, absently turning on the game console along with the television.

Rome had the standard sports and shooter games.

The ice hockey looked fun, but considering the T-shirt she was wearing, she'd figured Rome was a hockey fan and probably an expert. Not her game. She knew from personal experience that hockey players were definitely hotties. After all, she'd gone to a few San Jose Sharks games back home. But she liked the idea of being under the water, not skating on it. Plus, she wanted to win. So she picked out a popular football game instead and stuck in the disc.

There. Playing a game she'd already easily mastered should cool her down and focus her attention on something other than Rome. Who was quickly beginning to steal her attention in a strictly carnal way.

He walked in the room and plopped down on the folding chair next to hers.

Sitting very close, he almost brushed her thigh as he reached for the second controller. The muscles in his leg flexed against her. Maybe this wasn't such a good idea. Well, at least she was distracted from her messed up life.

"Football?" he asked, his voice lifting. "How about hockey?" She gave him a sideways glance and saw him shoot her a playful frown.

"You a big hockey fan?" She plucked at the North Stars T-shirt she was wearing with her free hand.

His gaze moved to her chest and she watched the clear blue of his eyes darken into deep swirling pools. She looked down to see whether she'd spilled something, but no, he was just ogling her boobs. A little smile creeped onto her face at the thought. Hadn't she just been doing the same to his butt?

"Um, no. I mean, yeah. Yeah, I am." Rome's voice was scratchy, and he cleared his throat with a little shake of his head. Raising his gaze, he met hers and smiled a tad guiltily. "I grew up in Minnesota." He gestured, not too close, to her chest and the team's old emblem. "I used to play in college at UM, but I busted my knee up really bad. I had to retire." He rubbed his right knee absently. She imagined a scar under the worn denim.

No wonder he was so darn sexy. And that explained the rolling r's that made her swoon when he said her name.

"Wow, you must've been pretty good," she said, remembering he'd said the same thing to her just a few minutes ago about her swimming.

"Pro scouts were all over me until my injury." He smirked.

As a former collegiate athlete, she understood the commitment that took. And the heartache his injury must have caused. She'd faced something similar.

"You ever get injured, Harper? I mean bad like that?" Was he reading her mind?

"About four years ago," she answered levelly. It still felt as if it were yesterday. "My first preliminary heat at the Olympics. The four-hundred-meter individual medley. My best race. I was so far ahead, I thought I would show off a little. I mistimed my turn and hit the wall. Tore out my shoulder."

"Ouch." He cringed in reflex. "But you bounced right back. Me, I was done. You never really realize how quickly your life can change. Well, I guess you would." He shot her a rueful smile that almost melted her insides with its sweetness.

"I was done, too." She shook her head, remembering how shattered she'd been. "I was a mess. I never wanted to go into the pool again. But Bobby convinced me not to give up. So I started over."

She thought of the long years in between her injury

and now. The endless rehab and the pain. The rigorous training. But it had been her dream to make the Olympic team once again. Only Bobby had known how badly she wanted it. Her ego was too big to let anyone else know just how much it meant to her. So when she destroyed her shoulder, no one was there to help her pick up her concealed pieces.

Except Bobby. She had wanted to forget it all ever happened. Forget all her wasted years of training just to have had it taken away in a split second on one greedy move. But Bobby wouldn't let her give up her dream. He said she had the strength to see it through once more. So she'd started over.

And now look where she was.

"Your brother's right. You are strong. Inside and out," Rome said, resting a warm hand on her knee. She could tell he was watching her carefully. "Besides, I'm not sure I would have had the focus and discipline for the pros, anyway. I don't have your drive."

"Oh, I think you do." She mentally shook off the futile thoughts of her swimming and thought about how strangely alike they really were. "You just channel it differently." She watched a smile crawl onto his face and then turned her attention to the television as the start screen of the game appeared. "So, how did you evolve from hockey player to government agent?" Her fingers moved on her controller, selecting a team.

"I have a degree in political science," he answered. She raised her eyebrows. He looked affronted. "What? Hockey players skate on the ice, not through the classroom. What was your major? Or did you even go to college?"

"Double major. Computer science and systems engineering," she countered with a disarming grin. "Stanford."

"Well, goody for you," he grumbled, turning back to the television. She laughed and watched him pick a team for himself. "Anyway, after I blew out my knee—and yes, I graduated—I got a job with the government, working for intelligence. My parents were both intelligence officers. But I was bored with just planning the ops. I wanted to be out there doing it. So I applied for field training. I had an excellent mentor who said I had great instincts. I then became an agent."

Harper noticed the fondness in his voice when he spoke of his mentor. She was beginning to think that underneath his tough-guy shell was an adorable softie she really wanted to explore. But right now, she just wanted to relax and forget everything and lose herself in his easy company.

"Are you ready to get your tushie thumped?" she asked, returning her attention to the game.

"What is it with you?" he asked through a chuckle. "Why don't you just say 'ass'?"

"Because I'm a lady," Harper answered with a grin, and pressed the Start button.

After a few hours, they were fully immersed in their second game. Harper had won the first and was now ahead by two touchdowns. To his credit, Rome wasn't too upset, as most guys she effortlessly beat usually were. In fact, she couldn't remember the last time she'd laughed so much.

"No!" The exclamation came from Rome after her player intercepted an ill-advised pass from his quarterback, sealing the game in her favor. He dropped his controller to the floor and held his head in his hands, groaning.

"It's okay, Rome," she said through her chuckling. "I'm a pro."

"Lady, my ass."

She full-out laughed now and impulsively reached over and threw her arm around his thick shoulders in a consoling gesture.

She could feel his warm body tremor through his T-shirt from his laughter. Then he turned his head to face her.

So close. His face was so close to hers. It would be so easy to just lean in. Her laughter sifted away as she was drawn in by the vortex of his powerful blue gaze. She could feel his soft breath against her face. She watched his glance move to her mouth.

Harper knew what he wanted. She didn't fight it. She wanted it, too. More than anything in the world. At this moment, all she wanted was to feel his parted lips against hers.

And with the slightest shift forward, Harper got her wish. Firm yet featherlight. The kiss seared and soothed all at once.

Then his mouth asked for more and she gave in without hesitation. She closed her eyes and opened her mouth, allowing his tongue to dive in, sliding and savoring. Sensual shivers of pleasure danced through her body, radiating from the sizzling bliss he was forging.

Her game controller slipped from her hand and hit her foot with a startling thud. A reflexive jump broke the kiss. Slowly she opened her eyes to meet his scorching gaze at very close range. Rome leaned back with a heavy, ragged sigh.

"I'm not sorry," he said with a rumble so deep, she felt it roll around inside of her like a pinball. Giving her a rakish grin, he stood up and reached to turn off the game. "I think we need to get some rest."

"Sounds good," she said, returning his smile with one of her own after a few calming breaths.

You know, she wasn't sorry either. Goodness, that kiss felt nice. More than nice. The thought that she'd had her birth control shot a few weeks ago quickly passed through her mind.

"You take the bed. I'll take the couch." He gave her the sexiest wink she'd ever seen and strutted out the door.

Pressing her fingers to her moist lips, she was sorely tempted to invite him into bed with her or follow him to the couch. Her body didn't seem to care that she didn't trust him. But she knew he was right.

Exhaustion washed over her, only this time it was mixed with a warmth from the lingering essence of the man who had decided to be her ally. And who let her have the comfy bed.

Harper didn't know what the future held, but for the first time since she stepped onto the bus for this fateful trip, she was looking forward to it.

CHAPTER EIGHT

Music floated from the large speakers in his Land Rover as Rome drove carefully through the crowded streets on his way to meet with Jeff. He was pretty sure no one knew yet he'd helped Harper escape. He'd find out for certain the moment he stepped into the facility. If he was seized and dragged down to the romper room for some of creepy Dr. Andy's lovin', chances were Jeff knew.

He tapped his fingers against the steering wheel in time to the ABBA song on the radio. A smile cracked his face when he recalled Harper idly doing the same just days ago while sitting in the seat next to him. Only then it was "Dancing Queen," not today's "Super Trouper."

Hmm, they had similar taste in music. He wondered what other tastes they had in common. He had certainly enjoyed the taste of her lips against his. Deliciously sweet and savory. He hadn't meant to kiss her. He had sure as hell wanted it. And he knew without a doubt she'd wanted it, too. But knowing the crazy, unstable situation they were in, a kiss should have been the furthest thing from his mind.

Only the kiss, plus planning future ones, was the foremost. The more time he spent with her, the more he was drawn to her. And not just physically. Something in her strong and spirited soul called to him. And something in her sinewy and sexy body roared to him.

Shifting in his seat, he mentally slapped himself. He had to focus, or they could both end up dead. He wouldn't be able to explore Harper Kane and her luscious lips if that happened. And that was more than enough incentive.

After their much-needed sleep earlier, they had spent more time hashing things out over grilled cheese sandwiches. She'd told him everything that had happened to her after her bus ride, up to the point where they squared off in the lab. Seeing her brother murdered, the inadvertent injection of the serum, unwittingly using her powers. Everything she'd gone through had just seemed to fortify her fierce determination to resolve this whole mess. And it reinforced his belief that Harper was an unbelievably remarkable woman.

But he'd also realized that Harper didn't trust him. Prudence had tinged every word she'd spoken and those she hadn't. Her emerald green eyes were full of caution. He knew he couldn't have expected her to trust him right away, but now he was certain it would take a whole lot to win it back. If he even could. His betrayal, regardless of his duty, had cut her deeply. And now she bled vigilance.

Rome had decided that it was imperative he talk to Jeff. He wasn't sure how much he trusted his boss anymore, but he and Harper needed a lot more information. He would talk to Jeff under the ruse that he'd heard the woman had escaped and see whether there was anything he could do to help find her once again. He hoped he could gain some more knowledge about the situation they were in.

It was a chance he had to take.

Harper had grudgingly agreed to stay put back at the warehouse. She'd wanted to come in case he needed her. That had made him laugh. He didn't need anyone to take care of him. Then she'd said she was responsible for the fact that he was in this whole disaster in the first place. The heartfelt sentiment had touched him deep down and had almost made him cave in.

But no. She was safe at the warehouse for the time being. If he brought her near Jeff again, he wasn't sure she would be. Or really, if Jeff would be safe from her.

Truth be told, the damage she was capable of still scared the life out of him. But underneath her strange powers lay a charming and strong woman. One he felt an impossible connection to. So he had to do what he could to keep her out of sight as long as he could, until he got more answers.

She hadn't argued his appeal for her to stay put. Well, not too much. But strangely, the one thing she did ask for was a laptop. And the flash drive he kept in his top desk drawer at his condo. How did she know where he kept his spare drives? And why would she want it?

He didn't ask what she'd needed them for and assured her he'd honor her request. Harper was a programmer. A programmer with a computer when they needed data couldn't be a bad thing to have around, he'd surmised. Plus he had a feeling her technological talents were more substantial than she had let on, if the subtle twinkle in her gorgeous green eyes was any sign when she'd revealed her bill-paying job.

A rare parking space on the street opened up about two blocks from the facility. Rome maneuvered the Land Rover into the tight spot, deciding to walk in. The more people around, the less conspicuous he'd be. Especially if he had to make a subtle yet quick getaway.

The tempting smell of freshly baked cookies forced him to detour into a hole-in-the-wall bakery. He selected a couple of warm oatmeal chocolate chip cookies, then walked out the door and resumed his mock unassuming stroll, savoring the home-baked taste.

Years ago in college, after he'd been injured, he'd been so angry at his inability to move around and his dependency on others, he'd hunted for something he could do on his own.

Cooking. He'd found an inexplicable peace when he baked and loved the fruits of his labor. He'd never told anyone about it. He'd even told his dates the food he'd served was takeout. But not Harper. Apparently she loved to eat as much as he did, so he knew his hidden talent would be appreciated.

Biting into the chewy cookie, his mind readily pictured Harper sucking on the dessert they'd had last night. Oh, how he had wanted to be that spoon in those moments. To feel her tongue all over him. Heat surged through him, making him smile at the delicious thought, which made the chocolate chips buried in the oatmeal all the tastier.

Harper. Why was he so willing to risk everything for her? His job. His life. All he could come up with was that he had an instinct about her. He'd told her that. And it was the simple truth. If he didn't help her, he would be going against everything he stood for.

Rome had a vision of how life should be. What was right and what was wrong. If he didn't help Harper, that vision was dumped on its ass. And the bad guys would win. He couldn't let that happen. Harper hadn't meant to become what she had. This was bigger than she was. And he had to make it right.

Finishing the second cookie, he brushed his hands

together, ridding them of crumbs, and steeled himself for his reconnaissance mission.

Approaching the building, Rome didn't notice anything out of the ordinary. Though very minimal, he knew the surveillance had to have picked him up by now. Now all that remained to be seen was to find out what was waiting for him behind the nondescript door to the facility. He entered and shut the door securely behind him.

The hallway was quiet and dim, as usual. Making his way through the winding walls to Jeff's office, he began to feel a little more confident about his status.

But it did pay to be paranoid. Years of harsh experience had instilled that belief. Folks were rarely paranoid for no reason. There was almost always a kernel of truth to their fear. And being suspicious had saved his ass more times than he cared to admit.

"Rome." Jeff's voice from behind almost made him jump.

"Hey, boss." Rome turned to lean against the wall as Jeff slowly approached.

"What now?" His boss gestured him into the office he'd seen more of in the last few days than he had in the last few years. They both sat down.

"Word is the girl escaped." Rome injected a hint of amusement in his tone. "What's with her?"

"What do you care?" Jeff asked while riffling through some papers, his usual attentive disinterest intact, knowing full well Rome had contacts and resources everywhere.

"I'm just wondering why you couldn't hold her." Rome noticed Jeff tense at his feigned accusation. "She is freaky, but damn, Jeff, I was able to bring her in all by myself."

"Because she was unconscious." His boss's usually

impassive voice had an accusing lift to it. "It couldn't have been that hard."

Rome remembered he hadn't revealed the circumstances to Jeff or that he'd witnessed her powers. He'd just brought her in and dumped her limp body into their cold hands. Rome never had to be briefed. He did the job by whatever means he needed or chose. Jeff never cared about methods.

As far as Rome knew, Jeff had no idea that he and Harper had been at Bobby's house together. For sure, Jeff must have found out about the men Harper had killed there, but there wasn't any evidence that Rome had been there—of his own volition—too. For all intents and purposes, it appeared that Rome had apprehended her by himself.

"So then why was it so hard to keep her here?" Rome asked with a trace of mirth. Jeff expected this much bravado from his agents, so he gave it to him, just like always.

"Tell me, how did you capture her?" Jeff leaned back, now giving Rome his full attention.

"I knocked her out," he lied, thinking he had to get Jeff talking about Harper. "She's kind of different. You know what I mean?" He watched Jeff closely. "Like she has some power or something."

"What do you know about it?" His boss narrowed his eyes, giving him a direct stare. Good. Jeff wasn't going to be evasive. Now he could get somewhere.

"Nothing really." Rome leaned back as well, keeping his gaze locked with Jeff's. "Like the force or something. Maybe she's a Jedi." He added a skeptical laugh. Pretending that he cracked himself up. Which was true, anyway.

Jeff quirked his mouth. Even better. His boss was loosening up. Well, what was loose for him.

"She's not." Jeff let out a long breath. "But I need her back to figure out what she is. Can you find her again?"

"Probably." Rome's answer was laced with indifference. Gotcha. "But I need the truth about her. No bullshit, Jeff. I've seen what she can do. I want to know what I'm up against this time." He watched Jeff watch him. His boss was obviously deciding what to reveal. Which meant he had something to hide.

"There's a serum that a Five Watch scientist was developing," Jeff began slowly. He was choosing his words carefully. "The scientist went rogue and destroyed the lab, and with it, the formula. Ms. Kane has the serum inside her. We have not been able to replicate it." Well, that cleared up absolutely nothing.

"What does it do?" Rome asked, genuinely wondering about its intended use. "This serum. Why is it such a big deal?"

"It was being developed for soldiers," Jeff answered. "To enhance them biologically so that they could withstand severe situations." Was he serious?

"Like what?" What did that mean? Was Harper not giving him the whole story? She'd said she thought her brother worked with plants, not human subjects. Was she really part of the experiment?

"The serum needs to be tested." Jeff ignored his question. So that was off-limits. His boss leaned forward, pinning him with a glare. "It's not working the way it should. That's why I need her back. We need to find out why she's reacted to it the way she has." Rome couldn't discern how much of what he knew Jeff was revealing. But it seemed to follow what Rome did know. Sort of. "She's dangerous. And she's a danger to herself. It's for her own good, Rome."

The way Jeff said the last line chilled him. Did he

know Rome helped her escape? That he was helping her now? And what was that underlying current of censure that tinted Jeff's words?

Rome promptly decided that what little he had found out from Jeff would have to be enough. It was time to go.

The stories from Harper and Jeff, though similar, didn't quite seem to jive with each other. But then, the whole thing was annoyingly suspicious and had holes.

Rome was more confused than ever. He'd trusted his duty for so long, it was tough to think that Jeff was feeding him crap. Yet Harper honestly believed she was an innocent victim in this mess. He was committed to his job, but he'd committed to Harper, as well. Most of all, though, he was committed to doing what was right.

Torn as he was, he'd already betrayed her once. He wasn't going to do it again. Something very strange was going on and he was going to have to sort it out himself. He'd much rather do it with Harper. She was a phenomenal kisser.

And he wasn't sure Jeff was on his side anymore. His boss was always evasive, but this time was different. Almost like a warning. *Do your job or we'll find someone who can*, was Jeff's message.

"So if you find her, bring her in." Jeff tilted back in his leather chair and picked up his papers, dismissing him.

"Great." Rome nodded with a coolness he didn't feel and stood. He walked to the door and looked back to Jeff over his shoulder. "I'll take care of it."

"Yes, you will," Jeff said, evenly holding his gaze.

Jeff was so damn hard to read. That's what made him so good at what he did. And it's also what made Rome now question whether going there was as good an idea as he'd thought it was earlier. Maybe he'd just tipped his hand. Damn it all.

Quickening his pace without appearing to do so, he moved down the shadowy corridor. A couple of burly guys turned the corner ahead and moved his way. They were unusually huge. Shit. Were they after him?

They looked like the same guys who'd tried to stop Harper when he helped her escape. He was sure no one had seen him in the alley, but he had witnessed them use the same power as her, though a tad muddied. And it confirmed what Jeff told him about the experiments. Maybe these brutes were the subjects.

Rome gave them a cordial nod as they passed. Nodding back, the two hulks kept walking. He resisted the urge to turn around and see whether they were watching him. He didn't want to appear concerned, but his back felt as if it were on fire.

Walking out the door, he held his breath as if waiting for someone to yank him back inside. Or tackle him. But nothing happened.

Reaching his car, Rome quickly inspected the Land Rover. He was going to have to switch it out before returning to the warehouse with the items Harper requested.

He had to get back to her. Now. Someone was hiding the whole truth. And hard as it would be, he needed to make sure it wasn't her. He was so damn tired of secrets.

CHAPTER NINE

Jeff Donovan watched the secure feed from the three streetlight cameras on his computer monitor. Rome finally passed the last one and moved out of sight.

He sat back against the buttery leather of his chair, steepling his fingers against his mouth.

Agent Rome Lucian made him uneasy. He always had. And that uneasiness was what prompted this whole project.

Not too long ago, the agent had mistrusted his instincts and the falter had cost lives. Yet the incident sparked an idea. An idea that removed unreliable instincts and replaced it with raw power. With the powerful serum, his men could create the variables instead of react to them.

And failures like Rome's could be prevented.

But here the agent was, testing his instincts again. Yes, Rome knew something. The fact that he'd been to the facility twice since Harper Kane became an issue had reinforced that.

Damn her. Damn her and her goody-goody brother.

Dr. Robert Kane had wanted to use his formula for global assistance. So did Jeff. Only their definitions of "assistance" were slightly different. Jeff's vision of saving the world meant creating the ultimate warrior. It was his pet project. To mold a force that no one would be able to reckon with. The country and its allies would be invincible. No one would dare cross them ever again.

That wasn't Dr. Kane's vision. Jeff didn't understand why their dreams couldn't live in harmony. The doctor was part of Five Watch. Surely he understood national security and everything that went with it.

But Dr. Kane refused to share even a scrap of his precious formula. And with that refusal, the doctor had signed his own death warrant. Jeff couldn't tolerate associates who weren't on board.

The moment Dr. Kane had found out about Jeff's experiments using a replica of his serum, the bastard went wacko and destroyed it all. Torching his private underground lab at the Five Watch facility along with his precious plants and every single piece of research he'd ever created. And he'd destroyed every drop of the serum.

Or so Jeff had thought.

Then that damn woman had shown up just as his men were finishing off Dr. Kane. When Jeff had heard that, he'd been furious. But it hadn't compared to the rage once he'd gotten the report about the incident at the train tracks.

Apparently the sight hadn't been pretty. Decimated bodies everywhere. The damn woman had injected the last of the serum. Used the power. And left behind a useless flash drive, which had no doubt held the only surviving remnants of Dr. Kane's data on the formula. Why else would her brother have given it to her?

Harper Kane was a tough bitch, no doubt, but he'd been sure they'd be able to get to her eventually—especially in the main lab at the Five Watch facility for more extensive and invasive testing.

Then she'd overpowered his own test subjects to escape. Though he knew his boys were imperfect, he'd underestimated the power the true serum gave her. Good thing he'd kept her underground.

Although her powers were obviously superior, her escape was just a little too convenient.

The surveillance cameras in the alley hadn't revealed anything out of the ordinary, but that was before she'd used her power to tear up the area. Her shock wave had damaged the cameras beyond recall.

So he hadn't been able to see whether she'd had help. But Rome's visit today was a little too coincidental. And Jeff had never really believed in coincidences. Everything was planned.

Rome had agreed to find Harper Kane again, but something in his eyes seemed amiss.

Doubt.

Rome had never asked questions about a job. Never doubted what task he was given.

But there were definite questions in his casual interest as he'd sat there, asking about Harper Kane.

The agent had admitted to witnessing her power. Could he be trusted with that knowledge? Especially given the suspicious vibe Jeff had sensed?

Maybe Rome had come here to feel him out. Maybe he already had the woman and was going to use her for his own purposes. Maybe the two were a team.

No. Harper Kane and the serum that flowed inside her was his. Jeff wasn't going to take any chances. He needed that formula, and he'd get it from the bitch if it was the last thing he did.

And no one, not even his best agent, was going to stand in his way.

Picking up the handset of his phone, Jeff dialed the number for his enhanced task force. He tried to think of every hiding place Rome had. He knew of only a few. He'd never had to tail him before, but he was certain Agent Rome Lucian had unlimited resources. Rome was that good. So it was going to be a challenge.

But Jeff loved challenges. He knew Rome did, too.

So, it was war. The prize?

Harper Kane.

Another undead attacker exploded across the television screen as Harper maneuvered her computerized warrior through a dark forest, hacking and slashing everything in her way with her giant sword.

Ragged zombies continued to emerge from behind nearly every rock and tree, swarming around her character, grunting while they persisted with their all-out assault, trying to keep her from reaching the magical fortress.

It was a nice break to mindlessly play the video game, allowing her to set her troubles aside for blessed spurts of time. Immersing herself in the game also helped put her worry for Rome on hold.

But not entirely. She found her mind wandering while her hands intuitively operated the controller. She wasn't convinced that Rome was being prudent in chatting up his boss. He'd been confident that no one would be the wiser. She wasn't so sure. Was she just a skeptical Sally now that her life had been turned every way but right?

Maybe. But although she was new to this cloak-and-dagger stuff, she was pretty certain that you just didn't walk up to the people who ordered a hit on the girl you were now helping and ask them questions about it. What if they suspected she and Rome were a team? Would they kill him?

Dramatic music filtered into her thoughts. Eyeing

the television screen, she saw her warrior surrounded. How appropriate.

Harper completely empathized with her red-haired heroine, twitching while she turned her character in circles. She herself had been in the same situation. Though her attackers weren't slobbering zombies with staves.

She quickly activated her character's inventory to see what, if anything, she could use against her threatening enemies. A box flashed across the screen, showing her everything she'd found, bought, or stolen while on her journey. What did she have that could get her out of the potentially fatal circumstances?

The zombies closed in on her waiting warrior. Harper noticed that she possessed a magical spell that would raze the zombies for good. Well, it sounded cool. She'd do it.

Casting the spell, Harper watched her simulated warrior sheathe her sword and raise her hand as a sparkling silver hue encased the character.

A gleaming energy wave burst from the outstretched hand like a shimmering bubble. In flashes of computerized smoke, the hostile zombies vanished one by one as the wave swept through them, clearing the way to the castle for her digital warrior.

A muted *thud* drew Harper's attention away from the television screen. Glancing down, she saw the controller on the carpeted floor and her empty trembling hands. Realization swamped her senses. She actually had those powers.

But instead of obliterating simulated zombies, she'd killed real people. Actual human beings had died at her hands. Because of her inadvertent power. The inadvertent power she had purposefully used.

Harper felt sick. Her stomach churned like it was

folding into itself. She wrapped her shaking arms around her roiling torso, trying to ease the shocking pain.

She was a murderer. She'd killed in real life. Not in some video game.

Yet, the reason was the same. To survive. She had to make sure she remembered that.

Survival. She needed to keep going in order to get revenge for Bobby.

With effort, Harper uncoiled her body and sat up straight, sucking in several deep breaths and blowing them out slowly. On screen her character was ready and waiting for Harper to put her into action. Instead she reached to shut the game off.

Okay. Okay, Harper. She couldn't change the past. But she could shape the future she wanted. *Relax.* She wanted revenge. *Focus.* She began to take easy, measured breaths, just as she did before a race.

Yesterday she had been able to summon the power and control it. Well, not quite control, but she'd directed it. Though the brutes she'd been up against had somehow met it head-on with a power similar to hers, she'd been able to have a shred of command over her mind's energy.

But not inside the facility itself. Harper leaned against the back of her chair, deep in thought. No, it hadn't worked inside.

The trigger seemed to be related to her emotions. It had come unbidden the times she'd been in extreme pain from thinking about Bobby and her unthinkable situation. The first time she'd been able to temper it was at Rome's. She'd been upset but hadn't wanted to hurt him.

But in the facility, she'd wanted to get out, not caring who or what she might hurt. Yet her mind hadn't cooperated. The energy hadn't been there for her, no matter how much pain she'd endured.

Taking a deep, controlled breath, she focused on the stack of game boxes on the table and attempted to summon the energy in her mind and direct it toward the innocuous pile. Nothing. Okay, so what was different? Inside versus outside? No, that couldn't be it. She'd been inside Bobby's lab and the power had come without command, from an overload of grief.

Shaking her head in frustration, she stood and walked out of the room. Heading to the refrigerator, she pulled out a bottle of water and twisted off the cap. Taking a long sip, she relished the cool liquid as it refreshed her body and settled her mind.

Rome had told her to stay inside, but she decided she needed fresh air. Suffocation was clutching at her.

She had changed into her own clothes now that they were clean, but she stopped by the bedroom to pick up one of Rome's well-worn gray sweatshirts. Smiling at the cozy oversized fit and the big maroon and gold M on the chest, Harper pushed the long cotton arms up past her wrists and walked to the front area of the warehouse.

Only the one sliding door faced her. The entrance was just large enough for the Bug to creep through. Walking across the empty space, she glanced toward the security box on the wall. Red lights warned her that some sort of alarm was activated. She smiled. Was he trying to keep her in or everyone else out? Most likely out, given that she'd told him she was a programmer, and surely he'd figured she'd be able to deactivate it.

Programmer. Right. Hacker was more like it. Her part-time job at the video-game company included programming, but was essentially hacking into the games to see how much code she could dismantle and how imaginatively she could mess with the so-called security measures. Then she would create hidden layered logic routines to keep other hackers out.

So as she stepped in front of the alarm panel she was pretty confident she could easily disarm it. Snapping the plastic cover off the mechanism, she peered at the exposed wires. Rome had obviously rigged the thing himself, given the concealed plate that hid a tiny keyboard and screen and the level of complication. Data streamed across the minute display, as Harper watched the shuffling code sequences for patterns.

There. She found a common string and studied it closely for a few minutes. She was able to identify figures that appeared to represent the broadcasting of the alarm signal without actually disarming the alarm.

Hmm. Close enough. Harper placed her fingers on the Blackberry-sized keyboard and entered a command to disrupt the data flow. Without hesitation, she hit the Enter key. The constant stream came to a slight pause and then flowed again, with an ever-so-minor modification. She doubted that Rome would even be aware of it. Besides, she'd change it back once she returned.

Smiling, she replaced the plastic covering and walked to the sliding door. She grabbed the handle and pulled. No sound. A long breath escaped her lips, one she didn't even know she was holding.

The autumn sunlight was sluggishly waning, but still coating every surface in its path. She took several deep breaths of crisp air and began to pace around outside the warehouse to the area that faced the dense forest, stretching her muscles as best she could.

Harper rolled up the sleeves of Rome's sweatshirt a little more and rubbed her bare arms. The sun's warmth invigorated her, as did the fresh air, sending light pulses of energy through her veins.

Strange. She experienced the same revitalizing sensation as soon as she stepped outside the facility right before she escaped. Harper peered at her arm, running her fingers gently over the tingling skin.

She swept her gaze around the area, looking for something she could practice with. She wanted to try to harness this power. Control it. If she could, revenge would be a lot easier. Quicker.

Shielding her eyes from the sunlight, she squinted to see a bunch of empty milk crates stacked against the wall of the adjacent warehouse to her right. Recalling the image of the warrior in her game, she raised her hand and focused on the crates.

The ice-cold sensation that preceded the scorching heat was now becoming familiar. Even welcome. Fiery power blazed through her blood, filling her mind and surging down along her outstretched arm. A small wave of nearly invisible energy rippled toward the crates, originating from her prickling hand.

Harper kept her gaze locked on the stacks, watching in amazement, and a little satisfaction, as they began to vibrate under her power.

A distant rumbling broke into her focus. Uh-oh. Rome's Bug.

Harper quickly dropped her hand and raced around the building to the sliding door she'd left slightly open, shaking off the power swelling inside her body.

Harper was just slipping inside when she saw the Bug come to a halt only feet from her. Peering through the flat windshield, she spied Rome's striking, narrowed blue eyes staring crossly at her.

She was busted.

Slinking back out, she mustered the most sheepish look she could manage. Maybe there was a way to spin this so he wouldn't be too upset with her. Then again, he was supersexy when he was angry. Maybe she could get him madder instead.

Rome had barely stepped out of the car before he went on the offensive. "What the hell are you doing out here?"

"I needed some air." She gave him a half grin. Well, it was the truth.

"How?" He stiffly gestured toward the sliding door with a wave of his hand. His kissable lips were tight with frustration.

"I altered the code." She held up a placating palm. "Don't worry. I'll reset it."

"Altered the code?" His anger turned to intrigue.

"I told you, I'm a programmer. It's what I do."

Rome didn't really have anything to say to that, but his gorgeous face, bathed in the fading daylight, cracked the most admiring and alluring smile she'd ever seen.

He walked over to her, stopping just inches away. She flushed. She could see every blue swirl in the eddy of his eyes. Smell every spice of his lingering soap. Feel every breath that brushed her face.

"Show me," Rome whispered as he leaned in. His mouth was so very close to hers. He licked his lips. She wetted her own. Harper almost closed her eyes, just waiting, desperately wanting the touch of those lips against hers once again.

Then she was flat on her back on the ground.

Well, that was fast.

"Somebody's here." Rome's whisper was nearly silent, just a tickling breath away from her ear.

Rome covered her body with his as he frantically searched the area. His intense blue eyes at such close range were a sight to behold. *Stay here*, he mouthed, rolling off her body easily and moving into a crouch, gun drawn. Wow, she hadn't known he was even carrying one.

Creeping around the dented front bumper of the Bug, Rome disappeared from her sight. She sat upright and tried to listen for whatever had startled him. And stopped their imminent kiss. Darn it. Her lack of trust in him hadn't diminished his allure. Double darn it.

After counting to sixty without hearing a sound, Harper decided to check things out herself. Rome should know by now that she was no good at waiting. She used the car for cover and took a quick peek out toward where Rome had vanished. She felt a little strange with all this creeping around, hunkering down like a spy or something.

Another minute went by with no sign of danger. What could he have heard?

Then she saw him walking her way. His shoulders were stiff and he kept looking around as though ghosts swirled around him, prickling every one of his senses.

"They're gone. We'd better discuss our next move," he said without preamble. "I'm not sure we have much more time here."

"Okay." Harper caught his grave tone and altered her mood. Kicking herself, she realized she had to remember this wasn't some weekend fling with a hot guy. This was her messed-up life that she needed to right somehow, and he was the only person who could help her. "Did you get the flash drive?"

"Yeah, it's in the car," he answered, moving to the driver's side. He opened the door and popped the hood.

Harper moved to the front of the Bug. Inside was a black duffel bag. She reached in, unzipped the bag, and pulled out a slim laptop. She shoved it under her arm and poked around inside for the small drive. Rome must have brought extra clothes, because she had to fish around for the drive through layers of soft fabric. When she found it, she quickly checked to make sure it was indeed the flash drive she'd asked for.

"Why that?" His close voice made her jump. She hadn't seen or heard him step beside her.

"C'mon, I'll show you." Harper reached to close the hood, then had to slam it a couple times before it latched. She turned around and sat on the concrete with her back resting against the front bumper, then booted up the computer. Rome joined her on the ground with a grunt, their thighs lightly touching.

"We should go inside," he said as he turned his head, alternately looking at her and their surroundings.

"I need some air," she countered, shifting the screen slightly to lessen the angling sun's glare. A password request popped up once the computer finished booting.

"By the way, how did you alter the code and get out without setting off the alarm?" Rome asked, peering at the laptop screen while she typed in a few commands.

"Kind of like this," she answered absently while she hacked into his computer, bypassing his imposing password protection schemes in under a minute.

Giving him a sideways glance, she noticed his slack-jawed expression. His mouth moved, but no words came forth. Smiling, Harper patted his rough cheek and continued to peck at the flat keyboard.

Once she was in, she plugged the drive into the USB port and waited.

"What are you doing?" Rome finally found his voice.

"That's a blank drive." He leaned closer so that their shoulders brushed. She noticed that his astonished look had morphed into one of confusion.

"It's not blank," she had to admit quietly, relishing the warmth where their bodies touched.

"I don't understand." He covered her hands with his own to still her fingers. He sounded outraged, perplexed, and fascinated all at once. "What aren't you telling me, Harper?"

She closed her eyes. *Here it goes.* The one secret she had kept from him. Here was where he got furious with her. Lost his trust in her. Maybe even took her back to the bad facility.

No, he wouldn't do that. But she needed to tell him the truth. Harper took a deep breath and let it out slowly. She opened her eyes and squarely met his gaze.

"Before Bobby died, he hid a flash drive for me," she began, watching for a reaction from him. There was none. Yet. "I found it, but I had to break it apart, so that it wasn't taken from me by the people who are after me. They thought it was destroyed, but I kept the data chip. When I was at your condo, I found your flash drive and replaced the chip inside with mine."

Rome blinked and looked away. After a few moments, he shook his head slightly, and then returned to meet her gaze.

"Impressive," he said with a wry grin. His blue eyes softened. "Why didn't you tell me?"

"If I had, we probably wouldn't have it anymore," she replied seriously. Most likely Rome would've handed it over to his boss when he dropped her off. And they both knew it. "I wanted your help. But I wasn't sure I could trust you." Pain flashed in his eyes for a split second, and then it was gone.

"I guess I can't blame you for that." His quiet tone scraped at her heart.

Harper was silent. She had no idea what to say. She couldn't trust him. Yes, he was helping her, but she wasn't about to put her life in his hands again. She couldn't chance that he'd take care of it this time.

"So what's on this thing?" he asked a little louder, probably trying to break the heavy tension. Trying to brush over her silence.

"I have no idea," she answered with a lopsided smile. "But it's time to find out."

Harper opened a code-authoring application and quickly wrote a scanning program for the flash drive to make sure it was intact. Pressing the Enter key, she watched the program read the little drive and caught Rome squinting at the screen while he did the same. She quickly explained what she'd done.

"Damn, if you're half as good a swimmer as you are hacker, I'd be surprised if you didn't win every medal at the Olympics," he said offhandedly.

Her breath caught. The Olympics. She should be getting home to train, not sitting here trying to figure out how to stay alive. A strong hand rubbed her tense shoulder warmly as if reading her thoughts.

"Don't worry, Harper." His voice was soothing as he continued his reassuring strokes. "You'll get that chance. I'll make sure you do."

If only he knew what that meant to her to hear that. Even though she knew she wouldn't get the chance. Heck, she'd already had her chance at the Olympics, and she'd blown it. She'd been looking forward to a second chance for four long years.

Because Bobby had been the one to convince her not

to give up swimming and take another shot, it had become his dream as much as hers. And now? Well, now that dream was all but over.

A soft beep from the computer snapped her out of her leaden thoughts. She read the results of her program with an incredulous shake of her head.

"Oh, for crying out loud." She sighed and ran her fingers through her hair in frustration.

"What? The data's gone?" Rome asked, looking at the screen along with her, a tad frantic. She was grateful he was still rubbing her shoulder, albeit a pinch faster now. The touch was sending nice little beads of sensation floating through her body.

"No, the data is intact." She turned to look at him and let out a big sigh. My goodness, his lips were so close. "It's just buried under layers and layers of jumbled code." He blinked away his apprehension.

"Can you decode it?" Rome laughed as he said it. "Wait, of course you can."

"Yes, I can," she confirmed with another long exhale, smiling at his belief in her. "In fact, I think I'm the only one who can." His brows furrowed, so she explained further. "Bobby knew what he was doing. There are so many levels of convoluted code here, yet it's a specific pattern. Something only I would know to look for. Kind of like his personal signature in the code itself."

"He wanted to make sure that you, and only you, would be able to decipher it," Rome translated. "Wow. Genius."

"He was." Harper fondly thought of how smart her brother was. And knew that he'd been smart enough to put the answers under all those layers of protection. For her eyes only. She just had to dig around for them. But it was going to take some time.

"So how long do you need?" Rome asked. She loved his absolute confidence in her. There was no doubt in his question that she could decode it, just how long it would take.

"I'm not sure." She thought hard. "Three, four hours, maybe. I won't know until I get in there and start poking around. And even then, things may be, probably are, embedded."

"Okay, well, get to it, then." Rome squeezed her shoulder and stood. "Inside, Harper." And then he held his hand down to her with a supportive smile.

She secured and closed the laptop after pulling out the flash drive. She stuck it in her front pocket and hauled herself up with the help of his strong hand. Brushing off her rear, she started toward the door, following Rome through the trickling sunlight, her hand still secure in his.

Shots rang out.

Bullets pelted the warehouse door just above their heads with a startling crack. Crouching to the ground, they looked at each other, bewildered. Rome had been right. Somebody was out there.

"Damn it." Rome seethed. She watched him pull out his gun and prepare it.

The gunfire ceased. Were they repositioning? Reloading? Not for the first time, she realized just how inept she was at these spy-game situations. And how grateful she was that Rome was with her.

"Shouldn't we go inside?" Harper whispered as Rome looked everywhere. She set down the laptop.

"No, we'll be trapped inside," he answered with a quick shake of his head. "We need to be mobile."

"Where are they?" she asked, glancing around the area through the dusky sunlight.

"My guess is they're surrounding us." He grimaced. She noticed his fingers flex on the handle of his gun. Their gazes locked and she saw the troubled intensity in his eyes. It mirrored her own.

It was Bobby's house all over again. Besieged. No way out. Images of the video game she'd just played flashed through her mind. Her virtual warrior. Lifting her digital hand. Commanding her power to save herself from her enemies. Living to fight another day.

Did she dare? Would Rome think her an abomination once again?

No, he believed in her, didn't he? So she decided to do it.

"Let me try something." Resting her hand against his stubbled cheek, she implored him with her steely gaze and her tender touch.

He looked away for an instant and then turned back, giving her a confirming nod. In return for his confidence, she surprised both of them with a brief yet intense kiss.

Harper stood to face their hidden attackers, completely exposed in the fading rays of the sun. It was very surreal to be standing there, just her against these unknown enemies like some superhero. Curiously, she kind of liked it. As though it were her own personal video game.

Several large men moved out of their shadowy hiding places. Slowly, three of them approached, monstrous rifles drawn.

Three thin red laser beams pierced the sun's rays from their scopes to rest in a triangle on her chest, directly over her heart. She sucked in a quick breath as spikes of panic prickled under her skin, spreading like a wildfire until she burned with fear.

Wait a second. This *wasn't* her own personal video game. There was no Restart button. This was true life. And these large men had every intention of killing her for real.

It seemed as though time slowed and she could see every millimeter of their fingers squeezing the triggers. She willed her chaotic nerves to settle as she'd done countless times before a race. Cold, then hot flashed through her body. She brought up her hand, palm out; just a sharp crack of gunfire echoed in her head. She shoved all fear aside, inviting the energy and focusing on the incoming ammunition.

The rain of bullets halted mere inches away from her hand, frozen in midair.

It worked. It actually worked. What next?

Calling upon the power again, she tested her mind's fortitude. Her body felt none of the draining effects she'd experienced before. With a concentrated effort, she summoned another swell of energy and directed it at the threatening shells that hovered at the edge of her shield of energy.

A fresh burst flowed through her arm and prickled into her hand, propelling the bullets back toward the three men at lightning speed. Their eyes filled with shock and then pain as they all staggered backward, crumpling to the ground, lifeless.

Harper lowered her hand and gulped a lungful of cool air. *Holy cow!* Not only had she controlled the power, but she'd been able to direct it, too. What else could it do?

She looked at her hand as if seeing it for the first time. A heavy touch descended on her shoulder. She jumped and swung her elbow backward. Rome caught it just before it hit his throat.

"Are you okay?" he asked, his voice breathy.

"I'm fine," she answered, realizing it was true. Her vision was clear, and she didn't have the detached wobbly sensation. Honestly, she felt invigorated.

He kept ahold of her elbow and pulled her over to the three prone men in a cautious approach. Blood seeped out of the bullet holes in their thick black vests. Harper bent down with Rome as he removed one of the garments from the closest body. Amazed, she gawked at the damage as Rome held it up for inspection. The bullets had penetrated the armored vest, killing him instantly.

"I'm sure there're more of them," Rome said tightly, dropping the vest onto the ground. "We need to move. Now."

"Rome," Harper pleaded, gripping his shaking hand from her kneeling position. "Please don't be scared of me." She shook her head sadly.

"Harper . . ." He gave her a crooked smile and twisted his hand to grip hers back. "I won't leave you again." He tugged her up to face him and grabbed her other hand as well. "I won't leave you." He leaned forward and planted a feathery kiss on her forehead. "But we do need to leave. Before more of these guys come."

"They're already here," she said dryly, peering past him to see a group of similarly equipped men pacing toward them with definite purpose. Rome turned to see them just as they broke into a jog, aiming their guns.

"Shit!" He pulled out his gun and dragged her to the nearest cover, behind another warehouse. "Can you stop them again?"

"I think so," she answered slowly, giving him a look she hoped conveyed a confidence she wasn't sure she had. He nodded at her.

She stepped out from behind the wall to face the oncoming group, noticing they were a bit bigger and bulkier than the other three. Like the men she'd escaped from at the facility. Uh-oh. They probably had powers, too. That could make things interesting. She moved forward a few more steps into the last rays of the setting sun and extended her arms.

The heat cascaded over her. Reliving the rush of power in her mind, she called upon it once more and pitched the energy toward them.

The lead man raised his hand, shooting a murky barrier ahead of him. He ran through her wave of energy unscathed. But two of the men behind him were knocked to the ground. She couldn't tell whether they were unconscious or dead, but they were still. Only four more to go.

She sent another pulse of power their way. One more down. The other three ran through it like going through a waterfall, slowed but ultimately unharmed. She peppered them again and again, cutting up the air as if sending harsh ripples through a serene pond.

Just before the leader reached her, he was attacked by a different power source: Rome.

But before she could do anything to help Rome as he grappled with their attacker on the concrete ground, the air was knocked from her lungs. She hit the ground hard right next to Rome. Another body piled onto the one already on top of her. The harsh ramming forced a grunt from her lips as she struggled to breathe.

The tussling to her left paused for a moment, then resumed.

A strange sensation flushed over her, a weight heavier than the two men, as though a solid screen pressed against her. Trying to crush her.

Her body strained against the unseen force. After unsuccessfully shoving against the obstruction with all her strength, she suddenly recognized what was happening. These two men were propelling an energy force at her, just like she had at them. Her breath came in strained spurts as panic and anger invaded her senses. Every wrenching intake was tinged with dusty asphalt.

Tilting her head, she saw Rome fighting two men now. They had him pinned and were delivering vicious blows to his body while he flailed and kicked at them.

No. She couldn't let them take Rome. He'd sacrificed too much for her. She had to do something.

She focused her energy while the men who held her captive tried to force her to turn over, facedown. Molten heat roared through her body, blazing in her blood. Prickles of fire danced under her skin and flashes of gleaming white light sparkled in her vision. An inferno of force swelled from every corner of her mind, racing to her limbs and surging outward, heaving her enemies off her.

They landed several feet away, against the wall of an adjacent warehouse, stunned but not out for the count. Harper shot to her feet and stalked toward them. Angry. Primitive. Hating them with every fiber of her fiery being.

One of the dazed men reached behind his back and pulled out a gun. A cracking sound reached her just before the bullet snapped into the muscles of her shoulder. Harper flinched from the sharp contact but ignored it, continuing to close in on the shooter and his woozy partner.

Stopping mere feet from the two of them, she held out her hand and channeled the power once again without hesitation. She wanted this. Wanted them dead. Surprise was the last look on their faces as the pure energy from her mind crested and tore through their cloudy shield of resistance, killing them easily.

Harper spared them one last glance; then she whipped

around, cutting the distance between her and Rome with determined strides. His assailants had frozen momentarily to follow her approach.

The two men shoved away from Rome and stood to face her, obviously regarding her as the bigger threat. Good. She was.

They raised their hands and she felt the displacement of air as their combined power rushed toward her. Unlike her clear wave, theirs was definitely visible. Curious. Spreading her arms palms out, Harper met their energy head-on with her own. A moment of forces colliding, creasing the space between them in nearly invisible wrinkles—then hers ripped through theirs, decimating the two men in an instant.

Blinking the stinging sweat out of her eyes, she tried to take a deep breath of the light evening breeze into her heaving lungs. Looking up, she saw the sun had set and the clear sky behind the trees was daubed in brilliant pink hues.

Her strength drained and she bent over, resting her arms on her thighs. The fierce exertion had finally caught up with her.

A slight pain in her shoulder claimed her attention. She peered at the spot, seeing a small bloodstained hole in the gray sweatshirt.

Harper tugged at the neck of the shirt, exposing the wound, wincing at the pinching sensation that crawled over her shoulder. Her bloodied skin started to itch something fierce. As she scratched it, a tiny object spurted out and dropped on the concrete with a light *clink*.

It was the bullet. The shell was stained with a rusty liquid. Her blood.

Harper took a closer look at where she'd been shot.

Though a tiny red spot marked her skin, the entry hole was very shallow. Poking at it with her index finger, she felt the tingling under her flesh seep away. After a moment, the tissue wasn't even tender and the skin was almost whole again.

She shook her head, lacking the energy to even try to process this newest development.

Rome lay on the ground. Blood ran from his nose and a mean cut across his forehead. "Thanks," he rasped, splaying his hand across his right ribs as he tried to roll over. "Again."

She gave him a crooked smile in answer, relieved not to see any censure in his eyes. Though fully exhausted, a curious sensation of exhilaration coursed through her, prickling her muscles. Their attackers had the same kind of powers she had, but hers were somehow stronger. And purer. Dominant. She felt empowered. Invincible. And she liked it.

Rome grunted and leaned on his side in an attempt to get up. Harper straightened and took the last couple of steps to his side. She bent down, placing her hands under his arms to help scoop him upright. His grunt turned into a deep groan as he stood, a bit wobbly. She leaned close, allowing him to slide his left arm across her broad shoulders to steady himself. Their glances brushed over the bodies that scattered the warehouse site like driftwood on the beach.

He reached over to touch the red splotch on her sweatshirt. She watched him stare at the fabric, examining it from every angle with a frown.

"This shot wasn't meant to kill," he said, shaking his head. "That's not good."

That wasn't a good thing? They weren't trying to kill her anymore?

Wait, she knew what that meant now. They didn't want her dead because they wanted to do more experiments on her.

"I think you're right," she agreed. *Big bullies.* Well, it wouldn't be long before she turned the tables. She had Bobby's data now. Soon she'd have the information she needed to take down her enemies. And with Rome's help, they'd be darn near unstoppable.

"Let's get these guys taken care of," Rome said with a sigh, and broke away from her, walking to the nearest body. "Then we need to see what's on that flash drive."

"Good idea," Harper agreed, walking toward the two slumped forms by the warehouse entrance.

She and Rome needed those answers now more than ever. Obviously she wasn't alone in her powers. But she was finding out she really was different from the others and needed to find out why in order to command the power and get her revenge.

And the more she was able to control it, the more that revenge was becoming a reality. A smile broke out across her face. Harper couldn't wait.

CHAPTER TEN

It was almost ten o'clock when Harper set down her mug of foamy hot chocolate, her gaze fixated on the bright screen of the laptop.

After taking care of their attackers' bodies, they had collected a few necessities, laptop and flash drive included, and hit the road. They drove a few hours away from the bright lights of Portland, then circled back near the city's suburbs to cover their tracks.

She and Rome had taken turns in getting some much-needed sleep. They made a quick stop at a rest station for some food and to clean up a bit. But most of the drive had been silent, save for the rattling of her fingertips on the keyboard. Eventually, the battery started to run low, and they pulled over at a quaint café where she could plug it in.

Knowing how well Bobby understood her hacking capabilities, she had to be careful and meticulous when collapsing each level of convoluted code. Most likely, he had created frequent fail-safes along the way in case anyone else attempted to unravel the data. She imagined that it would automatically corrupt everything if there was any tampering other than the precise decoding executed by her own hands.

She stopped for a moment when the figures on the

screen started to blur. Rubbing her eyes, she glanced away from the screen to peer around the friendly café.

The café wasn't too crowded, being just near ten at night. A few patrons sat at their own laptops, taking advantage of the free wireless Internet while having steaming cups of coffee and home-style food.

Two other tables were pushed together, surrounded by a group of teenage girls who seemed to be gossiping their young hearts out. She overheard that Emily was going to break up with Josh because she saw him kissing Felicia.

A wistful smile broke across Harper's face at their simple problems. No doubt the girls thought it was the most complicated thing ever. She'd trade for Emily's boy troubles in less than a heartbeat.

Speaking of kissing boys, her tired gaze wandered over to Rome, who was standing patiently at the marbled counter while he waited for the matronly server to make another iced tea. He appeared to be mindlessly studying the chalkboard menu, but she knew he was hair-triggered for danger. She was beginning to recognize that he always had an aura of tension surrounding him.

But you wouldn't know it unless you were looking for it. His fingers were in a half fist. Knees slightly bent. Shoulders hunched slightly. Clear eyes that saw everything.

He turned his head and locked that clear gaze with hers. The blue in his eyes sparkled as he turned one corner of his captivating mouth up in a half smile. She swore she could almost feel a current of desire radiate from him and reach out to her.

Or maybe it was her wishful thinking slapping her upside the head.

He shifted to pick up the full tray that held his glass of iced tea along with two heaping plates and a glass of ice water. It was difficult to decide which looked more appetizing: Rome's muscular bulk or the plates of delicious-smelling food.

As he set the plates down on the table with a small clattering thud, Harper noticed the conversation at the gossip table had stopped. All the teens, gaping, were watching Rome's every movement.

Yep, she knew exactly what they were thinking, because she was thinking it, too. Only she would bet all her gold medals that her thoughts were well past the R-rated version.

"What have we here?" she asked, shifting her glance back to their table as the clanking and shuffling sounds of the café receded with his presence.

"Club sandwiches," he answered as he removed a plate from the tray and set it down in front of her beside the laptop.

Her stomach growled at the mouthwatering smell of toast and turkey. She pushed away the laptop and pulled the plate closer, picking up half of the sandwich. Biting into it, she closed her eyes and moaned at the luscious burst of taste filling her mouth. Swallowing, she grabbed a napkin and wiped her lips.

"Have I told you how much I love you?" Harper said absently as she took another hearty bite and looked across the table at him, moaning, savoring the sandwich. She forgot the napkin this time and just licked the crumbs off her lips.

Rome's sandwich was frozen in midair, just in front of his mouth. He was staring at her with a peculiar look on his face and a twinkle in his eyes, but it disappeared just as quickly as she saw it.

What was that all about? Did her voracious appetite scare him, too? Maybe his usual dates were the side-salad type and never actually ate.

"I'm glad you like it," he said after he took a big bite of his own sandwich.

"What can I say? I like to eat." She tried to guess what he was thinking. Impossible. He shook his head at her and went back to his sandwich.

Being an athlete for most of her life, she knew the importance of the energy food provided to keep her body healthy. Nutrition was just as important as physical training. Moderation was the key, and she had been careful not to overindulge her chocolate tooth, but she was never one for abstinence when it came to good food.

After practically inhaling her sandwich, she placed the empty plate back on the tray and dragged the laptop back in front of her as she sipped through the bendy straw in her glass of ice water. It took less than a minute for her to get back into decoding mode, her mind and body now replenished.

"How much longer?" Rome asked.

"Not much," she answered, keeping her focus on the display. She could tell she was very close to unraveling the data by the way the level of complexity had skyrocketed with her last directive.

After ten more minutes, Harper sat back and ran her fingers through her hair. She stared at the blank screen, which was blinking a solitary cursor back at her.

One more command.

With her next move, she and Rome would know whether she'd deconstructed the code correctly. If she had, Bobby's data would be accessible. If not, it would be gone forever.

Harper was confident in her programming and deprogramming skills, but she'd had little sleep and her stress levels were beyond measurable. She'd gotten this far, but any single wrong command along the way could still destroy it all. She knew Bobby masked lines of code and she wouldn't know for sure whether she'd unmasked them properly until this last entry.

"All done?" Rome's deep voice broke into her thoughts. She glanced over the laptop at him. He was watching her closely but with an encouraging smile. He scooted his chair around the table to sit right next to her and glance at the screen.

She was afraid. Afraid that she'd screwed up the decoding. Above all, she was afraid that even if she had cracked Bobby's code correctly, it wouldn't contain the information she desperately hoped was there. Information that could sort this all out.

But Bobby had stashed this flash drive for her. His last dying words were for her to get it. The answers had to be there.

And then there was Rome, sitting quietly next to her, his warm thigh resting snugly against hers, looking at her with all the confidence in the world. This man who'd chosen to stand by her and help her, risking his own life and career in the process. She just hoped she hadn't let either of them down.

"I guess we'll find out," she said ruefully, and typed in the last command. Her finger hovered over the Enter key in a moment of tight hesitation. The she pressed it and held her breath.

The screen went blank.

No cursor. No data stream. Nothing but a black void.

Harper silently counted to sixty and still nothing.

She let her breath out and shook her head slowly. She couldn't even find the words to describe the misery threatening to overtake her; she felt as if she were underwater, unable to break the surface.

She chanced a sideways peek at Rome. His intense blue gaze was glued to the screen. Watching. Waiting.

"I guess I messed up," Harper said quietly after another eternal minute passed. Rome reached over and pulled her hand onto his thigh. Enveloping it in his grip, he gave it a comforting squeeze and let out a long breath.

A flicker.

Both she and Rome straightened, gawking at the monitor.

A cursor began to dance among the blackness like a frenzied shooting star. The display went black again. Then they watched in sheer fascination as manic data streamed down the screen, drizzling characters like the northwest rain.

And it stopped abruptly once more.

Once again, the empty black screen flashed bright characters and then morphed back to the original innocuous blue desktop.

With a new yellow folder in the bottom right corner, simply titled *Harpie*.

Harper dragged her finger over the keyboard's touchpad to open the folder. With a click, the folder opened and showed two subfolders. One named Research and the other generically named New Folder.

Harper clicked on the Research folder first to open it. The screen lit up with subfolders of various natures. They were organized by type and date, all with titles that included dates. She randomly clicked on one, opening a document inside.

Trial 1517.5.

Vegetation subjects 6–7 under incandescent light fail to respond to serum. Dosage immaterial. Vegetation subjects 15–17 under fluorescent light fail to respond to serum. Dosage immaterial. Vegetation subjects 4–5 under simulated sunlight respond to serum. Dosage immaterial.

Harper narrowed her eyes. Vegetation subjects responding? What was that all about? She closed the document without reading further and opened one dated later.

Trial 2761.5

Vegetation subjects 3–6 survive deep freeze. 4 of 25 branches frozen. Deep freeze duration 361 hours. Survival span 167 hours current. 3 of 4 frozen branches fully regenerated.

"These are Bobby's research notes," she explained, her mind in turmoil. "Considering the number of files, it must be everything he was working on. The serum mentioned here must be what's inside me."

"I'm sure it is," Rome agreed, deep in thought. "We're going to have to read through all those to figure out just exactly what he was doing."

"Thank goodness Bobby's notes are concise." Harper sighed, but cracked a smile.

She was happy for the first time in a while. Actual for-real happy. The information about the mysterious serum that flowed through her blood, that was now part of her essence, surging in her mind, was all there. It was just going to take some time to read through it all.

"Open the other folder," Rome suggested. She closed

the Research folder and opened the nonspecific New Folder.

Inside was a single document. She started to read from the beginning.

Lower Interior Five Watch facility Section 21–244. Witness to testing on human subjects. Using serum derivatives.

A crash made them both jump, startling them out of their reading trance. A young server had knocked over a mug while clearing the two tables that had seated the group of teenage girls. Its white shards, among dark droplets, sprinkled the hardwood floor. The matronly woman strolled out from behind the counter with a dustpan and broom, calmly bending to sweep it up.

Harper rubbed her weary eyes and stared back at the screen. The typed words were in Bobby's crisp voice, but uncharacteristically rushed and clipped. She wanted to keep reading, but as she turned to watch the unhurried cleanup, she realized they needed to get somewhere private to go through it all as carefully as they needed to. She didn't want to miss a single detail.

"Maybe we should take this somewhere else," Rome suggested, reading her mind.

"Sounds like a plan." Harper closed the files after protecting them with several encrypted passwords. She saved the Harpie folder to the flash drive and erased any remnants of it from the computer. Then she pulled out the drive and slipped it into her jeans pocket. She shut down the computer and stood, smiling at Rome. "Let's go."

"Drive safely, kids," the elder woman called out to them as they reached the door, giving them a hearty wave with the broom. "Have a nice honeymoon," she added with an exaggerated wink.

Rome gave her a friendly wave back. Harper stopped abruptly in alarm, but was shoved out the door by his strong hand at her back.

"H-h-honeymoon," Harper sputtered as they reached the car, almost stumbling over her own feet. "What was that all about?"

"She asked about us," Rome answered as he held the Bug door open for her and then slammed it shut. She watched him get into the driver's side and then turn to face her. He took a deep breath that sounded a tad strained. "I couldn't very well tell her that I'm a covert government agent hired to hunt you down because you suddenly have superhero-like mind power that came from a mysterious serum that your secret scientist brother developed and was then murdered for. But now we're working together and on the run to find out what it's all about, how it works, and how to stop the bad guys who keep trying to kill us."

A moment of silence.

"You could've just said we're friends on a road trip," she suggested quietly. That sounded simple enough to her. The idea of that kind of commitment almost made her want to forget this all and run away into the night.

"Yes," he said quietly. "I guess I could've just said that." She saw his grip tighten on the steering wheel before he reached to shove the keys in the ignition and start the car. The Bug rumbled to life and he pulled out of the newly paved parking lot onto the street just as raindrops started to splash against the flat windshield.

CHAPTER ELEVEN

The bright beam of light cut through the darkness, illuminating the quiet scene. The flashlight's trail was garish against the stark ground as Jeff Donovan searched for anything that could lead him to Harper Kane.

And Rome.

Jeff hadn't wanted to believe that the agent was a part of Ms. Kane's desperate actions, but he couldn't deny the facts. This was Rome's warehouse, and it was apparent that the two of them had spent time there. And now were gone.

A shame, really. Rome Lucian was an exceptional agent. One of the best. Jeff had even considered Rome for being a subject, but hadn't wanted to use the serum on him until the formula was perfected. The agent had invaluable skills. Now Rome would be another necessary sacrifice to the imperative project Jeff was trying to implement for the military sector.

But he had to find the two of them first. And his enhanced troops were proving to be less than adequate. Case in point, Jeff had no idea where their bodies were. He was getting very tired of Ms. Kane killing his men. Just one had survived the encounter, barely escaping, only to die soon after he'd relayed what had happened here at the site.

Jeff paced toward the dense tree line, looking for any lead. But again, Rome was very, very good. And obviously so was Ms. Kane.

His toe kicked something that made a hollow *clink* and skittered across the pavement. Jeff darted the beam from the flashlight around the immediate area, searching the ground for the source.

A bullet. Not just any bullet, though. He recognized the sleek and sharp ammunition his men stocked. Twisting it between his fingers, he could see a dark film coating it.

Blood. This was her blood.

His lone survivor, who had been the unnoticed backup, had told him they'd shot the woman. And she'd just pulled out the slug as though nothing had happened. He'd thought the man had been delirious.

She'd survived a powerful gunshot wound as if she'd never been hit. This was a new development. A very interesting and even more encouraging development.

Jeff smiled and squeezed his fist tight around the shell. The bitch was truly dangerous. He wanted her. Wanted her power. And he'd stop at nothing to get it.

Rome pulled into the potholed parking lot of a dingy motel. If it could even be called that. He'd been in worse places, but this spot was a dump. At least it was a surprisingly clean dump, miles from civilization.

Surrounded by leafy trees and a sprawling, overgrown hayfield, the ten-room, one-level motel was the perfect point in the middle of nowhere to hole up and spend some time going through the data that they hoped could answer a lot of their questions.

Harper was convinced it would. He trusted that she trusted her brother's foresight, so he was also convinced the information would be valuable.

He'd dropped Harper off here with explicit instruc-
tions to stay put this time, then left to get some provi-
sions. He'd had to drive for a while, finally finding a local
all-night superstore, which thankfully had a little bit of
everything, from clothing to groceries. There was no
way they'd be staying at the motel for long, but they'd be
there overnight for sure, given that midnight was fast
approaching.

Rome felt a curious thrill while shopping for extra
clothes for Harper. Her requests were simple, but actually picking out her cotton underwear seemed extremely
intimate.

He'd never bought lingerie for any woman. He'd
never understood the purpose of it. He wanted his partners naked, not clothed, even in just scraps. And he was
very glad he'd never wasted any money on the superfluous garments.

All Harper wanted were a pair of jeans, a couple of
T-shirts, and a hooded sweatshirt. Rome sighed as he
hefted the plastic bags.

He'd never met a woman quite like Harper. She
wasn't apologetic or embarrassed when she rattled off
the sizes of her clothes. She loved food. She was athletic,
sported an honest tan from the outdoors, and was right-
fully proud of her lean muscles. She was also extraordinarily intelligent.

And she wasn't ashamed of any of it. The woman was
completely confident and comfortable with herself.

Almost every other woman he'd encountered had always been on some kind of fad diet and would never in a
million years have eaten a full-sized salad, let alone a
whole sandwich.

Harper was the complete opposite.

Most of the women he'd dated back when he'd had

time to date wore glitzy designer clothes. Any muscles were carefully sculpted for looks without much actual substance. His usual type was celebrity gorgeous, with long midnight dark hair, pale skin, and petite frames. He'd always thought their insecurity was appealing and liked the fact that they were just plain shallow—like a pill, glossy on the outside but acrid on the inside.

It kept things simple. It kept things neat and orderly. He couldn't stand the drama of a relationship. His world of shadows, violence, and corruption had more than enough of it. So he didn't need it in what little personal life he allowed himself.

And it had been a while. Almost two years since he'd lost himself in a woman. Which was just fine with him. His work fulfilled him like nothing else ever had. Even hockey. Besides, he didn't want the complications of falling for anyone.

But he was falling for Harper. Hard. It was completely insane and a logistical nightmare, but he couldn't deny it. She was everything he'd never thought he'd wanted, and something he should never have.

And when she'd said she loved him at the café, his heart had pounded so loud, he thought she must have heard it. Though he knew it was just a fleeting quip, involuntary sparks of joy had shot through his chest, warming his every fiber.

Harper was all wrong for him, yet he wanted her. Bad. For more than just a night. More than just however long this mission took. Knowing she didn't fully trust him, he knew he needed to keep some distance.

Despite her apparent lack of trust, he was sure Harper wanted him, too. But for how long?

Stopping outside the thick wooden door to their motel room, he knocked on the door in the prearranged sequence that would assure Harper it was him. After a few seconds, the door opened a sliver and he saw a sea green eye, near his eye level, peer at him from above the jingling door chain. He gave her a smile. Then the door shut and he heard her fiddle with the chain.

And fiddle some more.

After several clatters, he heard a "for crying out loud" and something that sounded dangerously close to "gosh darn it."

Something else about Harper that was undeniably enchanting. She never swore. At least, he'd never heard one bad word come from those luscious lips, and she certainly had many reasons to rattle off some doozies.

After a heavy *thud* and splintering *crack*, he distinctly heard the clinking of the chain and the door opened wide.

She greeted him with an innocent smile. He stepped over the threshold and pushed the door shut with his boot. Glancing over his shoulder, he saw that the chain slider had been pried off the back of the door and now dangled harmlessly, still attached to the chain.

He raised his eyebrow at her in question. Her smile grew bigger with a shrug of her broad shoulders.

"How goes it?" Rome chuckled at her resourcefulness and gestured to the laptop resting on the lone queen bed. He dumped the bags next to the computer on the golden-flowered comforter.

"There's a lot of information there." Harper's voice sounded throaty and tired. He heard a slight squeak from the bed as she flopped down on it. "You were right."

"About what?" he halted his rummaging through the bags for a moment, giving her his full attention after feeling, more than hearing, her weary tone.

"Bobby was a Five Watch scientist," she said, rolling over to lie on her back. She crossed her hands over her flat stomach. Damn, she was hot. "He worked in a classi-fied bioengineering division. Apparently, he's not just a normal genius government scientist."

"Okay, tell me about it," he said as he resumed un-packing the bags, starting with the food he'd gotten at the grocery section of the store. He'd been surprised to find that the tiny room had a modest refrigerator. Even more surprised to find that it worked and was nearly spotless.

"I'm not through it all yet." Harper sprawled at the head of the bed and repositioned the laptop in front of her. "But from what I can tell, Bobby was experimenting with plants, developing—well, actually, he did develop—a serum for them. A superserum of sorts."

"The serum you have in your body," Rome said, con-firming more than questioning.

"I'm sure of it."

"So it's for plants," he said as he bent over to put some cans of soda in the fridge. "What's it supposed to do?"

"Augment and fortify global vegetation," she an-swered with a heavy sigh. She moved over to lean on her side, just watching him, her gaze raking him.

"What does that mean?" he asked, emptying the food bag and riffling through the heap piled on the top of the comforter.

A couple of chocolate bars slid across the bed and hit her in the thighs. His gaze followed her hand as it reached near her crotch to grab one of the king-sized bars. A rush of heat flushed through him straight to his groin and he had to clear his throat. She tossed the long bar back onto his little pile of food.

"The serum sounds amazing, actually." Her voice was tinged with pride. Obviously she and Bobby had been very close. She'd never talked about any other family and he wondered just how alone she really was now. "The primary intention was to enhance the plants to generate more oxygen for the environment."

"Wow, that sounds pretty damned remarkable," Rome said. And it did sound remarkable. He had to admit that Bobby really was one of the good guys. Not that he had fully doubted it in the first place.

"It is." She flung the other chocolate bar next to the first. "But what's really amazing are the other effects of the serum. The formula basically reengineered the plants' genetic coding to make them stronger and healthier. Also, self-repairing."

"Is that possible?" Rome halted his food sorting to look directly at her. He almost laughed, seeing Harper seriously eye the chocolate she'd thrown back.

Usually this kind of Science Channel stuff bored him to sleep, but this was actually fascinating. Maybe because he was smack-dab in the middle of it. Or maybe he just craved the sound of Harper's low, husky voice. He'd listen to her recite the entire dictionary for no reason.

"Bobby must have found a way to make it possible," she answered, finally giving in and fishing one of the giant-sized chocolate bars off one of his food piles. She tore the wrapping open to break off some squares. "He tested all different batches of plants, different types, to see if the serum was able to make them withstand severe weather conditions. Droughts, floods, fires, arctic freezes . . . You name it, the plants held up."

"So the serum was working," he said, reaching out to take the chocolate she was handing to him. Their fingers brushed, causing a tingle to shoot up his forearm.

"Right," she confirmed. "The damaged plants were able to heal broken or missing stalks and repair themselves. If the cold froze the plant, it went into a sort of hibernation to slow down the decomposition and build itself back up."

"Kind of a rehab," Rome mused.

"Self-preservation at its finest." Harper nodded and tossed another square of candy bar in her mouth, sucking on it lightly. "Plants that used to get pulled up by stormy winds were able to endure with stronger roots. None of the simulated hurricanes, typhoons, or tornadoes was able to tear them from the ground. Plants that would normally shrivel up from intense desert heat were able to keep rehydrating themselves."

He could imagine the creamy chocolate melting on her hot, wet tongue. *Oh, to be that piece of candy. Shit.* He was staring and not listening. She was smiling. And he was sure she saw him flush. What was it about her that made him lose his composure? Some damn agent he was. He cleared his throat, tilting his head to indicate she should continue.

"Each folder contained the data for every experiment," she went on. "Every detail on a given date. Bobby was meticulous about his notes. Each plant that was given the formula developed a keen hydrologic system that merged with is native plumbing. Developed its own filtering system, kind of like your brain filters a need or a threat. The superior new system adapted to its climate and other conditions."

"Superplants," Rome said, quite in awe at the brilliance of the formula her brother had developed.

She shrugged. "Bobby called it a variation of psionic power, meaning that through the complete force of genetic will, the plants actually desire to flourish. To find ways to survive. He found that a psionic plant could set off a power of sorts unto itself that would oppose any physical force or energy. The plants' modified molecular nervous systems basically commanded their enhanced muscle tissues to survive adversity and hostile climates."

He watched her finish her report and pop more candy bar into her mouth. Then he thought hard about what she'd just said.

Imagine. Food wouldn't be scarce in places where vegetation couldn't grow right now. Air quality could vastly improve. Forests could be replenished quickly. His mind reeled in absolute awe.

Bobby hadn't just developed a revolutionary brew; he'd saved the world.

"Harper, that's seriously incredible." He brushed the boxes and packages aside so he could lounge on the bed near her. Reaching across the hideous but surprisingly cushy bedspread, he snapped off another piece of Hershey's.

"He was incredible." Harper's voice was tinged with sadness. "Apparently this was a very top secret project within the Five Watch. Only Bobby and a handful of people knew about it. For security reasons, his notes indicated. They didn't want it going public until Bobby deemed it was ready for implementation. The last files were part of his final testing. But then they just stopped."

"A few days ago?" Rome asked.

She nodded, and then turned her gaze away from him, seeming to look at nothing.

She'd been alone here, in this cheap and seedy motel room, for about an hour while he had run their errands. He hadn't really realized until now just how tough it must be for her to sit here and read her brother's posthumous notes, the wording and diction familiar to her in a way he couldn't understand.

But, because she did understand Bobby's language, she truly was the best choice to go through it, in spite of the grief it may trigger.

"Harper, I'm sorry." Rome reached for her hand and held it in his, trying to convey both sympathy and encouragement in his touch. "I know this must be hard for you. But we're making good progress. This is the information we need."

"I know." She sighed heavily and squeezed his hand back. "I just . . . I hear his voice saying these words." Damn, how he wished he could erase the pain he saw in her intense eyes. She lowered them as she took a deep, unsteady breath. "I'm okay. I just wish he were here." She gave him a sad but sure smile.

"I know," he said soothingly, moving his hand to rub her bare arm just below the cuff of her short-sleeve T-shirt. Damn, she was steely solid under that silky skin. Strong yet all woman.

All he wanted to do at this very moment was to shove the food and laptop off the bed and draw her body against his, just to feel her against him. And from the swirling typhoon in the green of her eyes, he wondered whether she was thinking the same exact thing.

His fingers began to itch in anticipation and he quickly lifted his hand away from her enticing flesh. Mentally slapping himself, Rome sat up and resumed organizing the food pile.

"So, um, what went wrong?" Rome heard the hoarseness in his voice and cleared his throat. He jumped off the bed to put some needed distance between them. Well, as much distance as he could, which wasn't a lot in the small room.

He was never going to make it through the night if he didn't stop thinking about how damn much he was attracted to her. He imagined those lean tanned arms clamping his back. Those long legs wrapping around him. Those luscious full lips he was familiar with, running all over his . . .

Damn it all. Rome raked a shaking hand over his face, struggling to clear his roving thoughts. He peeled his attention away from her and to the plastic clothing bags. Reaching inside one, he pulled out a pair of new cotton panties. And stared at them, imagining them on her. Off her. *Damn. Damn. Damn.*

A husky chuckle floated from the bed. A hand flashed in front of his gaze to snatch the panties out of his grasp. She rolled the material around in her hands, checking them out. He almost moaned out loud. Maybe he had.

"Bobby's last phase of research was to test the consumption of the enhanced vegetation," Harper said, answering the question he'd asked before his fantasizing. "To make sure the plants weren't harmful to ingest and all that."

"Sounds reasonable," Rome said, continuing to unpack the bag, trying to impersonally sort between his and hers. He tossed Harper the rest of the clothes he'd bought for her and then organized his own, tearing off tags and stickers.

"He was preparing trial experiments for volunteers when he stumbled across test data he referred to as 'suspicious,'" Harper continued as she folded her garments neatly, then set them aside. "So Bobby dug around a little and found some files that outlined experiments that had been run on human subjects. Using copies of his serum. He also found that some of his plant inventory that he thought had been destroyed was missing."

"Missing?" Rome asked as he picked up his small pile of clothes and set it on top of the dented thirteen-inch television. He had yet to see whether it worked. "You mean someone stole them?"

"Bobby's notes said he'd found out about a faction within the Five Watch." Harper lolled on her side. "From what his notes say, Bobby didn't know who they were, but he did uncover their less-than-scrupulous work."

The Five Watch, though on the shady side, didn't seem like a mutinous group to Rome. On the contrary, they seemed very tight within their obscure walls. Besides, who could pull off that kind of mutiny without other Five Watchers knowing? There weren't a whole lot of them as far as he knew. Fifty, maybe sixty people within the elite group itself.

"According to my brother, this faction was hoping that the genetic alterations Bobby made for plants would have the same effect on human beings," she said. "Hoping to make people stronger and self-healing. The data he uncovered suggested they wanted to create bio-enhanced spies and soldiers."

"Holy shit." Rome sighed as a somber weight dropped onto his shoulders. They needed to find out who was the mastermind. Who engineered this faction and who turned against Bobby. Could Jeff really be a part of it? Maybe this was what had been making Jeff so antsy. Damn. The suspect list was vast, but narrow all the same. "That complicates things. There are limited people who even know about the Five Watch, but none of those people really knows what anyone else knows. It's the stuff that's made for conspiracy theorists."

Anyone could be behind this and no one would know about it. The only person who did know was now dead. This amazing woman's remarkable brother was snooping around in places he had every right to be and was killed for it.

"These people, this faction, killed Bobby because he found out," Harper stated quietly, watching him closely.

"Most likely, yes," Rome confirmed.

She closed her eyes and bowed her head for a moment. Then she nodded and looked up at him again, a hard resolve behind her gaze.

"Harper, we'll find them." He tried to instill every ounce of certainty he had in his voice. No matter how vast this sinister trek was going to be, they at least had a starting point now. And each other.

"I know we will." Her low voice chilled him. The tone was filled with more than the confidence he'd come to expect from her. It now contained a touch of . . . hunger.

At the very beginning, she'd told him she was going to get her revenge. And from the way she lounged there—like a lazy jungle cat, resting now, but primed to kill in an instant—he knew it to be true. Her vow for vengeance was very much alive.

"There's more," she said after a quick shake of her head. Great. More. "The human experiments didn't work quite right."

"What the hell does that mean?" He was getting very tired of bad news getting worse.

"The human subjects would develop the psionic power and be able to heal minor injuries, just as the plants could repair themselves. But soon after . . ." Harper's voice trailed off.

"What?" Rome asked, lying down on the bed, mirroring her pose to face her. Whatever was coming was the worst part. He traced his fingers over her shoulder lightly. "Tell me."

"Soon after they used their powers"—she looked away for a silent moment and then returned her gaze to his—"they died."

CHAPTER TWELVE

"You're not going to die," Rome said firmly, shaking his head. No. He wouldn't even begin to think about it. "You're different from them."

"How?" Harper asked quietly, narrowing her eyes in what looked like terrified but controlled anger. "How am I different? Those men did the same things I could do. I have the same serum flowing through my body. In my blood. Just like them. The subjects would die when they used their power to the fullest. The energy basically overpowered their bodies. Burning them up inside. Killing them."

"You were able to overpower them." He ran his hand down her arm, grabbing her hand and holding it tight against his chest, twisting his fingers through hers. "Not once, but twice. That has to mean something." She kept silent, just staring at him. "How long is 'soon after'?"

She just shrugged. "I don't know, but it doesn't matter. I just need to stay alive long enough to make them pay for what they did to Bobby."

"No," Rome said fiercely, clutching her hand tightly to keep her with him. "You need to stay alive for more than that." He leaned in closer, just a breath away from her lovely face, every pinpoint of green in her eyes lancing into him, cutting away every line of defense around his heart. "You need to stay alive for me."

The biting thought of losing her terrified him more than her violent powers ever could. He closed the brief distance between them and sealed his lips against hers, willing her to taste his basic primal need for her. In the short time since she'd literally blasted into his life, she'd come to mean everything to him.

Releasing her hand, he brushed his fingers along her smooth cheek, her neck, her bare arm, down her ribs to her hip, all the while enjoying long, soulful kisses.

Slanting his body slightly, he rolled across the bed, fitting himself against her sinewy length. The heat from her body blanketed him as he cupped the rounded firmness of her tight rear and reached lower to tug her powerful thigh across his, nestling her closer into him.

Deepening the kiss, Rome moaned and pressed against her. He felt a shiver pass through her body as she curled her thigh around the back of his leg, encouraging further contact. Frenzied contact.

His body grinded into hers in response, answering her call. She pulled him closer and swept her tongue into his mouth, making him dizzy with desire.

He broke away, desperately needing air, and then returned to trail hot kisses along her neck to the hollow at her throat. She gasped and writhed beneath him.

A soft chime floated through his aroused haze.

What the hell was that? It sounded again, and Harper stilled.

"Oh, for crying out loud." Harper's low voice was raspy. Her chest heaved against his. "My download is done."

Her what? Rome glanced menacingly over his shoulder at the damn laptop near the bottom of the bed, blinking an innocent cursor at him.

Damn it all. He almost kicked the thing across the small room.

She shifted slightly and allowed her to untangle from their more-than-eager embrace. He backed away to watch as she stretched her perfect body across the bed to pull the electronic pest toward her. He gave serious thought to pouncing on her back. She then twisted around to lean against the wall and set it on her lap, her fingers running over the keys.

He sat there, staring at her, his body still tight with arousal.

Was it that easy for her? Weren't they just about ready to tear each other's clothes off and get their money's worth from this cheap by-the-hour motel room? Rome knew he had been more than ready. And he was pretty damn certain she'd been, too.

Rubbing the light sheen of sweat off his forehead, he kept his slowly cooling focus on her. Her face was tinged blue from the digital display, but it gave her eyes an ethereal glow. Unearthly sexy.

Her gaze broke away from the bright screen, meeting his own, softening and igniting all at once. A smoldering shiver laced his body. He wanted her as if he always had and always would.

"It's not over," she said. And then she gave him the sexiest wink he'd ever seen. Promising more.

And he'd be ready. Harper, more than anyone he'd ever known, was worth waiting for.

Clearing his throat, he rolled off the bed and grabbed two sodas from the minifridge, hoping the chilled cans would help cool him off.

"So, what were you downloading?" He walked to the other side of the bed and plopped down next to her, but kept as much distance as he could manage. Her fingers brushed his as she took the Coke, sending a sizzle down his arm. Pulling back fast, he opened the can and took a long, cool drink, ignoring the tickle of fizz as it burned down his throat.

"Some of the files in the Harpie folder had extra levels of encryption," Harper answered after a big gulp of her own. He watched her read as she pushed the laptop lower on her thighs so she could place the can between her legs. *Holy shit*. Didn't she know he was trying to simmer down? "I had to create a little program to decode and extract those files."

Rome stared as she leaned over and set the laptop on the floor. Then she stretched her arms high above her head, pulling the fabric of her T-shirt taut against her chest, clearly outlining her perfect-sized breasts.

His gaze fell to the hem of the shirt as it lifted an inch or two to reveal tight abs rolling under silky, tan skin. He couldn't wait to taste the tempting flesh there.

"This next download will take some time," she said, bringing her arms back down to rest on her thighs. He had to shift his position on the bed a little when she reached between her legs for another swallow. "Maybe we should get some rest. I think my eyes are about to stick shut from reading that screen." She scrubbed her face and turned those eyes to him, taking his breath away with their emerald allure.

"You're right," Rome said, looking for a place he could sleep that was a safe distance from her, where he wouldn't be sorely tempted to ravish her body. He couldn't find one.

"I'm showering first," she declared as she stood and sauntered to the tiny but surprisingly immaculate bathroom.

He tried so hard not to think about her stripping off those clothes and standing in that tiled stall, the hot water running all over her naked body. Shaking his head, he tried to change the subject in his mind to what they should be concentrating on instead of how much he wanted to jump in the shower with her. She obviously didn't need to trust him to have sex with him. But surprisingly he realized he wanted her trust first.

"Harper," he called softly. She halted, half in, half out of the bathroom door with a questioning look. "I think we need to get a second look at the facility where Bobby's lab was. Put some proof with that data. After we shower and rest, let's plan."

"Sounds good to me," she agreed, and laughed playfully. "I'll be out in a few minutes. Keep the bed warm for me." And then she gave him another one of those scorching winks that boiled his blood and seared his insides before disappearing behind the chipped door of the bathroom.

A deep moan escaped his lips. She was obviously flirting to lighten the mood, but just the thought had him very close to bursting through that door and joining her, keeping her warm instead of the sheets. He was going to offer to sleep on the floor, but it sounded like she planned on sharing the queen bed.

Lying flat on his back on the ugly bedspread, Rome knew that he wouldn't be getting much sleep with Harper's tempting body next to his under the sheets.

He just couldn't decide whether the night was going to be ecstasy or agony.

CHAPTER THIRTEEN

Harper crouched on the moist, leafy ground, waiting for Rome to return. Disabling the perimeter cameras of the Five Watch facility without anyone noticing was his task. He'd been gone for about five minutes and she expected to be alone for precisely five more.

Watery rays of sunlight gently filtered through the moss-draped trees around her. A misty drizzle cast a light sheen among the brush that was providing her cover.

She'd never been in this area in the daytime. The only two times she'd come to Bobby's lab, it had been the dead of night.

She hadn't even known there was a vast facility adjoining the lab in the front. Bobby's lab was underground and seemingly far from the gray buildings she could barely make out in the distance. Apparently they connected through a myriad of hallways. But there was another concealed bunker about a hundred yards from the entrance she'd used to get to Bobby's lab.

That was where she and Rome were headed.

Over a package of surprisingly tasty store-bought cinnamon rolls, they'd decided this morning that they needed to find some tangible evidence of what was going on. They trusted Bobby's notes, but wanted to see for themselves exactly what they were up against.

She glanced at the timer counting down on her digital watch—4:30 blinked back at her. Rome had been very specific about the timing. And gone over and over it before they'd even left their tawdry motel room this morning.

Mmm . . . this morning. Waking up with Rome spooning her had been, well, heavenly. The combination of warmth and strength and the vulnerability in his sleep had nearly undone her. When he'd been kissing her the night before, she'd never wanted anyone or anything more in her life than she'd wanted him. Not even an Olympic gold. She still didn't fully trust him, but my goodness, she was fully attracted to him. But when they made love, she wanted plenty of time to explore his delicious body. And this morning they'd had other things to contend with.

Another glance at her watch—2:10. She had to clear her mind or she'd jump him the second he returned.

As much as she'd initially wanted to claim vengeance on her own, she'd come to realize that she couldn't do this without Rome. Harper knew nothing about this spy stuff other than what she'd seen in movies and the video games she played. She desperately needed his expertise and endless resources.

And not only was he trained in this kind of stuff, but his steadfast support was beginning to mean a lot to her. She'd lost so much already. She didn't think she'd survive losing Rome, too. Even if she did have a limited life span.

His betrayal still stung. And she still wasn't ready to forgive it. Yet she was smart enough to know he was a real asset. She needed him to help her get revenge for Bobby, given she didn't know how long she had to live.

She knew she should feel something about her imminent death. But somehow, she felt that the moment she'd decided on revenge, she realized it would end in a one-way ticket to mortality. And surprisingly, she was okay with it. As long as she got vengeance first.

A slight rustling of brush to her left spurred her out of her absorbed thoughts. Glancing at her watch, she saw the digitized numbers count down from ten. Rome slipped through the leafy barrier with hushed ease.

"I'm surprised I could even hear you," she said softly, flicking her gaze back to see the seconds tick down to zero. Amazing.

"It was on purpose," he said quietly with a smile, hunkering down right next to her. "I didn't want to scare you." He placed his hand on her shoulder, warming her through the fabric of the black microfleece coat he'd given her to wear. "Are you ready?"

Sure, she was ready to break into a supersecret underground government facility that, unbeknownst to everyone but the two of them, was being used by a traitorous faction with unscrupulous plans, willing to murder in order to keep their secret.

"Yes," she nodded, knowing it really didn't matter whether she was ready. They were doing this. For Bobby. For his research. For the good of everyone. They would put the wrongs of the faction right. "Let's go."

He returned her nod, taking her hand in his and pulling her up to stand with him. A light tug on her hand and she followed closely behind him, shifting out of his clasp to rest her hand lightly on the small of his back as they moved quickly yet quietly through the thick covering of trees.

A thrill of anticipation prickled through her blood, much like she experienced just before a race. Adrenaline pumped a sense of purpose into her, eliciting a confidence she knew she was going to need to get through this.

Sooner than she expected, they reached the well-hidden bunker. It surprised her to see just how close it was to the secret entrance she'd used not too long ago to sneak into her brother's lab.

Rome held up a hand, motioning for her to stay put. Nodding, she watched him move with ghostlike steps toward a rocky area covered with thick green moss.

Harper relished watching him and was impressed at how stealthily he could maneuver, considering his muscular bulk. She imagined it wasn't much different than the smooth way she cut through the water. They were more alike than they were different. She loved that.

Whoa. Love?

Where the heck did that come from? Wait. At the café, she'd said she loved him. In jest, surely, but she'd never slipped with the L word before. Ever.

"C'mon, we have sixty-five minutes." Rome's reminder shook her out of her shock, causing her to jump. "Hey, are you okay?" In an instant, he was beside her, rubbing her shoulder under the backpack she was wearing, sporting a sincere questioning look.

"Um, right. Yes, I'm fine," she stammered, and gave him a smile she hoped backed up her words. He narrowed his eyes at her, clearly undecided whether to believe her.

"You're sure?" he asked, his hand roving to her back in comfort.

She nodded crisply, gesturing for him to proceed as she reset her watch timer for the sixty-five minutes he'd bought them by shutting down surveillance. Or whatever he did.

He gave her a long, pointed look before turning toward the now-open door to the underground facility. After a quick shake of her head to clear her muddled thoughts, she followed him into the darkness.

Admittedly, she felt more than a little uncomfortable breaking into a facility like this. The worst she'd ever done was sneak into the living room while her parents were watching *Jaws*, after they'd forbidden her from seeing it. Yet, at the same time the fear spiked her adrenaline and got her heart pumping as though she were swimming a sprint.

Once again, Harper kept her hand on his firm back as they maneuvered down through the dimly lit corridor. The passage walls pressed in on them and the moist smell of packed soil sifted into her senses. Earthy dust grazed the back of her throat after she took a deep breath.

Every so often lightbulbs, enclosed by caged fixtures that had been secured to the dirt walls, illuminated the way for them. The slope wasn't too steep, but it was a definite tricky descent, making her grateful for Rome's sturdy presence just a pace ahead of her.

After a few moments of winding, the natural dug-out walls became smooth gray concrete and squarely structured. Their booted footsteps sounded deafening once on the level surface. Well, hers did, anyway.

This morning she'd hacked into several government provisioning databases to pull up the basic building plans of the facility to give them an idea of the layout. Then Rome had chosen this route when they devised this plan, thinking it would be the most deserted. He explained that the Five Watch was most likely confident in their anonymity and covert surveillance. So, he'd said with a wicked smile, they probably wouldn't be counting on a seasoned agent and expert hacker to come a-knockin'.

After running through several ideas together about where to head once they'd broken in, they'd concluded that the best option was to check out some offices or labs for files and hard evidence, then go through the ceiling's service ducts to see what they could witness firsthand.

Though their knowledge of the facility was limited, his familiarity with infiltrating secure organizations was considerable, so she didn't feel like they were going in blind.

But planning was one thing. Actually doing it was another. Especially with a novice like herself.

Rome stopped at a corner and peeked around it. His slow, easy movements were impressive. According to the building plans, offices were down this hallway, but Rome believed that the Five Watch may have made their own modifications by adding more laboratories.

She waited in silence, throwing an uneasy glance over her shoulder, chasing shadows. Ahead of her, Rome began moving forward again, rounding the corner as quiet as a summer breeze.

Following him closely, she once again marveled at how silently a tough guy like him could walk down a dim, sterile hallway. Every step she took sounded like a bass drum to her, but his strides were featherlight.

Rome slowed as they approached a closed unmarked doorway to their right. He flattened his hands against the surface and leaned in his head to listen. One of his hands brushed the door handle and tried it slowly. Locked.

He waved down the hall, signaling they'd try the next door, about twenty paces away. But that one was locked, too.

He gestured to a small panel on the wall with numbers and a tiny red light. Harper hadn't even noticed it. Pointing to it, he wiggled his fingers like he was typing.

What the heck? She wasn't trained in special-agent signs. She was winging it here.

Holding her hands palms up and shrugging in the universal sign for *huh?* she waited for clarification. Rome rolled his eyes and moved close to her, brushing his mouth softly against her ear.

"Disable this," he whispered; his warm breath against her skin caused her to shiver. He then pulled back slightly and gave her a questioning look, tilting his head toward the panel on the wall.

Oh. She nodded. She moved her fingers to the panel and pointed to the red light, giving him a cautious look. He nodded back, so she figured it was okay.

Removing the panel cover, she carefully fiddled with the wires, much like she had with Rome's alarm at his warehouse. In less than a minute, the light flicked to green and she heard the lock snick.

Rome moved his hand to the doorknob and twisted it slowly, opening the door just a sliver. He peeked through, then opened it wider and quickly moved inside, yanking her along with him.

He shut the door but didn't turn on the lights. The room was illuminated by two dim fluorescent bulbs, one hanging from each end of the ceiling.

Curiously, the room was very cold. It boasted several stainless steel tables and assorted laboratory equipment, not unlike the machines she'd been hooked up to while in captivity.

On the tables was a scattering of lab beakers, rubber tubes, and glass vials. Shuddering with unpleasant memories, she padded across the room to the laptop resting on the desk in the corner, careful not to touch anything along the way.

Rome was examining some of the equipment as he

moved toward a bank of large metal cabinets that lined half of the wall in the back of the room. She continued to watch as he reached for a drawer handle and pulled on it, raising his eyebrows at her when it unlatched easily. He gave it a good tug.

A body slid out.

Harper choked and covered her mouth with her hand. Considering all the dead bodies she'd seen—well, caused—in the last week, the grisly sight shouldn't have shocked her. But this one wasn't a victim of self-defense like the others. Against her better judgment, she went to Rome's side.

On a metal slab, the dead body was similar to the men who had attacked her—large and muscular, built for power. And almost familiar. But this corpse was withered and appeared annihilated, as though like it had been beaten thoroughly by some unbearable force of nature.

Then it hit her. This was the leader of the camouflaged group that chased her through the woods and cornered her at the Barracks.

And murdered her brother.

Her blood heated in rage, flushing her body. This corpse was a casualty of the psi-power war they started with her. This guy got what he deserved. And before this was all over, the rest of them would, too.

She blinked, then glanced at Rome and realized he was watching her, a probing look on his face she couldn't discern. She shook the greedy avenging thoughts from her mind.

Rome pulled out a folder filed in the small partition at the front of the drawer. He swung his backpack around and tucked the folder in it as he closed the drawer with a heavy click. She watched him open the next one

and take its file as well. He continued down the line until they heard an electronic beeping near the door. *Yikes.*
Someone was coming.

Zipping the backpack, Rome quickly replaced it on
his back and closed the drawer quietly. He put a finger
to his lips and pulled her with him along the wall to
crouch together behind one of the enormous machines
in the corner.

Blindingly bright incandescent light showered the
room, forcing her to squint. Peering through the thick
levers and pipes of the creepy apparatus, she watched a
tall man with a white lab coat walk in, his attention glued
to the open files he had in his hands. He hadn't noticed
the two of them at all.

A shrill ringing pierced the silence. Harper nearly
jumped out of her skin at the sound. In an instant she
realized just how foreign all this was to her. Rome laid a
calming hand on her thigh. The man reached into his
pocket and pulled out a cell phone.

"Yes?" he said, answering the phone, his voice a tad
nervous. "No, the latest tests failed." A pause as he listened to the caller. "You're coming here? Now?" He
sounded anxious, as though the person on the other end
was supremely unhappy at his negative response. "Okay,
I'll meet you here. Yes, at the lab."

Disconnecting the call, the man mumbled something harsh and slammed the folders on the desk next to
the laptop. He swiped his brow with a clearly shaking
hand, then stamped out the door.

Harper turned to face Rome. His blue gaze appeared
troubled and excited at the same time as it met hers.

"Let's get out of here and into the ducts." He glanced
upward. "I want to see who's coming to the lab to meet
with this guy."

She nodded in response and followed as he crept soundlessly around the side of the ugly machinery and headed for the door. He held up his palm, mouthing to her to wait, while he checked to see whether there was anyone in the hall.

At his signal, she followed him out of the room. They turned back the way they had come and tread quietly down the sterile hallway.

Another few steps and Rome stopped abruptly, almost causing her to collide with him in the cloak of near darkness. The comforting warmth of his strong body seeped into her while she watched his hands sweep along the flat surface of the wall. Looking for something.

Her eyes adjusted to the dark, and she saw the outline of a door flush with the wall, but no handle.

He reached into his back pocket, his hand brushing against her stomach, inadvertently causing little flutters.

"Not sorry." His low chuckle came from the darkness.

"Not a problem," she answered with a soft laugh of her own.

Harper heard a muted snap, then some scraping, and figured out that Rome was attempting to pry open the buried lock with his secret-agent-spy gadget that looked like a simple pocketknife, but had many special little tools inside of it.

With a faint click he pulled the door backward. She backed off slightly to allow him to replace it in the back pocket of his jeans, though she was sorely tempted to lean in for another indulgent fondle.

She took another step backward as Rome tugged harder on the door and stepped inside after a quick peek.

His nod was barely discernable in the dim entryway. She followed him across the threshold and pulled the door softly shut behind them, enveloping them in a close-fitting and slightly muggy passage.

As they moved cautiously upward through the enclosed space, she could easily see why he'd favored the ceiling ducts. According to the plans, these particular channels ran above the working laboratories, where she and Rome figured they could gather the most information in the least invasive way.

The shadowy duct was narrow and tight, with coiled wires snaking along the sides and underneath the thin, grated catwalk. Puffy silver-coated insulation lined the area above them.

Stagnant, warm air filled her lungs, making every breath heavy, and there was a constant low hum that tickled her ears. But among everything, including the various pipes that streaked above them, the space was blissfully empty and unprotected.

Carefully watching her step, she followed Rome's shrewd maneuvering. A few more paces and Rome stopped, kneeling to the floor. Crouching next to him, she watched as he pushed aside some of the wiring and pulled out his trusty little device to cut away some of the padding that layered the ceiling below them.

Harper admired his deft precision with the knife and the way his fingers balanced between strong and graceful. He passed the fluffy padding to her and she took it, placing the chunk on the metal walkway as he leaned down on his stomach to get into a good position to peer down below.

The ceiling tiles were unusually constructed. From the little green triangles printed on the corners, she could tell that they were made from recycled metals, creating a thin layer with tiny holes constructed for optimum air circulation.

The diagrams they had studied that morning had shown that the diamond-shaped holes filtered the flow of the recycled air, making it clean. The tiles also filtered out sound, which kept the noises that shrouded them up above silent to those down below.

Harper had actually been very impressed with the green-minded health consciousness of the Five Watch. Rome had explained to her that most of the government facilities in Oregon were constructed this way.

He'd also told her he'd noticed the same construction in Bobby's lab on that fateful night when they'd first met. Of course, he *would* notice everything. All she'd seen that night was her brother's workplace in shambles.

Shaking away her thoughts, she saw Rome slowly pull the wires back to their original position and then gesture for her to join him by lying flat opposite his prone pose on the catwalk. He pointed down and then brought his hand up to motion her to listen and watch.

The view through the shimmery metal tiles was hazy but workable. The room below appeared to be the same lab they'd just been in. Rome must have thought the man and the person who called would meet there, in the same lab. He'd estimated they'd have sixty-five minutes to investigate before his tinkering with the electronics was discovered. Checking her watch, they had about twenty-nine minutes left.

The door thumped open, almost startling a jump out of her. Harper cringed and glanced up to see Rome place a finger in front of his sensuous mouth in a shushing motion. With an apologetic smile, which elicited a sexy grin from him, she returned her glance to the lab below.

Crisp footsteps clacked across the hard floor out of her range of vision. She looked back down and saw a man wearing a white lab coat approach the table with the laptop. He faced her. She couldn't make out his features, given her high angle, but she was pretty certain it was the same nervous guy they'd hidden from. He had apparently returned to the lab in the time it took her and Rome to get to the ceiling.

The body that belonged to the clacking shoes came into her view, joining Lab Coat at the computer. Another man. He stood at Lab Coat's side, his face visible to her, but not one she recognized.

Harper sensed Rome tense. His face was tight with fury. Shoulders bunched, he appeared ready to pounce and tear something apart with his bare hands. And she didn't doubt that he could.

She reached over to carefully brush the back of his clenched fist with her fingers, trying to get his attention without startling him and blowing their cover. It took a long moment, but his stormy blue gaze met hers.

"Trouble?" she mouthed, watching him struggle to breathe normally. He was obviously rattled.

Rome shook his head firmly in answer, returning his concentration to the scene below, clearly dismissing any other distractions. Shrugging her shoulders, she did the same.

"How's the next batch?" Clacker's voice was muted, but understandable, and a touch irritated.

"The same as the others," Lab Coat answered with a sigh, sounding skittery and worried. "I don't think it's going to work."

"Think?" Clacker asked tightly, slamming his hand on the counter and causing the laptop to shudder. Harper blinked in surprise. "Dr. Blake, I'm getting tired of what you think. I need a working serum, not the knockoffs you're giving me. Stop thinking and start doing."

"It's not that easy, Jeff," Dr. Blake explained.

Jeff. Was that Rome's boss, Jeff? A quick peek at Rome's white knuckles and she knew she was right. Did this mean Jeff was in on all of this?

"I don't care whether it's easy or not," Jeff said, pressing. "Give me a good serum."

"You don't understand," Dr. Blake pleaded. "It just doesn't work that way. We don't have the original formula. We're trying to work from the plant extractions, but without the true formula, it will take time to recreate it. It's hit-and-miss."

"It's killing my men," Jeff countered, pounding his hand on the table once more. "*She's* killing my men." Did Jeff mean her? A small bubble of pleasure welled up inside of Harper.

"I know, and I'm sorry." Dr. Blake actually sounded remorseful. "But she has the original formula in her system. And trying to extract it from her blood is working the same way as extracting it from the plants. It's essentially diluted. Secondhand. Besides, I told you when we started that we shouldn't use human subjects until we reconstructed the original serum. My instincts are telling me this is never going to work."

Jeff moved closer to the doctor and grabbed him by his white lapels, bunching the fabric in his grip and pulling him close. Harper leaned forward in a reflexive response and noticed Rome did the same.

"Your instincts?" Jeff yelled, just inches away from the doctor's face. "Instincts are what made me launch this project. Agent Lucian's failed instincts killed good people. This serum will prevent that from happening again. So don't talk to me about your instincts."

Harper snuck a glance at Rome. His rugged face was strained with agony. Evidently Jeff had used Rome's one failure to prompt his own evil plan. And they'd both been caught up in it. She itched to reach over and soothe his suffering. But any movement would call unwanted attention.

"You knew what you were getting into, Doctor," Jeff said, rolling the doctor's coat in his hands even tighter.

"Losing the formula data in the fire has made my job very difficult," Dr. Blake sputtered.

"It's your job to produce the serum, so I can do my job by using superior agents." Jeff's voice was hard and controlled. "Dr. Kane was able to do it with the plants. You should be able to reproduce it for humans using those plants." The mention of her brother stung Harper to the core. Jeff released the doctor with a little shove, and then backed off to glare at him. "No more excuses. Do your job, Dr. Blake, or else."

Jeff turned on his heels and walked to the door.

"Or else what?" Dr. Blake asked with remarkable bravado.

"Or else I'll find someone who can," Jeff answered gravely, and straightened his tie.

"You'll murder me like you murdered Dr. Kane?" the doctor challenged.

Harper went rigid with crazed fury, just barely kept under her skin. Rome's tight reassuring touch on her wrist was the only thing that prevented her from crashing through that ceiling and strangling the filthy life out of Jeff.

"Dr. Kane was eliminated because he wasn't with the program," Jeff articulated solemnly. "Don't make the same mistake." And with that Jeff turned to open the door and step out of her vision.

Harper twitched as an angry chill flooded through her, causing her body to rock forward. Feeling herself beginning to slide ahead, she swung her arm around, trying to halt her abrupt movement. The catwalk creaked loudly with the sudden shift of her weight.

She glanced at Rome with an apologetic wince at her noisy blunder. His eyes were as wide as hers, and then they both looked down into the room at the same time.

Jeff and Dr. Blake were directly below, frozen and glaring at the ceiling. The two men couldn't see her and Rome through the tiles, but there was no doubt they'd heard the metallic groan. They knew someone was there.

"Go," Rome hissed, shoving her into motion.

He didn't need to tell her twice. Like a crab, she scrambled frantically across the grating to stand, as Rome rushed past her, already on his feet. He grabbed her hand and she stumbled behind him, racing as fast as the tight area allowed, their boots clanging on the catwalk, not caring anymore about stealth.

Just as they burst through the duct door, she ran smack into his hard back, almost causing both of them to fall.

Peeking over his broad shoulder as her eyes adjusted to the muted light of the hallway, Harper saw what had made Rome stop.

They'd been found.

Four huge men were barely visible in the dim lighting. Harper hoped there weren't more, but couldn't tell what lurked in the shadows.

Three of them had handguns pointed directly at her and Rome. The fourth stood holding a rifle across his barrel-like chest, but she had no doubt he was just as ready to whip that thing around and use it.

Harper was getting darned tired of big guys with guns.

The six of them stood there, facing off for what seemed like an eternity. She was sure Rome was planning something, the tightness of his shoulders and the twitching of his fingers warning her.

Was he thinking up something to say or to do? They hadn't really planned an escape strategy other than the gun in the holster inside his coat.

Well, that and her psi power, as they had referred to it since reading Bobby's notes.

Confident she was beginning to learn to control it, she decided that she'd use it on these guys. Placing her hand ever so slightly on Rome's back, she tried to signal her intentions. The muscles in his lower back tensed under her fingers. She hoped that meant he understood.

Focusing on the threat a few feet away, she concentrated sharply and reached inside every corner of her mind to call upon the psi power.

Nothing.

She closed her eyes and tried again, this time concentrating on remembering Jeff and the doctor talking about her brother while she and Rome were in the duct. She recalled her rage and fury at their words.

Struggling to direct the steep pain that flushed through her, Harper beckoned the white heat that would blaze within her body just before she unleashed her lethal power.

Nothing.

Glancing uneasily around the cool shadows, she wondered in a sudden fear whether she'd somehow lost her psi power. Panic flushed through her. Did that mean she was going to die now? Was she about to end up like the others?

She hadn't been able to use it when she'd been held captive, either. Maybe the power didn't work indoors. Yet she'd trashed Bobby's lab using it.

Before she could explore those thoughts, she sensed motion from Rome. Clearly he wasn't about to wait for her to save them again. Good choice, considering she couldn't, anyway.

Then all heck broke loose. Before she knew what was happening, Rome had rushed two of the men, slamming them against the concrete wall.

An instant later she went into action, kicking the gun out of the hand of the third man before he could pull the trigger, while ramming her body into the rifle-bearing brute with all her might.

Identical grunts sounded from both of them as they sailed through the musty air and thumped onto the unforgiving ground side by side. After a few seconds of wrestling and trading punches, she knew she had to do something about that rifle, but he was strong. Very strong. She wasn't sure just how much more scuffling she could take before he overpowered her or the others paid them attention. Plus she had no idea how Rome was doing with his battle.

Shifting her body to face him squarely, she clasped onto her enemy's shoulders, taking a couple blows to her abdomen for her efforts. Bracing her upper body on his, she hoisted her knee straight up to connect solidly with his groin.

Her attacker instantly froze and rolled to his side, grasping his crotch and wheezing. Hey, a girl's got to have some tricks, and she wasn't above fighting dirty when it came to her life. And Rome's.

Spinning away from the downed man, Harper peered through the dimness to see two prone bodies on the floor, and Rome fighting the third.

She scooted across the ground to kick the kneecap of Rome's assailant. The man crumpled and clutched his knee in agony.

"C'mon," Rome said breathlessly, grabbing her hand roughly and pulling her along the tunnel toward the entrance they came in.

Stumbling in haste, they raced through the winding shadows. At last they rounded the last corner of the dirt passage, arriving at the bunker door just as it crashed inward, almost banging into the two of them.

Bodies roared through the opening, taking advantage of their surprise. The door slammed shut, blocking the outside light, and they were once again shrouded in near darkness.

The rapid light and dark buzzed her vision for a quick moment, startling her into immobility. Someone thudded against her, forcing her back against the hard earth-packed wall. Her breath rushed out of her lungs, causing a momentary lapse of awareness.

Two solid punches hit her face, snapping her head backward, hitting the wall once more. Harper was sure she'd see stars if she could clear her vision.

A tackle at her thighs took her legs out from under her, and she tumbled to the uneven ground. Levering on her hands, she twisted her body around just as brutal hands yanked her up and pulled her to her feet.

She was then forced face-first against the wall while someone jerked her wrists around, trying to bind them together. She thrashed frantically to keep it from happening, tasting chalky bits of dirt that crumbled off the wall from the erratic movements.

Guns fired. The shots echoed loudly in the cramped space. Then the struggle with her hands stopped. And the large body behind her slid to the ground.

Swinging around, she watched a blur of forms grappling and shards of light dancing in the haze of gun smoke as the muted beams of the corridor flickered off the barrels of moving guns.

She also spotted the glint of a blade, which descended in a flashing arc to slice her forearm.

A searing burn stung her flesh. She reflexively reached for the wound. Pulling her hand away, she saw blood drip through her fingers. *Ouch, that hurt like a son of a gun.*

The knife ripped at her again. Harper backed away as the swipe passed just in front of her; then she lunged forward, knocking her attacker against the wall.

She heard the clang of the knife as it hit a rock on the ground. A quick backhand smacked her hard across the face.

Harper reeled back a few steps as her nose stung and tears welled in her eyes. Running her tongue along her upper lip, she tasted blood, presumably trickling from her tingling nose.

Enough.

Planting her right leg firmly on the hard-packed dirt, she recalled some of her kickboxing training and hopped onto her left leg, twisting her right foot through the air to land a solid roundhouse kick to the head of the brute who hit her. He flailed backward, knocking his head against the wall, and then fell flat onto the ground.

And stayed there.

The crack of gunfire ripped throughout the shadows again. She whipped around, watching bodies fall. More close-range shots rang and more bodies fell.

Silence.

She realized after a cold moment that she was the only one still standing. A murky haze from the gunfire and upset earth veiled the area as she anxiously searched for Rome among the prone figures.

The leaden tang of blood swamped her senses. She could taste it with every breath. Smell its thick stench. See the dark stains mingle with the shadows on every surface.

She found Rome lying facedown. As she turned him over, she gasped at the blood covering his face and drenching his coat.

Was it his? Had he been shot?

A blinking light and hushed single beep came from her wrist. No. The system that Rome had shut off was about to come on. Her watch warned their sixty-five minutes were up in sixty seconds.

"Rome," she whispered, shaking him gently. "Rome."

No response. They needed to get out of there. Now. Before more people came. Panic bubbled in her stomach. Were you supposed to move gunshot victims?

Maybe a little louder. "Rome!" she screamed in true fright, afraid he might really be hurt.

A strong hand seized her wrist. She jumped back, but the ironclad grip held her steady before she fell over.

"Stop yelling, Harper," Rome rasped, and groaned as he struggled to push himself up on his elbows.

"Sorry," she spurted, relieved beyond belief that he was okay. She hadn't started to think about what she'd do without him. She didn't want to.

She reached under his arms to help him. He groaned even more, but allowed her to support him. That spoke volumes to her.

Smiling, she began to stand and heft him up with her. His arm clenched her slashed forearm, making her wince in the dimness as her wound seethed from his heavy touch.

"Let's go before more come," Rome grunted through heavy breaths. Great idea.

He braced against her as he stood, a bit wobbly. She flung her arm quickly around his lower back, trying to hold him up. He was solid muscle.

Walking to the bunker doorway, his sagging weight almost knocked her over. Leaving him to lean against the dirt wall, she hurled the door open.

The bright daylight nearly blinded her, but she grabbed Rome around his waist and hauled him up the uneven stairs and outside with her. Sucking in a lungful of cool air, she relished being in the fresh outdoors and out of that rank corridor.

Rome moaned, and she chanced a sideways glimpse at him as they staggered away. He looked as if he were about ready to keel over, but lurched forward to snap himself alert. Thank goodness her years of training had made her legs strong; otherwise his jerky motion might have pitched them both face-first onto the ground.

A beeping noise startled them both. Her watch alarm. Their sixty-five minutes were up. Good thing they'd scurried far enough away for cover where they were hidden from the outside surveillance, just beyond her original hideout. And close to Rome's stashed motorbike.

He'd been the one to drive them here on the bike, but he was in no condition to drive now. They'd concealed the Bug about fifteen miles from this location and ridden over the uneven forested terrain to get here.

In other circumstances, she'd have been excited to drive the unusually quiet dirt bike, one of Rome's many resources. He'd given her a basic tour of the machine and how to operate it, but right now, she just hoped she could get back to safety without killing either of them.

Reaching the bike, she propped Rome against a tree

trunk. He was steadier now, but in definite pain, given his intermittent wincing and grunting. The slice in her arm was simply on fire, but she put the burning aside to pull the bike out of its camouflage of leafy brush.

She rolled it toward Rome and started it up just as he'd shown her. As soon as it rumbled to life, she pulled up next to him.

She helped him settle onto the back of the wet leather seat, and then quickly moved ahead of him to straddle the bike, grimacing at the sogginess that seeped into her jeans. About to reach behind to secure his hold, he did the job himself by wrapping his shaky arms snuggly around her torso.

"Rome, are you okay?" she asked softly, knowing she should've asked sooner, but also knowing she couldn't have taken the time. They probably didn't have the time now, either.

"Yeah. Okay," he said with a sigh, and leaned forward against her back, his warm breath reassuring against her damp neck.

Harper took a moment to pull his arms tighter around her middle, and then put the bike into gear. The drizzly wind streaked through her hair and the hazy sun energized her exhausted body as they sped through the rough forest in a light drizzle.

Reluctant to take her eyes off the terrain, she chanced a glance over her shoulder at Rome. His eyes were squinted but alert as they raced along.

Turning her gaze forward, Harper was just in time to see a big black Hummer barreling through the trees, headed straight for them.

Harper yelped as bullets whizzed past her head. A man was standing through the sunroof, aiming a rifle at them while the huge vehicle continued on a head-on course toward their little motorbike.

"Holy shit!" Rome's loud curse reached her ears as more gunfire rang out. "Turn!"

He didn't need to tell her twice.

She veered the bike to the left, nearly skidding the machine out from under them on the loose, wet soil. The Hummer flew past them and slammed on the brakes to angle around.

Her knuckles strained white with tension as she gripped with all her strength, trying to control the fish-tailing bike. Rome began leaning with the motions, which eventually helped her steady the wild twisting.

Sparing a quick glance over her shoulder, she saw the black monster tear up the earth with its spinning tires. Finally catching enough traction, it began to follow them.

Great. Just great. How was she going to lose them? She could barely manage this thing. Sure, she'd driven Jet Skis, but they were made to slide around. The bike needed solid footing. Something that was going to be difficult on the leafy, muddy ground.

Another round of bullets streamed past her as she turned back around. She had to focus on the jarring landscape.

"Weave, don't keep a straight line," Rome shouted.

One of his arms unwound from her waist. His hand shifted between them as though he was digging around for something. Something solid brushed against her lower back.

A gun. It was a little frightening that she was beginning to recognize it so easily.

"Keep it steady," Rome instructed, and started to remove his other arm from around her.

"What are you doing?" Harper asked, worried about his stability. She was fighting hard against the rocks and muck to keep from dumping them off the bike while he was wiggling it.

"I'm going to shoot back while you lose them," Rome explained simply.

Oh. Okay. No problem.

More rustling behind her was followed by a few grunts. She continued to wind across the terrain, zigzagging to keep from being hit by the bullets peppering the drizzly air and foliage around them.

Harper almost jumped out of the seat when Rome's arms encircled her to tie his fleece coat around her middle. She looked down to see his hands twist the arms into a tight knot. He tugged on it, pulling her a little with it.

His hands disappeared and she kept her eyes ahead. Then she pitched forward slightly when his arm snaked up her back to hold on to the coat, levering his body as she felt him twist to face the threat behind them.

Ah, Rome was using her as an anchor while he fired off a few shots at the Hummer. Though she doubted his one little gun on the back of the bumpy bike could do much.

"Got one," Rome called to her.

Despite the dire circumstances, she couldn't help grinning as she stood—well, sat—corrected.

Her body jerked a little as Rome shifted in the wet leather seat while she maneuvered over some slick granite. She glanced behind, hearing the deep rumbling of the Hummer's huge engine drown out the bike's own motor as the big monster began to gain ground on them, plowing easily through the jagged, muddy terrain.

Another smattering of bullets filled the air, and she knew she had to do something. She had a feeling the chase couldn't go on forever, and at the rate they were going, the Hummer would be on top of them soon.

She gave a fleeting thought to using her psi powers now that she felt a little stronger. Out in the open, it had never failed her.

Looking inside herself, she began to focus on the energy inside her mind.

"Harper!" Rome yelled as she skimmed a jutting rock, almost dislodging them.

"Sorry." She cringed, glancing around at the blurring greens and browns of the forest as the rain slapped against her face. Apparently not a good idea right now to try out her tenuous control of the power. She could kill the two of them before she saved them.

Taking a deep breath of the fresh damp air, she looked hard at the trees to their sides. At the cutting paths that crisscrossed through the course they were riding. At the hills that rolled ahead.

Harper knew this area. She and Bobby had hiked it many times before, though she had no idea just how close they'd been to the lab all those times.

The bike slanted dangerously from the harsh recoil of another shot from Rome's gun. Struggling to keep it under control as they raced over moss and mud, she tried to recall everything she knew about this area.

Where could she lose the Hummer? The metal beast was mowing down the vegetation, but she didn't dare try to slalom the trees to the sides. She was afraid she'd land them smack-dab in the middle of a solid trunk, so she'd stayed on the rough trail that traversed the dense tree line.

"Do you know this area?" she called over her shoulder to Rome.

"A little." He paused to aim and shoot once more. She anticipated the shot this time and swerved along with the motion. "Just from the map." He sounded a little breathless. A lot breathless, actually.

Goodness, she'd forgotten about his wounds. And hers. She flexed her arm to test the slice in her forearm. A little tight, but not the heavy stinging of before.

"I think there's a small gorge up ahead," Rome hollered, jerking her body backward while he reloaded his weapon, his arm still looped through the coat tied around her waist.

Gorge? Oh, holy cow. Rome was right. But it wasn't a small gorge. It was a wide ravine. Wide and deep.

Sharpening her focus, she peered through the spitting rain, looking forward for the signs of the fateful ravine that just might save them.

Or kill them for good.

Harper recalled that the only warning of the ridge was the thinning of trees and a small hill that dipped just before the edge. If she remembered correctly, the drop was about the length of the Olympic pools she swam. Probably even a touch more than the fifty meters.

The distance across the ravine was the real problem. She wasn't sure. Twenty or thirty feet. Maybe farther.

She noticed a rise in the terrain as she swerved around a thick section of a downed tree. The ravine was just ahead.

Now what?

She flirted with the idea of jumping the chasm, then shrugged it off with a smirk. Was she crazy? She was barely keeping the bike stable on the ground. How in the world did she think she could run it off the ledge and make it to the other side? Could this bike even do something like that with both of them on it?

She'd seen motocross commercials where they did flips and jumps. So maybe . . . Oh for crying out loud. Was she seriously thinking about jumping?

Another barrage of bullets whizzed by her, smacking the large rock in front of her, the sparking chips of granite nearly showering them as she sped past the boulder at close range.

Yes. Harper was seriously thinking about it. She didn't really see any other option. The Hummer was gaining on them and seemed to have an unlimited arsenal, so they couldn't stop. The trees were too thick to try to weave the motorbike through. Turning around would be suicide.

Rome was too injured to fight or run. And she didn't know whether she could chance revving up and releasing her psi power before it was too late.

"Damn it all," Rome yelled. "I'm out of ammo."

Her body jostled forward, and then back as Rome dislodged his arm from the coat loop. He twisted around with a grunt and settled against her back, locking his arms around her waist.

"Where are we going?" His warm breath huffed against her ear, tickling her damp skin. "I thought the gorge was ahead."

"It is," Harper confirmed, turning her head so he could hear. Should she share her idea? Sure, why not. He had to come with her anyway. "We're going over it."

She waited for him to yell at her in disbelief. No sound came. She shifted to glance over her shoulder. No wonder he was quiet. His jaw was clenched so tight, she was surprised he could still breathe. She could have sworn she saw smoke come out of his ears.

She faced front again to see the hill quickly approaching. Just beyond it was the ledge. And beyond that, the ravine.

"Harper, I'm not so sure about this." He tightened his grip on her body.

"Me neither." She grinned against the drizzle blowing against her face. It was crazy. "But what choice do we have?" She was crazy.

"There's always a choice," Rome roared at her, just as a bullet hit the left side mirror, blowing it off the bike. She turned to meet his wide gaze with her own. "And it's a good choice." He nodded at her.

Harper laughed and turned back around to face forward. Rome's grasp tightened, almost squeezing the breath from her gut.

Gripping the handlebars tight, she twisted the throttle, giving the motor all the power it could manage. The bike lurched forward with the extra speed. Rome stiffened behind her and moved forward so close, she doubted any speck of air could fit between them.

Her stomach dropped as she shot the bike down the last decline at full speed. The bike caught a little air as it snaked across the ground just ahead of the ledge.

Here we go. Harper's knuckles whitened as she held tight to the bike. One last pull of the throttle and she watched the slick rocks that bordered the edge of the ravine fall away to nothing.

And she and Rome soared.

As if looking at herself from outside her body, a perfect lightness overtook her as she savored being suspended with Rome for this one moment in time.

Then the descent. The ground on the other side rushed at her at an alarming rate.

They made it. As the tires hit the hard earth, they swerved and reeled. Harper barely—*barely*—held on, struggling against the natural forces trying to sweep the bike out from under them.

But she did. And Rome was right behind her.

Steadying the bike, she skidded to a stop, mud and leaves kicking out from the strain on the tires.

She took a deep, steadying breath and gazed toward the ravine they'd just miraculously jumped.

On the other side, the Hummer's front wheels were hanging over the edge, the back tires squealing against the ground, trying to reverse the heavy truck fully onto the solid land as it teetered dangerously.

The decent human being in her hoped they could right the vehicle. The fallen fugitive in her, sick and tired of being chased, beaten, and shot at, really didn't care whether they succeeded.

Peeling her fingers from her death grip on the handles, she turned to look at Rome, rubbing the circulation back into her stiff wet hands. He appeared stunned and invigorated all at once. Just like her.

He leaned forward to pull her into his shaking arms, giving her a hard and deep kiss. Primal. Natural. Full of adrenaline. She kissed him back, tasting sweat and blood and the sexy tang that was all Rome.

They broke apart and stared at each other for a long moment, just glad to be alive and in one piece.

"Let's get back to the Bug." His low suggestion severed the charged air. She nodded in agreement.

As the adrenaline of their thrill ride started to wear off, reality set in and the aches and pains came in droves. She realized that they did need to get back. Back to the Bug and back to work.

Harper grabbed control of the bike and started off in

the direction Rome pointed. It would be a longer drive now, but at least they were alone.

And once they were back to relative safety, they could assess their wounds. And the information they'd over-heard. She just didn't know which was going to hurt more.

Chapter Fourteen

Rome straightened his aching body as Harper pulled the Bug into a tree-shaded space behind a mercifully remote log cabin.

Before they'd left that morning, he'd paid up their cheap motel room for a few more days. And added extra to pay for privacy. The front desk attendant/owner of the motel had simply pocketed the money, saying something sleazy about Harper that almost earned him a broken nose.

As Rome glanced at her long fingers turning the keys to kill the engine and her other hand reaching down to pull the lever to pop the hood, he was enormously glad they had decided to move locations. For many reasons. Mostly, he didn't need leering assholes ogling her. Plus their situation seemed to be only getting worse, so he'd told Harper it would be best to not stay in one place for too long.

But right now they were about to hole up in a very nice and very private log cabin. The owner had four rental cabins that were spread out over acres and acres of family land. This particular cabin sat enclosed by the majestic woods, with a swift-moving creek just steps from the front door. One simple phone call from Rome had secured the heavenly place.

He'd had to hide away here several times before, both professionally and personally. After a long history being acquainted, Rome trusted the owner understood the meaning of "discreet."

His most recent trip to the reclusive spot had been just after the loss of his team two years ago. The serene retreat possessed a cleansing spirit. The simple joy of fusing with nature had helped him send some of his demons to their lair and pacify the rest of them just enough so he could return to his job.

The slamming of the driver-side door broke into his thoughts, and he watched as Harper closed the door again. And again. The door clicked shut for good on the third try, and he couldn't help smiling at her fresh familiarity with the old car he loved so much.

She disappeared from his sight around the front of the car as she lifted the hood. He guessed he'd better get out of the car and find the key the owner would have stashed under the wooden porch. He hauled himself out of the car and had to shut his passenger door several times before the latch caught, as well.

He sucked in a deep breath and blew it out slowly, the crisp air from his mouth fogging as he tilted his head back to glance at the bloated dark clouds. It definitely looked like a hard rain was in the forecast.

"I'll get the key," he said to Harper, walking gingerly toward the porch, his boots clomping against the damp, hard-packed dirt. A wave of exhaustion tingled through his body as he reached the wooden stairs.

He was surprised Harper didn't look ready to drop, too. Clearly she'd been through hell in their escape from the facility. He'd been so proud and admittedly a little surprised at the way she had fought alongside him. And even more surprised at how right it felt. Whatever fear she must have had, she'd masked it with a fury and resilience he'd never seen. She was a damn trouper, that was for sure.

Case in point: She had decided to jump the gorge. It had been a lot bigger than it had appeared on the map. He thought she'd been kidding around. But the woman had guts of steel. He'd instantly realized that jumping the gorge had been their only real chance at survival. He didn't kid himself when it came to a fight. And that fight was one they couldn't have won.

The only thing he could do was hold on and trust her. And one risk later, they were safe. A pure ecstasy beyond any he'd ever experienced had filled him then, almost to the point of bursting. He'd kissed her, trying to convey all that she was to him.

Life with Harper was going to be one wild ride. And he suddenly realized he wanted it to last forever.

But they didn't have forever. Harper's life was a ticking time bomb. Plus, though they'd been through a lot, he wasn't sure he'd regained her trust.

Rome shook the unsettling thought away. They had more immediate problems. Such as their damn injuries. So Rome figured he'd better get their asses inside to start the mending in order to find a way to make forever happen.

He bent to one knee, briefly wondering whether he'd be able to get back up, and fished through the weeds and cobwebs to pull out a little metal box. He retrieved the old brass key, then put the box back under the stairs.

It took all his remaining strength just to stand. The muscles in his legs cried out in protest at the motion. He was losing it. Fast.

Turning around to check on Harper, he saw her standing there quietly, waiting for him with a quirky smile. He nearly swooned at the sight of her, partly because of his fatigue, more so because she looked like a sexy battle-worn goddess surrounded by mighty Mother Nature.

Her T-shirt was covered with dark stains of blood, sweat, and dirt under her unzipped coat. Angry scrapes and splotches marred her weary face, and her blonde locks were mussed like a pile of strewn hay.

But she'd never looked better. He'd known her only a short time, but he was sure he'd seen her at her worst. And that didn't even compare to anyone else's best. The raw energy and natural essence of Harper were thrilling in a way he'd never experienced.

"Can we go in?" she asked with her eyebrows raised. She held their duffel bags, one in each hand.

Rome realized he was staring like an idiot and blinked to snap out of his haze. Rubbing a weary hand over his face, he nodded and waved her forward.

Every one of the four wooden stairs was like a moun-tain hike. Reaching the door, he heard the creak of the weathered wood of the porch, and then felt the comfort-ing warmth of Harper's body beside his.

He slipped the key into the sturdy lock and twisted the knob to push the door wide-open. He cautiously peered inside the shadowy room, the only light coming from the windows and the open door. Everything was just how he remembered it.

The cabin was basically one large room, built of hearty cedar planks from the forest outside. In fact, the founding trees that built the cabin had stood in the same spot, providing a sheltered and natural aura.

A sturdy kitchen to the left was outfitted with stain-less steel appliances and white tiled countertops. An is-land sat in the middle of the kitchen area with wooden stools standing on the open side.

Behind the kitchen in the corner was the sizable bathroom, complete with an inviting octagonal shower. The one closet just outside of the bathroom housed a stacked washer and dryer.

On the right side of the cabin, just inside the entryway, was a sunken living room with a cozy fireplace and cushy sofa. A bedroom in the back right corner held an enormous bed with a thick down comforter.

Rome smiled at the thought of spending time here, in this haven, with Harper, even if it was for just a day or so.

"C'mon in," he said, sweeping his arm in a grand gesture, instantly regretting it when a dull twinge trickled up his forearm. Was there any place on his body that didn't hurt? Strange. He'd never let anyone see his pain before, but in front of Harper, he didn't feel the need to be so damn tough. She never doubted he was.

She had to have the same draining aches, if not worse ones than he did. He knew by now she wasn't the type of gal to really worry about pretense. And he very much appreciated that right now.

"I had the power turned on when I called," Rome said, closing the door behind her after she dropped the two bags on the sofa. He tossed the key on the island and moved to the wall to turn on the lights.

"Does that mean there's hot water?" Harper asked hopefully.

"It should." He chuckled. Honestly, as much pain as he was in right now, he had almost told her she'd have to wait until he was done with the shower to find out. Damn manners. "Go ahead. There should be plenty of towels in there. I'll get the rest of our stuff."

He left her inside and walked out to the car to bring

in the rest of their supplies and the laptop. And a gun from the small but effective arsenal kept under the hood in a hidden compartment.

After gathering what he needed, he slammed the hood shut, then returned to the cabin to find Harper stooping by the fireplace, arranging some kindling around a couple of logs.

Her filthy jeans were pulled taut against her firm thighs and rear. Admiring her curves, as dirty as she was, he easily remembered the feel of her grinding against him. The perfect way she fit in his arms. The wetness of her mouth.

A spark snapped and he nearly jumped out of his skin. She had struck a match and was lighting the fire. How was it possible that he was very close to collapsing, but he wanted her with a hunger he'd never tasted?

Rome watched her poke the fire around, then stand and turn to warm her backside. She rubbed her forearm, something he'd noticed her do in the car as he had floated in and out of consciousness. Walking over to stand in front of her, he gently clasped her arm and held it up for his inspection.

She flinched as he peeled apart the fabric of her sliced coat. Looking inside the flaps, he saw a sweeping gash, maybe two inches long. Prodding it with his fingertips, relief warmed him as he saw it wasn't deep. She wouldn't even need stitches.

As a matter of fact, as he peered a little closer, he noticed the skin was already closing.

He glanced up from her wound, questioning her with his gaze. A chagrined expression graced her lovely face. They'd stopped at a gas station restroom to wash off the obvious blood, but he'd been in so much pain himself, he hadn't even noticed her serious injuries. Or lack of them.

Sure, she had scratches, but now that he looked closely, those were healing, too.

"Pretty handy, huh?" Harper half grinned. He couldn't tell whether she was happy about it or not. But he was ecstatic. Hot damn, she could self-heal at record pace. Wasn't that a good thing? A great thing?

"Harper," he whispered, raising her hand to brush his lips across her lightly scraped knuckles.

She shifted her hand out of his grasp and placed her palm against his cheek. Her touch comforted him like hot chocolate with marshmallows, warming him from the inside.

He couldn't help himself and leaned in to capture her lips in a much-needed kiss. But his audible wince made her pull back. Damn those bastards.

"Rome, we need to check you out." Harper took his hand, and he allowed her to lead him to the huge bathroom. Why would he want to fight it, anyway?

He noticed the tremble in her touch and wondered whether she was scared. Scared about things her body was doing without even trying. Hell, he'd kill for her newest power right now. He stood still while she turned on the bright light and faced him with suffering in her eyes.

"Harper, I think I'll live." Rome gave her a reassuring smile and took both of her trembling hands in his, holding them loosely. "I think you will, too." He wanted so much to believe that.

Harper lowered her head and gripped his hands tight. She held on for a long moment. He tried to think of something to say that would make the raw tension in her body go away. Then she let go and moved her hands under his coat to rest on his shoulders.

"Apparently I will live," Harper said, her voice a little

stronger as she lifted her head and slipped his coat off. "For now. But let's just make sure about you."

He heard the soft *thud* as the garment hit the tiled floor, and her surprised gasp. He looked down at himself, seeing what all the fuss was about. His T-shirt was liberally ripped and had a few slices on the side from a bullet's graze. He wasn't sure whether that had happened while on the bike or in the facility. The pain had just kind of run all together.

Strong hands pulled at the hem of his T-shirt, drawing it out of the waistband of his jeans. The fabric brushed against his bruised skin as she pulled it up and over his head.

Another loud gasp reached his ears, and then she whirled away from him to open the shower door and turn on the water.

A light film of dried sweat coated his skin, and angry red marks dotted his rib cage, just waiting to color and bruise. Sticky smudges of blood were caked in some of the hair on his chest.

On his right side, he saw the ruptured flesh from the gunshots that had ripped through his clothing and grazed his body. Luckily, he'd twisted the right way at the right time to avoid the lethal fire. The bleeding had long since stopped, but the skin was torn on the surface and tingling. It definitely looked worse than it was. He hoped she saw that, too.

"I don't know much in the way of dressing gunshot wounds," she said, rallying, as she turned around to face him after she checked the water's temperature with the back of her hand. "But, I do know that a hot shower always makes the aches go away." Sweeping her hand toward the burgeoning steam billowing from the open shower, she gave him a saucy wink and stepped toward the bathroom door to leave him. "At least it does for me."

"Then why don't you join me?" That damn wink had made his stomach flip.

Her eyes hooded slightly, and she gave him a low, throaty chuckle in response as she pulled the door shut behind her, leaving him alone among the warm vapors.

CHAPTER FIFTEEN

Damn, the woman knew how to flirt. She knew how to kiss, too. He wondered whether he'd ever get to find out just how much else she knew how to do.

Shaking his head and chuckling, he unwrapped the brand-new bar of soap on the counter. Rome removed the rest of his clothes, a few grunts escaping with the effort, and stepped inside the hot shower. He closed the steamed-up door, sealing the hazy heat within the eight high walls of glass.

Standing completely still, he reveled in the constant torrent of hot water raining down onto his beaten body. He lathered the fresh-scented bar of soap in his hands and then ran it across his solid chest and abdomen, stinging his cuts.

But Harper was right. The aches and pains seemed to flow down the drain like the frothy bubbles from the soap, reviving his strength and clearing his head. He turned slow circles in the wide stall, soaping every inch of skin, and then just allowed the water to rinse it away.

Setting the soap on a corner ledge, Rome braced his hands against the misty glass wall in front of him, bowing his head under the spray and closing his eyes.

Images flashed behind his eyelids. His mind raced with the dark thoughts of the facility. And the experiments. And the men who continually tried to kill him and Harper.

And Jeff.

That's what hurt the most. More than any of the bruises that covered his flesh, it was the stark betrayal he felt inside from learning Jeff was the one who orchestrated all of this. The one who had Bobby Kane murdered because the scientist had found out what a bastard Jeff was.

Damn him. Rome had never really trusted his boss, but he'd always figured they were on the same side. Yet Jeff had twisted Rome's single failure into a sick experiment that killed more people than he ever had and hurt Harper beyond repair. Now more than ever, he wanted to make the bastard pay for what he'd done.

The hot water pounded the back of his neck, seeping warmth into his beaten body. With great effort, Rome cleared his mind, not even wanting to deal with it all right now. The only thing he wanted at this very moment was outside the bathroom door. He knew he should fight the attraction, given they had a limited future at best, but he couldn't fight the way she'd planted herself into his soul.

Everything else in his head washed away and the only thing that remained was Harper. He could imagine the shower door opening, steam whirling as she stepped inside to share the cozy, misty space behind him. Her strong swimmer's hands gliding over his wet shoulder blades and slanting around to spread across his chest.

Rome pulled his hands away from the walls. Standing up straight, he felt his lower body tighten in response to his vision of Harper naked, her sleek wet breasts pressing against his back.

Keeping his eyes shut, he ran his hand down his solid

stomach to slide over his hardness. Closing his fingers, he stroked himself slowly again and again as the shower spray soaked his body and the fantasy of Harper flooded his mind.

A heavy groan rumbled behind his back.

His eyes snapped open. His moving hand stilled. Looking down, he saw her hands clawing across his chest. Shifting his gaze over his shoulder, he saw her stirring green eyes were searing into his. Hungry and primitive.

It wasn't a vision. Harper was really here. In the shower. Wanting him, too. A sharp desire spiked through him, igniting his entire being.

One of her hands slid down to cover his and resumed the unhurried stroking. Rome kept his stunned gaze locked on hers while the motion continued, setting fire to his blood. He watched her eyes darken as his breath hitched with the sensations radiating from their joint movements.

Her tongue poked out slightly, licking her lips, sending a powerful shiver through him. He was near bursting when she suddenly stopped the caress. A deep groan escaped him as she pulled him around to face her, a sultry smile creasing her gorgeous face.

Rome had to admit that he was more than a little nervous of what he hoped was about to happen. He'd never made love to a woman like Harper. He wasn't quite sure what to do with her. She was so sure of herself. He wasn't. It had been a while, and he'd always had to lead. But following her was something he thoroughly wanted to experience.

He watched her flaring green eyes fill with a playful yet sexy glint. Then she pushed him back a step and bent down to kneel on the smooth, tiled floor of the shower, facing him.

The shower spray pelted her slicked-back blonde hair as she moved closer, clutching his behind with one of her strong hands. The other hand gripped his thigh, kneading the muscles there.

Running his hand through the wet strands, he guided her to his thick hardness. She went willingly, running her tongue and lips along his shaft as though licking a Popsicle on a hot summer day.

Rome shut his eyes and tipped his head back, holding on to her head while she took him in and out of her mouth, over and over again. The breathtaking pressure built to unspeakable levels as he neared an earth-shattering release.

Then she stopped.

He opened his eyes to see Harper standing in the wet haze, raising her lengthy arms to grasp the top of the shower walls and spreading her legs while she stood, inviting him to take her.

There was absolutely nothing in the world he wanted more.

Raking a thorough glance over her long, athletic body, he marveled at the perfection of her sleek muscles and womanly curves. As in a dream, he raised his hands to brush his fingers across the hardened points of her breasts, amazed by the groan his touch elicited. He did it again, smiling at the identical response.

Taking a step forward, he reached his arms around her torso and grabbed her hips with slightly shaking hands, lifting her to him. Pressing his chest to hers. Her upper body strained against him as she hoisted her body upward, just enough for him to slide into her waiting center.

Her heated slickness clenched around him, their bodies setting a frenzied pace his mind could barely handle. Powerful legs twisted around his middle, pulling and pushing him. He crushed his arms around her tightly, holding her lean body as he thrust hard and wild, his confidence growing as their gazes linked like lasers through the shower's steam.

Fiery sensation poured through his every fiber, igniting every inch of his flesh, boiling his blood. Her aggressiveness chased away any hesitance he had left. Rome wanted this flawless moment to last forever, but craved the climax she was drawing from him, wanting to share it with her.

Rome watched the green of her eyes brighten and spark. Could feel her searing center tighten around him, seizing his hardness as she neared her own release.

And as she gave him a radiant grin, his heart split into countless pieces, filling his entire being with an honest passion he wanted to give to Harper.

He loved her.

Against all rational thought, he loved her. He knew he shouldn't. Their lives had just intertwined for this one blip of time. What would they do once this whole thing was all over? When *she* was over? He had no business falling in love with her.

But he loved her. And he realized in an alarming yet certain instant that he wanted this one blip to last for eternity. He had to find a way to make it so.

Her low moan reached through his thoughts, grabbing his attention. He watched Harper throw her head back and gasp, locking her thighs tightly around him, wringing from him everything he could give her.

Fiery sparks exploded inside of him, splintering through every muscle, shaking his vision. Riding out the powerful climax, he continued to thrust, savoring the feel of Harper's undulating body against his until her urging relaxed and his breathing slowed.

Lifting her to stand once more, he relished the lazy,

fulfilled look in her eyes and wanted to freeze it in his memory. Savor the knowledge that he put it there.

With a languid movement of his own, he placed one hand on her hip while the other reached around to turn off the warm water. She rested her hands on his wet shoulders, met his gaze with a charming smile that grabbed the hovering pieces of his heart, claiming them for her alone.

"I love you, Harper." Rome couldn't stop the words that poured from his soul.

He hadn't wanted to get close to her, to fall in love with her, because he knew she was going to die. Because regardless of the serum's healing power, it would kill her. And because he knew she didn't trust him. A distance had been between them ever since he'd turned her in. Yet his heart had somehow closed that distance in spite of everything.

Her smile twitched and she blinked, obviously stunned by his open admission. He didn't regret the words, but he second-guessed voicing them right now. He knew she wasn't ready to hear them. And maybe he'd jumped the gun.

But after the still moment, her grin widened.

"I know you do," Harper responded, and leaned in for a deep kiss, stealing his breath away.

She ended it just as quickly and twisted to open the shower door, taking his hand in her steady grip.

Apparently that was all she had to say. But it would be enough for now. He watched her reach for a towel, and then willingly went with her as she dragged him along to the big, comfy bed.

Then again, maybe it was more than enough.

Rome loved her.

He said he loved her. Harper had no idea how to react. No man had ever said that to her. Certainly not a man like Rome. A man she imagined she could love as well—a dangerous thought. That, even more than his words, had shaken her something fierce.

So, instead of making a fool of herself with some kind of hasty response, she'd taken his hand and led him out of the shower and they'd dried each other on the way to the foot of the bed. The superfluffy and cozy-looking bed. The kind of bed that made you want to make love to a man like Rome while on it.

Rome's confusing yet adorable hesitance she'd sensed in the shower was all but gone as he tugged on her hand and pulled her against his strong body, already stiff again with desire. Apparently the shower did have magical healing powers.

Under the intense spray of the water, she'd tasted his heated length, revered the power of him once he'd slid inside her. She hadn't even wanted any foreplay. Never before had her body been so fulfilled and her soul been so content.

But she didn't want to think about that right now. All she wanted was to lose herself in him for a little while longer.

He crushed his lips to hers, and she opened her mouth to him, allowing his hot tongue to sweep over hers. Back and forth, his hands glided over her energized flesh, searing trails that mimicked the movements of his mouth.

Moaning with a churning desire that was making her too weak to stand, she leaned back to lie on the bed and pulled him down on top of her. The brief seconds she was separated from him were pure agony, and the moment his sleek skin touched hers again was sheer bliss.

Running her hands down Rome's muscular back, she

shifted her head to the side as he nipped down her neck. His mouth skimmed across her collarbone, cascading feathery kisses on her shoulder, peppering the scar from her swimming injury. She vaguely remembered tracing the long scar on his knee with her tongue.

Harper's attention snapped back to now and she clutched his solid biceps as he levered himself up to cover one of her breasts with his open mouth. He pressed the flat of his tongue against her taut nipple, stroking and licking around the rigid peak, while the other was pinched with exquisite vigor.

In reflex, her hand shot up to hold his head in place, latching on to the short damp locks. Tiny bolts of lightning flickered from her breast to her groin, the delicious sensations wetting her easily.

Rome shifted his mouth to her other breast, pleasantly rewarding it with similar treatment. She wanted him to stay there for a good long while.

Then his lips trailed down over the ridges of her ribs and abdomen. Balancing above her, he spread her legs and paused, hovering his mouth over her heated center.

Rising up on her elbows, she chanced a glance down at his face, wondering what the holdup was. His blue gaze burned into hers as the sexiest grin she'd ever seen flashed across his face just before he lowered his head to her.

She dropped back to the bed with a short gasp as he flicked his tongue over her, alternately licking and nipping, as if lapping rich cream from a bowl. Only she was melting.

A coiling pressure continued to build, centering from his mouth and spreading through every fiber of her body at a staggering pace.

Against her will, her hips began to buck against his

fervent attention. Her body began to spiral and she immediately decided she wanted him inside her when it burst into a thousand glittering pieces as she had in the shower. She reached down to clasp her hands on each side of his head to pull him up before she lost it.

His body covered hers as he slithered on top of her, the hair on his chest grazing her oversensitive skin, thrilling her into a shiver, his thick hardness pressing against her tummy.

Bringing her hands to his shoulders, she pushed against him, flipping him over to straddle his solid abdomen.

A huff of breath escaped from his grinning mouth. He seemed to like her taking control. She did, too.

Running her hands over his chiseled chest, she shifted her hips downward. Harper lowered her head for a moment to dash her tongue across each of his stony nipples. His body jerked under hers at her touch, eliciting a low laugh from her. Rome brought his hands to her thighs and hips, running them up and down her scorching skin, leaving trails of fire behind his touch.

She grazed her slick center along his erection as she moved her breasts over his chest, the surge of sensations driving her absolutely crazy. Reaching a hand down, she circled her fingers around him, guiding his thick shaft to her and lowering herself to take him inside of her.

They moved as one, joined together in a timeless moment, sheltered by the resilient bond they'd forged.

The pace suddenly picked up by mutual consent. With a powerful joint thrust, the crest of the stormy wave came crashing down. The sheer force of their shared climax rivaled that of the energy that flowed from her psi powers.

He'd said he loved her.

And as Harper collapsed onto Rome's heaving body, spent and sated like never before, she believed she might be in bigger trouble than she thought.

Because in spite of everything, she had to admit to herself that she was falling in love with him, too.

CHAPTER SIXTEEN

Harper peered at the laptop, scrolling through the files that had finished downloading as she lay on her stomach on the rumpled bed, naked beneath the down comforter. As soon as they'd awakened, they'd engaged in another round of lovemaking. Well, honestly, really hot and mind-blowing sex. But this time it had been slow and easy, even playful. When it was over, they'd just dozed until her empty stomach growled for some attention.

Rome had made them something to eat, and then they'd gotten down to some more research to plan their next move. It was the first time she'd been able to get back to the laptop and finish scanning over Bobby's files. Reading the same paragraph for the third time, she rubbed her strained eyes, easily figuring out why she was so unfocused.

The reason was sitting against the sturdy headboard, his lower body covered by the other half of the comforter.

She'd known he was hurt at the compound, but it just now came to her how close he'd come to getting killed. Rome was willing to die for her. Yes, he'd betrayed her once, but even knowing that she didn't have long to live herself, he'd now risked death to protect her.

Shaking her head, she glanced over her shoulder and saw his intense gaze focused on her. She smiled at him, which earned her a matching grin. He added a heated leer and then returned to reading one of the file folders they'd taken from the lab. There was no longer any doubt that he was committed to helping her in a way she was just beginning to understand, and she was eternally grateful for it.

She reluctantly turned her attention back to the bright screen and switched gears. A few extra seconds and the data began to register. The picture and scope of what her brother was doing flashed by as if she were on an interstate highway, soaking in the landscape as it spoke to her.

The serum, once bonded with the plants, couldn't be transferred from them. Meaning you could eat the fruit, but not extract the formula. The plants wouldn't pass it along. No wonder the creepy woman torturing her couldn't get what they needed to replicate it. Bobby hadn't got around to testing that for sure, but she was living proof.

As normal plants, they needed the natural elements to thrive. That's why Bobby had constructed unique lights inside his lab to emulate natural sunlight. He'd built them sunshine. And it had worked. Perfectly. Plants that had received his sunshine had flourished just as if they'd been outdoors.

Just as she had. Her psionic power had worked in his lab and outside in the natural light. But in any dark confines, she'd been unable to summon it. And every time she'd stepped outside, she'd felt rejuvenated.

No damaging side effects had been found. Well, not to the plants. She, on the other hand, was in for a different fate given the results of Jeff's trial. But at least the plants wouldn't be shooting out angry psi-powered waves at people as they picked fruit or sprinkled water on them. She guessed that was a bonus.

Bobby had kept everything top secret so the serum wouldn't get in the hands of people who would abuse its power. People like Jeff. He had intended the test plants and serum to be delivered to a few hand-picked secret agricultural regions for trials, but nothing could move forward until the final tests proved the serum's perfection.

Harper smiled fondly. It was so like her brother to want to be absolutely, positively, one hundred percent, inescapably sure before he launched it.

The next folder she opened housed one lone document. She clicked to open it and was rewarded with a request for a password. Harper had to laugh. She should have known that Bobby would do the unexpected and make the final step straightforward instead of the most complex one of all. Any other hacker would be fooled. Sometimes she got so caught up in encryption and breaking codes that the basic password protection delighted her.

Until she realized she had no idea what that password could be.

Oh, for crying out loud. She closed her eyes and thought of her brother. Pictured Bobby sitting at his laptop securing this folder with the simplest of protection. Yet the most difficult to crack by her standards. She could hack it, but that would take time, and she was running low on patience.

Okay, so she wouldn't hack it. She'd reason it.

He'd probably been in a hurry, so it would have to be something that came to him quickly. And something he knew only she would know.

They had so much history to choose from. So many inside jokes. What would he think only she knew?

Maybe her name? It was simple enough. She typed it in but was denied. Darn.

Okay. Think. It would be a direct message from him to her. Olympics? Ever since she started training again, he'd e-mail her just one word: Olympics. Reminding her that he was with her every step of the way. That had to be it. She entered the word.

Denied once more. A simple password would lock out after three unsuccessful tries and she'd be back to square one. She had to get it right this time or maybe lose the data forever.

With a frustrated sigh, she glanced outside the window at the misting whitecaps of the frigid river.

A sudden memory flashed to her mind. A few years ago, they'd gone hiking on Mount Shasta. She'd slipped, slid down the slope, and splashed into a glacial pool at the bottom. Bobby had tried to reach her, descending carefully, but had ended up falling into the pool along with her. They'd laughed until their keisters began to freeze from the icy-cold water.

Ever since, whenever one of them tripped or fell, they had called out "Shastaboom."

With a fond smile, she shifted her thoughts back to the present.

Wait. Shastaboom. Could it really be that easy?

She typed the crazy word in and held her finger over the Enter key. Hesitating, hoping she knew her brother as well as she thought.

But no. She was sure. She had to be. Pressing the key, she held her breath.

And let it out slowly with a grin as the document opened without fanfare.

The formula.

Maybe now that she had the actual recipe, someone could develop an antidote. Bobby's notes mentioned that he hadn't yet reverse engineered the serum. He obviously thought he had the time to do it right. He'd been proven wrong.

She carefully committed his formula to memory, then closed her eyes and recalled it in her mind a few times. Opening her eyes, she peered at the formula again. She knew it now. And knew she'd never forget it. She erased the document and saved it, completely blank. Then she deleted it.

Closing the file, Harper rubbed her face with tired hands. The more data she uncovered, the more she resented the situation she'd been thrust into.

Bobby's research was beyond important, but she had no experience dealing with this kind of thing. Jeff and his faction were twisting the honorable research into an ugly vestige of its original intention. And before she could even begin to deal with her new life—whatever that new life may be—she was determined to avenge her brother.

The only thing she didn't resent was Rome. Though she hated that he was caught up in the fallout from the horrific situation his boss had created.

Shaking her fuming thoughts away, she focused on the data again, nearing the end of Bobby's entries. Every stark word seemed rushed. He'd known the worst was going to happen. Harper tingled with rage because he'd been right.

The worst had happened.

Bobby had given his life to keep his secret and make sure it got into her hands. By avenging his sacrifice, Harper would give her brother his rightful tribute.

After reading the last of Bobby's notes, Harper realized that her brother had no idea who was running the counter operation, only that he had discovered the faction and tried to find out as much as he could.

They hadn't taken any time to talk about it, though she knew it had to be bothering Rome. It would certainly bug her if she found out her coach was engineering bio-enhanced swimmers. Especially if it was driven by some mistake she'd made.

She peeked back at him. Earlier Rome had admitted to her that she'd been his first partner in two years. That explained his puzzling nervousness in the shower. Harper realized that his confession, and the fact that he'd let himself be with her intimately, really spoke volumes about the love he'd professed to her.

A gorgeous specimen of man like him, she would've thought he had women lined up at his bedside. She never lacked for partners, but Rome was different. There was a connection there that went deeper than physical gratification.

She had always wanted a man for fun, not a relationship. Relationships were messy and distracting. Something she couldn't afford while training. And she'd been training forever. So she'd never wanted more than a quick and pleasant rendezvous.

Until now. Maybe it was the extreme circumstances. Maybe it was the secluded setting. But maybe it was just the right man.

"Harper." He purred her name. She raised herself on her elbow and looked at him. His eyes darkened as his gaze moved from her face to her chest. Glancing down, she realized there was no comforter covering her upper body.

A smile cracked her face again. She'd never been an

exhibitionist, though she was used to wearing nothing but sleek racing bathing suits. And she was proud of her fit body.

A moan simmered from deep in her chest when she felt his strong hands cup her breasts and start to stroke them. Leaning into his touch even farther, she placed her hand on his lap and slipped on the paper files resting there. Losing her balance completely, she ended up sliding off the bed and landing on the hardwood floor with a solid thump.

Rome joined in with her laughter. She got on her knees and began to pick up the scattered papers. Looking at one of the sheets, she noticed a scrawled signature at the bottom.

Jeff Donovan. Her laughter faded as she glanced to Rome. He waved his hand for her to join him back on the bed.

She grabbed the rest of the documents and returned to the bed to sit beside him, showing him the paper. Reading it along with him, she could sense his gentle playfulness morph into serious work mode.

The paper was a gruesomely detailed report on what the faction had found up at the Barracks. The empty syringe. The bodies. The destruction.

The last paragraph was a requisition for additional force to track down the source of the damage.

Meaning her.

The last line of the requisition clarified the additional force.

Meaning Rome.

Jeff signed the order to hire Rome to track her down and bring her in. Dead or alive.

Harper just gawked at the paper, realizing just how crazy things had become. And just how much he'd given up for her. She was going to destroy his entire career. Because of her, he'd had to make a choice to go against his boss, regardless of the fact that Jeff was a horrible, rotten, disgusting person.

A strong hand settled on her thigh, halting her uneasy thoughts.

"This was my choice, Harper," Rome said quietly. "When Jeff gave me your picture, I knew. I just knew that something was off about it. But this, you and me, is right."

Harper looked at Rome's face. He was looking out the window, but his gaze seemed unfocused.

"I can't explain it, but I guess it doesn't surprise me that Jeff is behind this," he continued. "I just hate that for the first time in my life, I regret what I do for a living. Regret that my mistake provoked this. I knew that operations like Jeff's existed. I knew that innocents like Bobby were killed for knowing things they shouldn't. I guess it just never mattered to me." His gaze shifted to hers and burned in its forlorn intensity. "Until you."

She covered his hand with hers, not really knowing what she could say to make this better. Wait, yes she did. She just couldn't believe she was about to say it.

"I love you," Harper simply stated. The three words tasted strange and unfamiliar, but somehow right.

Rome turned his body to face her. Taking her hand, he brought it up to his lips and kissed her palm. "I know you do," he said with a sure grin.

She smiled back at him and shook her head at his response. The same one she'd had.

Rolling the other way, she swung off the bed and padded to her bag of clothes. Unzipping the duffel, she reached in and pulled out a few things to wear and slipped them on with a sigh.

Things between her and Rome were getting a little too close, a lot too fast. And ultimately had nowhere to go. But it felt nice. New and scary, but nice.

She needed air.

Besides, she needed to do something. Now more than ever, she wanted to resolve this whole thing and get her revenge so she could explore a real relationship with Rome. She had no idea how long it would be possible or whether life was ever going to return to a semblance of normal during her tapering life span.

"I'm going outside for some air," she said, bending over to tie her running shoes. Glancing over her shoulder, she saw him still sitting on the bed staring at her with a questioning expression. She tossed him a wave and walked to the door of the cabin.

Harper stepped outside the cabin, breathing in the fresh, crisp air. Thriving ferns graced the area, waving in the light breeze.

She moseyed past the Bug toward the rushing creek and began to walk along the side of the burbling water. The natural hum had a calming effect on her mind and body, as water always did.

Gazing around the lush green trees flanking the rough path beside the creek, she thought of the information she and Rome had gathered from Bobby's data and the files.

So. The formula flowing in her blood was the only true serum left. And she had the formula buried and locked deep inside her memory. Which meant she was the only pure fruit of Bobby's efforts. She was able to do things the other guys couldn't do. And so far, Jeff's faction had been unsuccessful in trying to replicate it.

It was a strange feeling knowing that she was one of a

kind. Strange and isolating. Even if—*when*—she did finish this, the psi powers would still be part of her. And eventually steal her life.

A life that was forever changed. And though she had Rome, what kind of life could they really have with her unknown and limited life expectancy?

She was scared to find that she needed him, more than just his help. Never before had she allowed anyone other than Bobby to get so close to her. Inside her soul. But Rome had somehow done that without her knowing.

The fact that they had learned she was terminal made her crave him even more. Her heart was breaking little by little just thinking that every second she spent with him could be her last.

She'd told Rome she loved him. How could she say that, knowing her world was falling apart? How could she think she even had the right to say it?

But no matter how she looked at it, she knew it was the truth. She couldn't help herself. He made her feel like she wanted to give everything she had to him in ways she hadn't even thought possible. Her heart. Her soul. He'd somehow been able to reach inside her and claim them.

Again, she wondered what kind of life awaited them. Always waiting for it to end.

She seriously doubted she could ever go back to swimming while possessing a psionic power. She couldn't even imagine what her coach was doing right now, wondering where she was, why she hadn't come back from her trip home. The meanie hadn't wanted her to visit Bobby in the first place. Was he mad? Worried? Kicking her off the team? How would she explain everything that had happened? No doubt she'd fail any drug test they'd administer, and who knew what kind of advantage she'd have in the water now?

So, no, she could never go back to competitive swimming. Also, she was sure she'd been fired from her job by now. All her friends—what would she say to them? Could she ever go back to anything she'd had before?

A slow fury smoldered in the pit of her stomach. No. She seriously doubted she ever could return to life as normal. Jeff Donovan had taken that away from her. Taken everything away from her. Her brother. Her swimming. Even her natural life.

It was a good thing she was going to die anyway. Her life as she knew it was gone.

The simmering fury threatened to blossom. Her mind began to swarm with rage at everything she'd lost. Glancing at the thick green foliage surrounding her, she remembered the solitary vow she'd made not long ago in a forest just like this one. Right after Bobby had died in her arms, the fury had consumed her and she'd sworn revenge. Now she had the means inside of her to enact it. Bobby had given her the serum. And she would use it for him.

She stopped walking and forced the anger to recede. Her heated vision cooled as she gazed at the swollen creek, misting and brisk as it rushed over cragged rocks. The fresh water was shrewd in the paths it chose to flow through the wild terrain.

Harper realized that's what she needed to be. Razor sharp and in command of her power. And not afraid to use it.

She scanned the majestic trees and foliage. The sentries stood tall and sure, branches reaching out to provide the unparalleled balance of beauty and power in nature.

Calling to her. Reverent and reassuring. Enticing

and elevating. Illuminating the energy that stirred within her body and mind.

Suddenly she wasn't afraid anymore. Like the protected undergrowth at the base of the trees, she knew she wasn't alone. She had Rome's savvy at her back. She had Bobby's creation inside her. And she had enough grit and confidence in herself to face what lay ahead.

Steeling her resolve, Harper swept her attention to the creek. She had to give in to the power. Control. That was the key.

Focusing on a rock under the swiftly gliding water, she beckoned her psi power. A familiar flush of cold filtered through her body, quickly followed by a rush of heat. She concentrated hard, imagining that she was lifting the rock out of its submerged home in the creek's bed.

Her vision tunneled, blurring around the edges and centering on the sunken stone. Almost in a trance, Harper raised her hand slowly and with it, the basketball-sized rock. It shimmied, the cold water cascading from its surface as it hovered in the air, mere inches above the racing creek.

Another rose. And another.

A surge of energy crackled from her head to her hand. With her open palm, she guided the rocks across the water's surface, bringing them just a body length from where she was standing. Her eyes widened as she watched the objects frozen in the air, just like the bullets before. But this time she was making it happen, not just reacting.

Raising her other hand, she beckoned the energy to erect a shield. Like a breeze ruffling her sleeve, the psi-power rippled down her arm and dashed from her hand to form an almost invisible bubble caging her body.

Cool. Very cool.

"Harper."

With a start, she whipped around to face the unexpected intrusion, swinging the rocks along with her. Rome ducked as they hurled just over his head to crash against the boulder behind him, shattering into small chunks behind him.

Oh, poop.

"Rome," she moaned, realizing she had almost taken his head off accidentally. "For goodness sake, please don't sneak up on me like that." At some point she'd have to break that habit of his.

"That was amazing," he praised, standing from his instinctive crouch, brushing the remnants of the rocks from his broad shoulders, clearly in awe.

She took several deep breaths, trying to calm her racing mind. She was practically gushing inside at being able to control her power. It was addictive. That would make revenge so much easier. "What's going on?" she asked, putting a lid on her excitement, wondering what drove him here after her.

"Nothing. I just missed you," he answered with a sweet smile.

She gave him a skeptical look, adding a smile to soften it.

"C'mon." He took her hand in his and kissed the inside of her wrist, sending pleasant little shivers up her arm. "We need to work on a plan before they can mobilize. And I made breakfast. Well, lunch." He looked at his watch, then at the overcast sky.

He was right. Though they'd escaped from the facility, the bad guys now knew she and Rome were onto them. The two of them needed to stay on the offensive. Plus she wanted to end this sooner rather than later. She was getting real tired of being on the run.

"Good idea. Let's plan." She gave his hand a squeeze. Besides, she was ravenous. The psi power seemed to give her an appetite now instead of fatigue. The quick self-healing must be kicking in faster as her body adapted to it.

And after a sideways sizing-up glance at Rome, she realized her hunger wasn't just for food.

CHAPTER SEVENTEEN

"Let's just round them up and kill them," Harper suggested mildly as she took a bite of her sandwich. Sounded easy to her. Especially given her newfound control.

"No," Rome said in flat disagreement, blunting her gusto. "There've been too many casualties already. Besides, we want them to be accountable. Make them pay." She watched him pop a corn chip in his mouth, keeping his clear blue gaze locked on hers.

"Right," she concurred while she chewed. "Make them pay. With their lives."

"No." Rome leveled her with a definite agent-type glare.

"Okay, then," she said, peering at the map they'd sketched of the facility and surrounding area. They pooled their knowledge and observations with the data from the laptop to create it. "What do you suggest?"

Rome's face became pensive and his eyes unfocused as he looked toward the window and the forest beyond. They were sitting on the high stools at the island in the middle of the kitchen while sharing a lunch of turkey sandwiches, corn chips, and fruit.

And fresh-baked brownies. To their utter gratitude, the caretaker of the cabin had stocked it to Rome's specifications before they'd arrived yesterday. Lucky for her, those specifications included brownie mix.

"Rounding them up is a good idea," he said after a few minutes of quiet contemplation. "It's a big place, but it has only a couple entrances and exits."

"So that should make it easier." She reached for a chip from the open bag. The salty crunch in her mouth almost made her groan in delight.

"Maybe." He picked out an orange slice and bit into it, licking the juice from his lips. She almost groaned again. "We'll need to draw them out without too much commotion. We don't want to provoke them or get trapped ourselves. If we can get them out front, it could be doable."

"Use me as bait." Harper shrugged and took a large gulp of water. That was the most logical thing she could think of. They wanted her. She wanted them. *Let's get together.*

Rome was silent. A tiny muscle twitched in his jaw while he stared at her. She turned her full attention to him, wondering what would make the clear blue in his eyes storm so violently.

"No," he whispered, and shook his head. Clearly the idea did not appeal to him.

"Why not?" she asked, ignoring his troubled look. "It's me they want."

"They'll kill you." He shook his head again. "We'll find another way."

"I'm already dead," Harper said, wondering at his adamant caution. Regardless of her imminent demise, she didn't think the faction wanted her dead as long as they thought they could squeeze the serum out of her. Maybe with Rome's experience with this sort of thing, he sensed they were through trying.

But she still didn't see the problem. Hadn't he seen her moving rocks? Plus she could heal fast. She was near invincible.

Taking the last bite of her tasty sandwich, she glanced at their sketched map again. When she went to Bobby's lab, she'd used his direct secret entrance. Yesterday she and Rome had used a back door.

But as she'd explained to Rome on their walk back from the creek a few hours ago, the one problem they were going to have was that her psionic powers didn't work indoors.

Rome had protested, citing their first encounter together. Bobby's lab was different, she'd clarified. He'd been impressed that her brother had crafted sunshine for them. And for the same reason the plants were able to draw strength from the lights, her powers had worked in there.

When in natural daylight, she flourished with vitality. So they needed to draw the faction outside to have a chance.

"Here," she said, pointing at a spot on the map. She circled her finger around the front entrance, which, according to the layouts, as well as to what Rome knew, was a square, concrete walled area with two small depots bordering an open patio, a mix between a square and a U shape. Almost like a gladiator pit from a Roman coliseum. How fitting.

"What about it?" Rome asked, peering at the drawing while he chewed the last of his sandwich.

"Isn't this a courtyard?" Harper tapped on the paper in the middle of the assumed structures, recalling the aerial maps they'd found on the Internet. "Let's lure them here."

She watched him focus intently on the map as he licked the crumbs off his fingertips. The spinning wheels in his mind were nearly visible in every flickering movement of his eyes.

He turned the map around several times, checking it out from different angles, and then sat back, raising his gaze to hers. Mimicking his pose, she leaned back in her bar stool as well, waiting for his competent assessment.

"It could work," he finally said, though with obvious reluctance. He rubbed a hand over his head, clearly distressed about something. "If we could draw them out somehow, they would essentially be isolated."

"And vulnerable," she added, thinking about just how exposed they would be to her powerful psionic mind energy. In one crushing swoop, she could take care of all of them.

"Right," he agreed, drawing out the word and giving her an odd look as he picked up a knife to cut the brownies in the pan. He handed one to her.

Holy cow, these brownies are good.

"Their only retreat would be back into the facility. The quad's formation would work against them. But we need to get them there first."

"So use me as bait," she said again. Watching him chew his little piece of bliss, she caught the troubled look in his eyes. Was he scared for her? She had to reassure him. "I'm not afraid."

"I am," he said simply, his intense gaze burning into hers. "I'm afraid of losing you, Harper."

Rome's vulnerability touched a chord deep inside as no other words had before. His stark concern was both reassuring and disconcerting at the same time. But it wasn't necessary.

"You won't," she insisted stubbornly. They would not lose each other. At least not this way. "I will not let them tear us apart like they did to Bobby and me."

He just looked at her, his uneasy gaze still swirling, beseeching.

"I won't let that happen to us." She reached across the counter to clutch his chilled wrist with both of her hands. "I promise you, I will kill every single one of them before I let anything like that happen again." She gazed squarely into his eyes and squeezed his hand in a silent vow, asking him to believe in her. "You won't lose me."

"I already have," Rome said, sadness and frustration coloring his tone.

"What are you talking about?"

Rome lowered his gaze and looked away for a long moment. She sat there, just waiting. He finally turned to face her, his hand almost twitching in her grasp, as though he wanted to pull it away. She wouldn't let him and tightened her grip.

"You're losing yourself, Harper," he said quietly. Well, that explained nothing. "You just want to go in there and wipe them out."

"What's wrong with that?" she asked, seriously wondering why he had a problem with the old eye for an eye. He should know much better than she did. This was his job, wasn't it?

"Do you want justice or revenge?" he asked, yanking his hand out of her grasp and sliding off the stool to stand, his motions jerky and tense.

"What's the difference?" She slipped from her stool as well to stand before him, nearly face-to-face. Anger simmered in the pit of her stomach, leaden and coarse. "I want retribution. I want each and every one of them to know just what they did to me. I want them to get what they deserve."

He took a step away from her, shaking his head and clenching his jaw.

"Harper, listen to yourself," he snapped, holding his

arms out wide, his eyes demanding. "You're consumed by your need for revenge. And frankly, it's really creepy." Taking a deep breath, he gestured at her in frustration. "And it's not you."

Harper was livid. More than livid. Heated anger raced in her blood, and she fought with all her might to keep it down. To keep from lashing out at the one person she thought for sure was on her side. She took a deep breath and two steps back, struggling to control her budding rage.

"How do you know me?" she asked in a calm, still voice, narrowing her eyes. "You don't know anything about me."

He looked as though she'd slapped him. She certainly felt like doing it, but his expression said she didn't need to. Her words had done the trick, cutting deeper than any knife could. She winced inside with the knowledge that she'd hurt him.

"I know that a few weeks ago, my life was hollow." His rich voice was quiet now, almost disenchanted. "I know that now you've become the center of my world. That's all I need to know."

"That's all you need to know?" she asked incredulously, comforted by his words and at the same time, restless from their message. But she needed to set him straight. "You need to know that a few weeks ago I was an Olympic hopeful, training for my swimming trials. Excited to spend some downtime with my brother. Now my brother is dead and I'm a fallen rogue with superhero powers, a fugitive from a covert and ruthless government faction that wants to dissect me like some lab rat in hopes that they can create supercommandos from the serum I inadvertently injected inside my body."

Breathing heavily from her long tirade, she just stood

there staring at him. A blank expression covered his
face, as if he had no idea what to say. Heck, she had no
idea what she wanted him to say.

Harper shook her head slowly, calming her tangled
nerves. She was tired. So tired of what her life had become. She wanted to end this once and for all so that she
could begin to move on in what little time she had. Was
that so wrong?

"I'm just becoming what I need to be to make sure
Bobby's murder gets avenged," Harper added after the
long minutes of charged silence.

"No." Rome's voice was low and unyielding, his eyes
brimming with anger and accusation. "You're becoming the very thing Bobby tried to prevent."

"How can you say that?" she roared, fury in every fiber of her being.

"Why can't you see that?" he barked back. Stepping
closer, he was now just a breath away, his steely gaze
drilling into hers. "Bobby risked his life, his last moments on this earth, to save the serum and make sure
you got that flash drive of data. He put everything there
for you so that you could take that information and do
the right thing."

She shook her head, fuming, wanting to lash out at
him yet knowing somewhere deep down that he had a
very good point.

She just didn't know whether she could let it go so
easily. She'd made a vow. But maybe Rome was right.
Maybe justice was the right thing.

Rome's strong hands clasped her upper arms gently,
rubbing her flushed skin with soothing motions.

"Harper, these are genuine," he said quietly yet forcefully as he gripped her biceps. He rested his hands on
her chest over her heart. "This is genuine." He then

lowered his hands to grasp hers and pull them up, hugging them to his chest. "Your strength comes from inside you, not some artificial serum."

Harper stilled, willing herself to believe what Rome was saying. Wanting so badly for it to be true. She knew her physical limits. And yet the psi power could extend those limits to cease this horrible nightmare.

"I don't know if I can believe that anymore, Rome," she whispered, desperately wanting to trust in herself, but not quite sure she could. Her need for revenge was a thirst she didn't think she could quench without destruction. She wanted to fight. That was her nature. But Rome's voice battled within her to be heard.

"Harper, this is the right thing to do," he said, his blue gaze boring into her. "Sometimes doing the right thing isn't always the thing you want to do."

His words reached out to embrace her as if a heavy cloak of responsibility. Though Rome wholly believed in her strength, she didn't know whether she could bear the crushing weight.

"Bobby trusted you," Rome continued, folding her hands tighter against his warm body. "He trusted that you'd do the right thing." He leaned in and placed a kiss on her forehead, the tenderest kiss she could ever imagine. "And I trust you, too. Isn't that enough?"

Was it? It would have to be.

"I guess so," she answered, still unsure. But knowing that Rome had such strong faith in her went a very long way.

She shook her head to clear away her anger and uncertainty. They had a job to do. And no matter what plan they came up with, she was going to make sure justice was had.

One way or another.

* * *

"I still don't like it," Rome grumbled, his gaze riveted on the map resting on his lap.

Her gaze was riveted to the same area, but for a very different reason, his being naked and all. They'd released some of their tension by spending some heated time in the big bed and were just now finalizing a plan to bring Jeff and his faction to justice.

"Your opinion is beside the point," Harper said, lounging on her side. Her head was propped in one hand while her other traced a scar on his sturdy knee. "It's the best option, and you know it."

Rome's searing glare nearly branded her. But she knew that he knew she was right. Revisiting the plan of using her as bait was still troubling him. But no matter how much it rubbed him the wrong way, it was the quickest and easiest solution to drawing the faction out of the compound. And he had to know it.

"I know it, but I don't have to like it," he said grumpily with a heavy sigh. He reached for a prepaid cell phone as it trilled, one of the many untraceable phones in his secret stash from the car. He pressed the button on the phone to answer it. "What?"

After a few seconds of watching his delicious lips as he talked in curt phrases, she rolled onto her back and thought about the plan they'd hatched.

Right now she assumed Rome was talking to a trusted contact to help with reinforcements. Bringing down the splinter group would take more than the two of them, Rome had said. They needed backup if they were going to round up and bring in the Five Watch faction, and Rome knew good people he trusted who could help.

The plan was simple. Harper would contact Jeff and claim she wanted to surrender and work together.

Whether Jeff believed her was irrelevant. Both she and Rome knew the call would be enough to entice the jerk to meet her. And she knew the magic words to make him agree.

With one phone call, she would set up a parley with Jeff. She was to walk into the open courtyard area of the remote Five Watch facility in broad daylight. That should lure Jeff and his group out soon enough. Then she was to give up willingly and turn herself in. Once they moved in to take her, Rome would come barreling in with the good guys to take Jeff and the bad guys instead.

Simple. Straightforward. But hardly satisfying.

"It's all set," Rome said confidently. She looked at him. "Tomorrow. One o'clock. Help will meet us there."

"Just like that?" she asked.

"I trust them to be there," he answered, and ran a hand through her hair. She almost purred. "I'll meet them, you'll go in; then we'll come and save the day. Just don't rile the faction up." He tweaked a few strands playfully.

"Okay, just don't take too long to save me." She gave him a half smile. "Or I'll have to save myself." Her half smile blossomed into a full-blown grin at the alluring thought of revenge. It was so close now, she could taste it. And she savored the flavor.

No, wait; hold on. She wasn't supposed to antagonize them with her powers. That would make the capture of the faction unpredictable. Rome explained that plans like this never quite worked how they were supposed to, anyway, no matter how simple and precise they seemed. But he'd asked her to stick with it for as long as she could.

And she would. For as long as she could.

The bed shifted as he set the map aside and nestled down to face her, side by side. His muscular arm snaked around her hip, tugging her snug against him. Clasping his arm, she leaned in for a languid kiss.

"I can't wait until this is all over," Rome said, his fingers caressing her neck, trailing along the old swimming scar that marked her shoulder.

Not knowing quite how to respond, she let herself get lost in the bluest eyes she'd ever known.

Resting her hand on his hard chest, Harper realized she didn't want to think about what would happen next. Because really, what would happen when this was all over? What did Rome expect? What did she expect?

Her mind whirled at the endless possibilities. And then stopped. When this all began, she'd planned on revenge. And, honestly, she hadn't planned to survive it. She hadn't cared.

Until Rome. Now maybe she actually had something to live for. Well, live as long as she could.

She had told him she loved him. And she meant it. But, she hadn't planned for it.

"Hey," he said, running a gentle finger across her cheeks to tap her temple, startling her. "What's going on in there?"

His honest concern snuggled inside her heart, warming her from within. Should she confess she still had doubts? Grave doubts about restraining from using her psionic powers once she faced Jeff, the man responsible for orchestrating her brother's murder?

Probably not.

And if they did make it through tomorrow, what then? What kind of life could she even lead? She was as good as dead. Her entire existence had been altered beyond repair. Her mind was reeling with questions she had no answers to and probably never would have.

"Nothing." Harper shrugged it off. She couldn't talk to Rome about it. She didn't even know where to begin. Didn't want to burden him with her doubts and fears. He said she had enough strength to handle everything. She wanted to prove him right. "Nothing." It was all she could say. "Let's call Jeff later."

Reaching with both of her hands, she pulled his face close, covering his lips with hers. Tasting. Memorizing. Hoping that this wouldn't be their last night together, but knowing it was.

CHAPTER EIGHTEEN

Jeff Donovan sat in the plush chair of his office within the drab confines of the downtown facility, running over the disturbing events at the remote facility two days before. Someone had been eavesdropping. Two someones, actually.

His best agent, Rome Lucian, and that damned bitch, Harper Kane. The men who had chased the two of them in the forest had confirmed their identities.

And the two of them had escaped.

His cell phone trilled, and he stared at it with a withering glare, willing it to shut up.

He was angry. More than angry. How had they gotten into the laboratories? How had they known what to look for? More important, how did they manage to escape? Together, they'd managed to become seemingly unstoppable.

Another trill, this time with a buzz, sending the little phone skittering lightly across his immaculate desk. He seized the annoying device, almost chucking it against the wall just to see it break and fall apart into little pieces, just as his plans seemed to be doing.

But instead he gazed at the display. UNKNOWN CALLER. Why not? Probably another inept scientist offering up a new excuse as to why they couldn't get the formula right.

Jeff was beginning to think maybe he shouldn't have killed Dr. Robert Kane. If only to use his sister against him. He had so loved to hear Harper Kane's screams when Dr. Andy had played with her in the romper room.

He opened the phone and pressed the green button to answer it.

"What?" he barked to the unknown caller on the other end.

"Mr. Donovan?" The cool voice was low and gravelly, yet very feminine. Speak of the damn devil. It was her. Harper Kane.

"Ms. Kane," Jeff responded cordially. Somehow he should have seen this call coming. "What can I do for you?" He knew exactly what he wanted to do. He wanted to dismantle her body and examine every single microscopic scrap, inside and out, to extract the formula, molecule by molecule. Instead, he decided to hear what she had in mind first.

"Well, you can start by calling off your men," she answered conversationally. Her tone was calm and together. "It never seems to end well for them."

Bitch. "I'll see what I can do," he countered, holding his anger in check. It wouldn't do any good to piss her off.

"Besides," she went on, "I can't see what good it would do, given that I have original serum in me. My powers are stronger. I'll always win."

He could just picture the smug look on her face. She obviously knew more than she was letting on. And she'd overheard him talking to the idiot Dr. Blake.

"So, what exactly do you want?" Jeff decided to stop playing games before he chose to just kill her himself. His project was too valuable to waste on one wretched woman.

"Why don't we get together?" she asked civilly, as if they were discussing getting together for tea.

"What did you have in mind?" She was obviously setting him up for something. This whole thing reeked of Rome. Having the skilled agent as an advocate was definitely a point in her favor. Several points, in fact.

"How about we meet back at the lab?" Harper suggested. Yes, she was undeniably setting him up. But why? She had to know he'd see through this.

"Ms. Kane," Jeff said, figuring he better fish around for some clues as to what she was planning, "as much as I'd love to see you again, I'm not sure that's such a good idea. After all, you left so hastily last time we met. Didn't you enjoy my hospitality?" *There, that ought to throw her off a bit.* Make her see that he wasn't to be trifled with.

Her silence was good enough for him. He didn't expect an actual answer.

"Not really," she rallied. The bitch had guts; he'd give her that. "But I think maybe this time I can be of some help. I have something you need. Something I'd like to give you in exchange for leaving me alone."

"Really?" Jeff was getting tired of this cat-and-mouse game. "And just what is it you think I need?"

"The formula," Harper answered simply.

It was Jeff's turn to be silent. She was lying. She had to be. The formula had been lost when Dr. Kane set fire to his lab, destroying every remnant of his precious creation. How in the world could she possibly have it?

"I take it you don't believe me," her complacent voice filtered through the connection.

"I find it hard to believe, yes," he managed. Damn her. If she really had it, a meeting was worth the risk.

"Well, I saw that you found your men from the train tracks." Her tone was confident. Not only had she overheard his conversation, but she'd dug around the lab as well. "I take it you saw what I left there. An empty syringe and a broken flash drive." Yes, he had seen those. What was she getting at? "I bet you know what happened to the serum in the syringe."

"Yes, I'm quite aware of it," he answered, an unusual sense of foreboding washing over him.

"I'm sure you are." She laughed, the arrogance grating on his stinging nerves. "But the flash drive wasn't quite destroyed. I kept the memory chip." The foreboding turned into dread. "And I have all of my brother's data. I know what he did. And I have tangible proof. Of everything."

Fear sank into his stomach like an anchor, latching onto the bottom. She wasn't bluffing. He could hear it in her voice. It was his job to filter out the lies and mine for the truth. And through his many years of experience, he knew she was telling the truth. She could ruin everything he'd worked for.

But she hadn't. Because she wanted to be left alone. Well, he could do that. For a short time. Time enough to get the formula out of her. And then he'd see to it that she was left alone. Alone to die.

"So, can we get together?" she asked once again.

"I'd like that," Jeff answered flatly. Let her think she had him where she wanted him. Yes, she had Rome, but she was a novice at the games he could play. He just needed her unaccompanied for a few moments. "The lab, you said?"

"The courtyard outside the lab, actually," she amended. "I'd like to stay outside, just in case. If you know what I mean."

"I'm sure you would," he snarked, unable to help himself. The woman needed the natural daylight to use her power. That much he knew. "Okay, I'll agree to that. But I'd like you to come alone, just in case. If you know what I mean." And he was sure she did.

"Of course," she stated evenly. "One o'clock. Tomorrow."

"One o'clock, tomorrow," he repeated.

"Bye, then." Her gravelly tone lifted a tad, and then the connection was severed.

He didn't even try to trace the call. He had no need for it. Besides, he knew Rome had her use something undetectable.

Harper had accepted his terms. Though he didn't believe her for one moment. He knew for a fact that she'd have Rome close by. For some unknown reason, the agent had decided to stand with her. Fine. Rome had clearly picked a side and would suffer dearly for it.

Once she stepped foot into the courtyard, Jeff would have her taken down. Yes, her power was superior, but he had superior numbers. And though not as strong, that many enhanced men would be able to, at the very least, subdue Harper and Rome.

And then he'd make them both suffer for choosing the wrong side.

CHAPTER NINETEEN

Twelve o'clock.

Harper's digital watch displayed the time in bold black numbers. A raindrop splattered on the small face and she brushed it off before she turned her attention back to the veiled position she'd staked out. The facility was just beyond the dense trees and thick brush that kept her well hidden.

In precisely one hour, Rome would show up with reinforcements. To bring Jeff Donovan and the Five Watch faction to justice.

But in a few minutes, she would face Jeff and the faction on her own. To bring vengeance.

She knew full well what her and Rome's plan was. The intricate timing Rome had established and every move she was supposed to make.

But this morning, as she lay awake in Rome's secure arms, rehashing the plan over and over in her mind, she knew she couldn't do it.

She couldn't do it and be whole with herself.

Rome had drawn a line and she was about to cross it. She refused to wait. Waiting meant justice, not vengeance. And the only justice she could understand was to avenge her brother's death by wiping out Jeff and his faction. That way, there was no chance they could exploit and murder anyone else. They deserved as much and more for all the lives they'd ruined.

Bowing her head, she closed her eyes and looked inside herself for a long moment. Was she doing the right thing?

Sharp visions of Rome flowed unbidden into her thoughts. Confident and honorable. Strong yet vulnerable. He'd allowed her to see his weaknesses just as she had shown hers to him. They'd seen each other at their best and worst. They'd shared triumphs and setbacks.

And they'd loved.

She'd never loved anyone as she loved Rome. Never thought herself capable of that depth of emotion. Of wanting to give everything she had been and everything she ever hoped to be to someone. She'd always kept her heart locked down somewhere deep inside herself.

But Rome had somehow unlocked it. Without her knowing. Or maybe she had known. Because from the moment she'd awakened tied to his couch, she'd known he was someone who could change her life. And not just because of her horrible situation, but because of the amazing man he was.

He'd told her he loved her. And he meant it. Of that she had no doubt. She just had to look at what he'd given to her and given up for her.

He had given her his heart, body, and soul. He was sacrificing his career and possibly his life. And he'd asked nothing in return except that she believe in him. And she truly did. She believed in everything he stood for and everything he was.

But she also believed that this was something that she had to do. For Bobby. Vengeance was the only thing that could make this right. She hoped Rome's love included clemency. Because no matter how much she wanted to believe, she knew in her every fiber she would die today. She just hoped Rome would forgive her for it.

Her life and love were sacrifices she would willingly make to see Bobby's killers revenged.

She opened her eyes and narrowed her focus. Ready to face whatever may lie ahead. She was on the block. Time for the race.

From her crouched position, Harper peered from behind a moss-covered log to study the outside of the Five Watch facility. It looked very different from the covert entrance to Bobby's lab and the other obscure entrance she and Rome had snuck into a few days ago. Plain. Ordinary. Like any other boring office park.

On the tree-lined hill, she was able to look down, unnoticed, onto the scene. A couple of guys were wandering around the courtyard, just going about their business. Anyone else might think they were just normal building security guards on their tedious rounds.

But she knew better. They walked with subtle purpose and were, no doubt, armed to the teeth with weapons and maybe even psi powers like hers.

Well, not exactly like hers, she thought with a wicked grin.

The layout was very similar to the map she and Rome had made. There were three sturdy buildings in a squared horseshoe shape. In the middle was a well-manicured grassy quad, lined with cherry trees, many of them bare, and wet cement walkways that were soaked from the steady rain.

Her own plan was simple. Walk right up and challenge them. The more armed men who came to take her, the more she'd be able to get rid of, until there was no one left.

Given that Jeff had kept her alive for experiments,

she was banking on the assumption that he wouldn't just have her shot on sight. He probably wanted to go another few rounds with her in the labs with the horrific equipment. But if they did start shooting, she'd just stop the bullets.

And even though she couldn't see all of them, she knew they'd be waiting for her. Her goading of Jeff had ensured he'd be there with practically an army. She knew she'd gotten a rise out of him by his way-too-controlled responses. Rome had been impressed.

Rome. She had to purge him from her thoughts to do this. She took a deep breath to calm her mind. Just as she'd done before a race.

She glanced up at the tumultuous, cloudy sky. Though an incessant rain was coming down, daylight was the key. She needed to stay out of the shadowy cover from those looming buildings.

Besides, she liked the invigorating natural shower and briefly wondered how much of that was her love of water or her need for it. Either way, she looked forward to what was about to come.

Checking her watch once more, she crept around the thick uprooted base of the log and headed carefully down the wet slope, weaving between the trees. Slick pine needles and moss covered the ground, and she slid several times on the moist, loose soil as she made her way toward the facility.

Harper reached the outskirts and ducked behind a cluster of nearby brush. The flanking two buildings loomed larger from the level ground than they had seemed to from her previous elevated vantage point. Though vacant just a few moments ago, someone could easily be on guard from up there without her knowing. She'd have to keep alert and stay aware at all times.

Taking a deep breath, she braced herself, knowing she was doing what she had to do. Then Harper stood and, with deliberate strides, warily headed toward the open entrance. The damp roadway was spongy under her sneakers, drawing little splashes with each step.

Harper reached the edge of her cover. She could see past the trees that made up the boundary. The two sentries were talking together, facing each other, rifles resting placidly on their shoulders. One more step and she'd cross the point of no return.

And she wouldn't return. She knew her time had to be just about up. And the last thing to do before she checked out was wreak havoc on those who had destroyed all that her brother had stood for.

Rome wouldn't be here for another thirty minutes. Enough time for her to pull back and wait to put their plan in motion. Enough time for her to move forward and take solitary action.

She took a step forward, moving ahead to seek revenge.

Rome smoothly crossed the threshold from slumber to consciousness. Eyes still closed, he rolled over and went to throw his arm across Harper's warm body. His eyes snapped open when all he felt was cool sheets.

Harper was gone. Leaning on one elbow, he ran his hand over her side of the bed. The flannel material wasn't just cool. It was cold. With a frown, he peered around the modest cabin, quickly searching and listening for any sign of her.

On the hardwood floor near the bathroom door, he spied a neatly folded pile of her clothes. He let out the heavy breath he hadn't even known he was holding.

His tossed the comforter to the side and climbed naked out of the bed. Long strides carried him to the front window. Frowning, he peered out the hazy glass, looked through the misty rain besieging the dense trees. The Bug was still there, but Harper wasn't.

Turning his back to the window, he looked around the cabin once more while his thoughts dashed with unthinkable possibilities. Maybe she'd been captured. Maybe she ran away.

Or maybe she just went for a walk to clear her head. Rome smacked himself upside the head for letting himself think the worst. That was it. The exasperating woman loved being outside. No doubt she was just taking some time alone to focus on her part in their plan to shut down Jeff's scheme.

Appeased, he headed for the shower to ward off the chill that had seized his bare body. Turning on the water, he couldn't help but remember the fun he and Harper had the other night as they stood under the spray. He smiled, hoping against hope that this would all be over soon and they could move forward. Together. Harper was more than a handful, but he was very sure he wanted many more showers with her in the future.

Rome finished his hot shower and pulled on his clothes, not wanting to miss a moment with her when she returned from her outing.

Striding into the kitchen, he began to boil some water for hot chocolate for the two of them, guessing she'd want something to warm up her insides. He'd take care of warming her body.

Rome figured that they had plenty of time to get ready for the afternoon. He had set the rendezvous with his handpicked special forces team for thirteen hundred hours. It was currently nine fifteen. He stole another look outside and then almost slapped himself again for being so anxious.

Removing the steaming boiling water, he fixed himself a cup of hot chocolate and headed toward the island and the laptop. Perching on a stool, he decided his mind could be put to better use other than worrying by the door like a father on prom night.

Rome sipped his hot drink while the computer booted. He chuckled at the complex log-on procedure Harper had orchestrated while he went through the methodical steps. She was really something else.

He'd admired her inner strength from the moment he'd decided to help her. He saw that strength mirrored in himself. In his instincts. He'd been right about her. And being able to trust himself was a gift from her that he could never repay. But he'd try.

Finally he got to the files they had combed through meticulously. But he knew it wouldn't hurt to browse one more time before they jumped in and did something about the information. He couldn't help thinking there was something in there that could give them an edge that would make a big difference. Countless times, the smallest detail had proven the largest advantage in his covert line of work.

He went through file after file. He and Harper had color coded the folders to delineate which one of them had been gone through so they didn't duplicate any work. Hers were green, his were blue, but all of the sudden, he came across one generic yellow folder. Had they missed one?

Damn it all, they couldn't afford to have missed anything. But it was entirely possible. Rome's mouth quirked into a grin, knowing exactly what reason made it entirely possible. Last night, their eyes had been prickly, tired of looking at all the data, but their bodies held plenty of sizzling energy. And they'd used every last fiery ounce.

Damn. Damn. They really couldn't afford any mistakes or faulty information. Maybe they'd just forgotten to color code it.

Ten forty-five. Harper still wasn't back.

Rome clicked the lone folder to open it. Definitely not something he'd seen. It was one of the files from Jeff's experiments that Bobby must have had time to go through. Bobby had inserted his own notes into the text. He scanned the words, though not as familiar with the tone as Harper would have been.

The more he read, the more he gathered he was reading an analysis of the men Jeff had injected with the replicated serum. The big question repeated throughout the data was why they had died from it. Rome shivered. That was the exact question he and Harper had tried not to face. But they sure the hell wanted to know the answer, too.

"Holy shit." He rubbed his head in shock. "Bobby figured it out." A smile broke across his face, chasing the chill away with vehemence.

Continuing to read Bobby's notes on the serum Jeff had used for the subjects, Rome's smile grew.

Harper's brother had examined Jeff's reports on the trials. Because the faction stole the infused plants, they had only derivatives of Bobby's formula. "Offshoots," Bobby called them. Rome remembered Harper saying that her brother was possessive to the point of paranoia when it came to his plant experiments. There was no way the faction would ever have gotten ahold of the true serum unless Bobby had let them, which the notes in the file showed he distinctly had not.

Bobby had examined the formula the faction used. Because that applied formula was from the dissected plants and not the authentic formula, the effects were diluted. Bobby included notes on his own experiments with his own plants that had obviously been conducted months before he'd discovered the faction.

The test plants that had been given the original formula had flourished. The plants that had been given a diluted serum had deteriorated and eventually died in less than a week. They did age, even though they were able to repair themselves throughout their lifetime. The only things that killed them was their natural life span or if they were intentionally uprooted. Those were the limitations. The natural order of things remained untouched.

The serum had to be administered to the seeds, and then the seeds had to be planted. And it would stay with them as long as they lived their healthy green lives. Or until someone cut them down. Like the faction was trying to do to Harper.

But Harper had the pure genuine serum inside of her. Not the offshoot.

Rome's heart soared. Harper wasn't going to die like the others.

He quickly reread the data to be sure he was interpreting it correctly. There was no mistake in Bobby's findings. The formula that flowed through Harper was pure. And therefore, she'd survive its effects.

Hopping off the stool in an ecstatic frenzy, Rome dashed to the door of the cabin and ran outside, practically bursting to tell her the good—no, great—news.

But Harper wasn't anywhere to be seen.

His buoyant mood began to deflate rapidly. Eleven seventeen. Well, she'd survive if he didn't kill her first. Where the hell was she? They had to leave soon. Very soon.

Damn it all. She had a watch. A fancy Ironman watch

she used when she swam. She knew they were supposed to leave at noon. Was he going to have to find her again like yesterday? They didn't have time for that.

He let out a ragged sigh, watching his breath plume in the cool fall air. Excitement drained to anger as he stomped back inside to drag on his coat. Shoving his hands into the coat pockets, he trudged back outside, nearly growling with each harsh step.

And stopped still.

His fingers jammed against something cold and hard inside the left pocket. An eerie sensation shivered through his hand and settled uneasily in his gut.

Before pulling it out, he knew exactly what it was.

Harper's first gold medal. The medal she'd said she treasured over all others. The medal they'd found at Bobby's. The medal he'd returned to her.

And now she'd given it back to him.

Rome sank to his knees in the wet gravel, the grainy mist shrouding his slumped form.

Harper was gone.

Clutching the medal against his bowed forehead, he knew.

She'd gone to bring Jeff down herself. She thought she was going to die anyway. It was a sacrifice she wanted to make. He thought he'd convinced her that they could do this together. That whatever was between them could keep her safe and alive until they found an antidote. She didn't need to surrender her life to take Jeff's.

Yet she had already made up her mind. Last night, he thought they had solidified a promise to see it through together. As she lay in his arms in the late hours of darkness, she'd said a breathless good night. But what she'd really said was good-bye.

The gold medal was covered with dull scratches and

beads of mist. It reminded him so much of Harper. At one time full of shine, now tarnished and changed forever. Yet like the gold, she still glowed under it all.

And like the cherished medal, she would endure. Even if she didn't know it yet.

He had to stop her. Had to let her know she had a life worth fighting for. And a love worth giving a chance.

Shoving himself up, Rome raced into the cabin and got the things they had planned to take. Five minutes later, he was in the Bug speeding to stop her from making a horrible mistake.

He couldn't blame Harper for doing what she thought she needed to do. But he was downright furious with her for thinking she could leave him behind so easily.

Damn it all. He just hoped he could get to the compound in time to let her know she was going to have a lifetime to make it up to him.

CHAPTER TWENTY

It took longer than she thought for the guards to notice her as she walked inside the walls. She was near the courtyard grass, almost to the walkways before they turned their heads in her direction. *Idiots.*

They stared for a few seconds, then snapped out of their surprised trance and marched toward her, pulling their weapons around. She maintained her leisurely pace, steeling her body for the fight of her life.

Harper stopped halfway down the wet cement walkway just as the two guards slid to a halt, mere feet away from her, the barrels of their rifles pointed directly at her chest.

"Hello, boys." Her voiced dripped with a menace that coursed through her entire being, welcome and rousing.

She raised her right hand and called upon her psi power. The rush of ice through her blood was instantly replaced by a swell of heat. Then a surge of energy shot from her mind to her hand and toward the two men, the near-invisible force propelling them off their feet to land far on the other side of the courtyard grass.

Two other men materialized from the building on the left, charging toward her at full speed. She brought her left hand up and flared another wave of energy at them with the same satisfying result.

She reveled in the addictive energy that pumped through her body and mind, just waiting, thirsting to unleash it again. A rustling of motion from above drew her attention to the roof of the building on the right. Guards on the roof. The load cracks of their rifles sounded. So much for her theory of their keeping her alive.

Harper whipped around and brought up both hands, palms out, creating an ethereal shield, freezing the bullets in midair as they shot toward her.

She pushed another wave of energy against the barely perceptible buffer, sending the bullets back at the shooters high above. Short screams reached her ears as her targets were hit by their own ammunition.

A group of men poured out of the main building and lumbered toward her, their boots kicking up splashes with every step. They had no weapons, but that didn't keep them from looking dangerous.

No, they didn't need guns. They were bio-enhanced. But not like her. She was stronger. Singular. Pure.

She grinned at her confidence. At the unparalleled power of her mind.

Two men shot a surge of energy at her. She could see the air displace as the cloudy wave swelled toward her like an oncoming flood.

She effortlessly met the surge with a clear one of her own. The space between Harper and her targets crackled like lightning as the crushing forces collided.

A handful of other men behind the two at the forefront added their power to the psionic fray. She met their energy as well with more than enough of her own. Her grin widened. Maybe she wasn't suicidal. This was going to be easier than she thought. And fun.

More footsteps in the soggy grass of the courtyard behind her. She spared a quick glance over her shoulder to see another group of brutes briskly approaching her position in the center of the quad. For crying out loud, did Jeff seriously have an entire army at his disposal?

Narrowing her eyes, she turned sideways and moved one arm behind her, launching powerful waves toward the newcomers to hold them off while she continued with the other arm to battle the men she'd already engaged.

Harper's blood was on fire, sizzling through every fiber as her psi power raged like a ravenous caged beast inside her mind. Her body became a giant dynamo, radiating improbable power inside and out, searing her muscles and singeing her skin.

Closing her eyes, she saw red sparks flare behind her eyelids. The blazing heat threatened to overtake her, engulf her body in an unearthly inferno. If she could open her eyes right now, she wouldn't be surprised to see her clothes in flames.

So she did. And her superior psionic power was wearing her adversaries down.

Incredible. Harper couldn't help the heady sensation of invulnerability. Rather, she greeted the feeling as though it was finally coming home. If the psi power was going to kill her, what a way to go.

Focusing on the men in front of her, she decided to crank it up a notch. When she swam in a race, she had always been able to tap into her strength for a little extra boost when she'd needed it. She decided to use a trace of those reserves now, but also save some for later. If she'd even need it.

Reaching inside her mind with a fiery talon, she sent a shock wave down to her hand and willed her psi power to tear through the onslaught of pounding force the men were bringing from the front.

And it did. Cutting through their resisting murky energy like a razor to silk. Barraging through their bodies in a ghostly surge and dropping them as if they were rag dolls. Dead. For Bobby.

With a pleased smile, she turned to fully face the enemies behind her. Using both hands now, she centered her mind's focus on their substantial attack. There were more of them than she'd just killed, maybe ten or twelve, but it was hard to discern through the heated fury coloring her sight.

Bringing her hands back toward her chest, she quickly pressed her open palms toward them, again and again, pushing the men back with swells of energy.

With each forceful thrust, she drove them farther and farther away, until she broke through their defense completely and hurled them through the air. Their limp bodies fell cruelly to the damp grass. Unmoving.

More spattering footsteps on the pavement trickled through her concentration. She whirled around to face the entrance of the complex once more. Four men walked toward her, but without the hostile intent of the others. They held guns, but they weren't aiming them at her.

A greeting party? Finally.

Harper stepped forward to meet them, stopping when they halted about twenty paces away from her. Maybe they were giving up and this was some sort of parley. Somehow the thought disappointed her. She had so been looking forward to tearing through each and every one of them to get to Jeff Donovan and destroy the horror that he'd created.

"Enough," she snarled. "Where's Donovan?" She waited, half hoping they'd make the slightest move. Wanting to unleash more fury upon them.

"Ms. Kane." They parted like a curtain, revealing the source of the strangely familiar voice.

The man from the lab. The man who had murdered her brother. The man who had ordered Rome to hunt her down.

Jeff Donovan.

She knew he'd be here. And she also knew he wouldn't keep their bargain. That was okay. She hadn't intended to keep it, either. There was no way she'd ever give this vile piece of filth her brother's formula.

"Nice to finally meet you face-to-face," he continued as he strolled forward to stand just in front of his four guardians. She noticed a large wooden crate behind the spot he'd just vacated. Probably for her. Because if she was out of the natural light, her powers would be useless. "An impersonal phone call just isn't the same. Nor were you really in any condition to chat the last time I saw you."

She just smiled in response, keeping a lid on her burgeoning hatred for him at the moment. It was more than satisfying to finally confront the mastermind behind all of this. She nearly twitched in anticipation of ending this once and for all.

"You've made quite a mess out here," he said genially. She watched him leisurely glance around at the crowd of bodies that littered the courtyard like confetti.

"You've made quite a mess yourself," she shot back, her gaze locked on him. The rain increased its pounding from the sky. Much like her psionic energy pounded against the walls of her mind. Itching to be set free.

"No, your brother did." His voice turned cold and condemning. "Dr. Kane created a revolutionary formula. But instead of exploring its full potential, he hoarded it like a spoiled child."

Harper seethed at his words and wondered why she wasn't cutting him down right that very instant. Maybe she just wanted to hear why he'd done it. Why someone would choose to destroy the lives of others. Though in the end, it wouldn't really matter.

Jeff would die. And so would she.

"Ms. Kane, you are the proof." He sauntered toward her. His unhurried steps ate up half the distance that separated them before he stopped.

"Proof of what?" she couldn't help asking as she shook violently inside, just waiting for the right moment to open the gates of her emotions and allow her fierce power to rip his world apart.

"That the formula has a higher purpose," Jeff answered. He didn't appear to be afraid of her. He should be.

"And what's that?" Harper decided to humor him.

"Vengeance," Jeff stated simply.

He had that right. She did plan to use it for vengeance. What higher purpose was there?

"You want to avenge your brother's death," he continued, holding her captive with his words. "He was an unfortunate casualty."

"Casualty?" She fumed at the term, taking a threatening step forward. "He was gunned down in cold blood. I was there. I saw it."

"It didn't have to end up that way," Jeff countered in a sensible tone. This man was insane. He acted as if Bobby had asked to die. "Your brother assumed the worst and pulled his research. He didn't take the time to find out the real intent of my program. Instead of joining my team, he shunned it. His research was important for more than just his beloved plants."

The man was talking in circles. Trying to confuse

her. Maybe trying to buy some time, because he knew he was running out of it. And yet, why was she allowing it? Why was she holding back?

"Get to the point," she demanded, heat simmering just under her skin, tingling and ready.

"The point is, Ms. Kane, the serum you have inside your body can be used for more than just a trivial payback for a tragedy," he said, taking another step forward.

Motion flickered in her peripheral vision. She chanced a brief glance to her right and saw a solid line of men form on the roof of the building. Weapons all trained on her. A look to her left revealed the same thing. If she looked behind her, she knew she'd see them, as well. She was surrounded.

"My intention is not to create monsters," Jeff said, his hard voice commanding her attention. "My intention is to create a superior soldier."

Harper's eyes narrowed. She knew this. Knew what he was trying to do and the lethal experiments he administered. Knew their horrific results. She would be one of the failed statistics.

"Ms. Kane, you could be the ultimate weapon." Jeff's intense eyes bore into hers as his voice sank into her mind, unbidden and unwelcome.

What on earth was he talking about? She didn't want to be a weapon. She wanted to be herself. She wanted her brother back. Her life back.

"You have an extraordinary power that can be used for good," he said, pressing on, moving another pace closer. "An invincible power. Think of all the injustices of the world. You could seek vengeance globally. Right all the wrongs." Jeff was now just a mere body length away from her.

Uncertainty flooded Harper's mind, bringing with it

an unsettling rush of confusion. She had come here to right the wrong. To seek vengeance for the injustice. Precisely as he said.

"Just like your brother would have wanted." Jeff's words were quiet. But they thundered louder than a sonic boom.

Was he right? Harper searched deep inside herself, hoping to find the answer buried deep in her soul. Needing the answer.

Is that really what Bobby would have wanted?

No.

Bobby had given his life to stop this. To keep his precious formula secret. Whatever his reasons, her brother hadn't wanted Jeff Donovan and his team to succeed.

That was enough for her.

Bobby had died to stop them. And she'd do no less to stop them, as well.

"No." Harper's voice was low and still. The quiet calm before the deadly storm. "That's not what my brother wanted."

She was going to kill them all. Starting with Jeff.

Chilling, bitter ice raced to her mind. Then in an instant, vibrant heat scorched her vision as she called upon all the hatred and resentment she felt for this man and what he'd done. Her body blazed unmercifully, her flesh barely able to contain the inferno that seared every fiber inside.

She grabbed his neck. Her grip a searing vise. Sizzling flames prickled in her muscles as her mind began to launch flares of energy through her arm, just waiting to unleash.

Through high-powered binoculars, Rome watched Harper face off against Jeff in the middle of the rainy courtyard. *Damn it all.* She was supposed to wait for him. Lowering the glasses, he slammed his fist into the moist soil, the mud sucking at his fingers. *Damn it.*

"That your girl?" someone to his right asked. "She's quite a looker."

Rome clenched his jaw and turned his head, narrowing his gaze at the trusted special forces operative to his right. Holding a similar pair of binoculars, he was watching the scene unfold, as well.

"She was supposed to wait," Rome growled, shifting his attention back to Harper while he yanked his hand out of the muck with a muted *glorp*. The operative chuckled.

What the hell was Harper doing?

He, along with the planned reinforcements, had arrived precisely on time, only to find Harper not at their meeting point. He'd hoped to talk her out of her personal vendetta. But all they'd found were blaring cracks and heavy thuds that had drawn them to the sheltered hill above the courtyard, where they watched her use her powers to easily dispose of all comers. Rome's team had been markedly shocked, but curious at the same time.

Upon meeting up with the trusted group at a more distant rendezvous point, Rome had explained the situation. But to see it in action . . . he knew that was a different story.

The special forces team had all been wholly impressed with the scientist's noble creation and believed in the project and the universal environmental vision that accompanied it. They all wanted to be a part of assembling a worthy group to complete Bobby's revolutionary work with plants.

It was exactly what Rome had wanted to hear. And he

had thought Harper would be more than thrilled to hear the team's intentions.

But now, the only thing Harper was doing was throwing her life away. Giving in to the hatred and revenge she so deeply believed she needed. Rome knew that she did need vengeance, but not this way. Not by becoming a cold-blooded killing machine.

Knowing the extraordinary kind of person Harper was, he couldn't believe that her brother would've wanted that.

Add that to the fact that she thought she was going to die anyway, and she'd likely figured she had nothing to lose. But she was damn wrong. She had everything to lose.

He saw Harper move at lightning speed, roughly grabbing Jeff by the neck with one rigid hand. Rome twitched at her unreal strength.

Gunfire rang out, causing him to jerk again, but Harper merely raised her free hand to freeze the charging ammo in some type of near-invisible shield. Damn, she was getting good at controlling her powers. Too good.

Rome shook his head with a profound sadness. He thought he had convinced her to bring Jeff and his faction to justice. To make the bastards accountable for what they did, not just decide to kill them and be done with it, losing her precious humanity in the process.

He couldn't stand by and watch her go down that dark and desolate path. It nearly tore him apart to see her shatter his belief in her. To take the easy road of a vigilante instead of the tough route of responsibility.

She'd chosen to break the rules and, for everyone's sake, he couldn't let that happen. The cost of her personal vengeance was too high a price to pay for the rest of the world.

He had to stop her somehow. If she killed Jeff, he knew he'd lose her forever. Maybe he had already.

No. Rome refused to believe that. And he refused to let that happen to her.

"I'm going in," Rome told the operative next to him as he resolutely jumped up and raced down the slick hill, the rain stinging his face.

Through her fury, Harper heard the crack of gunfire. Raising her other hand, she freed up a small corner of her writhing mind and formed an energy field, blocking out everything except Jeff and her, essentially encasing the two of them in a bubble. The bullets pummeled but didn't breach her psi-powered defense.

Harper was heady with spiking power. And she liked it. Craved it. Her body filled with sultry energy, consumed with the hate for this man and his monstrous actions.

All it would take was one small shift of her mind and that energy would surge from the hand wrapped tightly around his neck into his body, searing him from within. Less than an instant would pass before his death.

She was that strong.

Bobby had known her strength. He'd seen it when she decided to fight back from her swimming failure. That's why he'd left the serum and the data for her. Because he knew she had the inner fortitude to see this through.

Even Rome had said the same thing. He, too, had faith in her inner strength.

Rome.

Harper blinked as recent memories flashed across

her vision, merging with the energy that swirled in her head. She and Rome fighting side by side in the darkness. Perusing Bobby's data together over sandwiches.

Falling in love.

The rigid hand around Jeff's neck trembled. Rome had said he loved her. He had said her strength was genuine. That he trusted her as much as Bobby had, to do the right thing.

The right thing.

And what was that? She thought it was revenge. But Rome told her she was losing herself to that craving for vengeance. He demanded that she believe it.

He'd said that the right thing wasn't always what you wanted to do. But what had to be done.

Make the hard decisions. And usually the hard decision was the right one.

Evil was easy. There were no boundaries. No rules. But also no honor. Doing the right thing consisted of doing the honorable thing and making the tough choices.

Like Rome and his steadfast dedication to duty. No matter what he did, he always tried to do what was right. Even if it meant going against his boss. Even if it hurt. Even if he sacrificed something he wanted, he did it because it was the right thing.

After knowing her for mere days, Rome had sacrificed everything he had, everything he was, for her, for the sole purpose of the greater good. Bobby's greater good. Her greater good.

Rome trusted her to believe she was more than just vengeance. Because he believed it. And because Bobby had, too.

And because it was right.

Harper blinked again, clearing her rage-clouded

sight to look closely at Jeff and everything the man stood for. Then she took a deeper look inside herself.

Did she have the right to play judge, jury, and executioner? Even if Jeff and his faction committed hideous and dishonorable wrongs, did she have the right to act out on her own to resolve it?

No. The answer was easier than she thought.

She was more than that. She was better than revenge. The inner strength she had didn't stem from the serum, but from passion. From the tenacious bond she had with Bobby, unbreakable even with his death. And from the unwavering love she'd found with Rome.

And that was enough.

The relentless heat roiling just under her skin receded slowly, like a bear pacing coolly back to its cave, alert but relaxed. Her mind calmly pulled back the power that radiated though her body, storing it for another time.

Harper peeled her stiff fingers from Jeff's throat and stared at him. Still hating him and everything he had arranged. Hating him for lying and using her brother to bait her. But sad for him as well, because he had no idea what real strength and power was. And probably never would.

She stood her ground, holding off the threatening barrage around the two of them with her protective shield while she just gazed at him. Jeff rubbed his reddened neck, staring back at her in fear and uncertainty.

"You're right. My brother would've wanted me to use my powers for good."

A sly grin creased his face. His fear morphed into hopeful triumph.

"I'm glad." He lifted his chin a notch and straightened his tie with shaking hands. "Glad that you understand what your brother really wanted."

"I know exactly what Bobby wanted." Harper smiled with solid and sure belief. And for the first time in a long time, peace. "He wanted you stopped and brought to justice. And that's what I'm going to do."

The moment held still.

And then he lunged at her.

CHAPTER TWENTY-ONE

Jeff tackled Harper to the ground. She wasn't fast enough to stop his onrush. Her head snapped hard against the wet turf, causing sparks to flash across her vision and pain to explode inside her skull.

Straddling her hips, he smacked her cheekbone sharply with a solid backhand. Twice.

Chaos rang loud in her ears as she realized her protective psi-powered field had dropped at the same time she hit the grass. A frenzy of heavy boot steps and loud voices filtered through the ringing, and she saw frantic blurs of movement out of the corner of her eye.

Another hard whack connected with the other side of her face, shocking her fuzzy focus back to the madman on top of her.

"Coward," Jeff seethed, lowering his face just a breath away from hers, his cheeks fuming red. "You have no idea what justice is. You could have had everything." His eyes turned wild. "But now you've chosen to lose it all."

He swung his hand back again, now with a cruel blade clasped in his severe grip, ready to strike. Harper thrashed and managed to loosen Jeff's hold on her.

As she struggled to free herself, a slight motion to her left caught her attention. A tall dark figure raced down from the hill where she'd been not too long ago. Rain lashed at the runner, but he sped on, boots kicking up splashes of standing rain and mud.

Rome. What in the world was he doing?

Gunfire filled the air. Followed closely by deafening yells and splashes. A fierce wave of black-clad figures rushed into the courtyard and clashed with camouflage.

Rome's group of special ops attacked Jeff's army, half of which were supersoldiers. Skirmishes swamped her vision. Bodies battled and dropped. It was war.

Jeff took advantage of the distraction and pinned her again, raising his knife above her chest.

He was going to kill her. And the moment Rome took one step inside the compound Jeff would kill him, too.

She lashed out, anything to get free and find Rome. A hot slash pierced her skin. Jeff's knife had missed her neck, but found her shoulder.

The searing pain throbbed, giving her mind a shot of clarity. Rome needed her help.

Untangling her arm from under Jeff, she thrust the heel of her hand upward and heard a satisfying snap as it connected with his jaw. She took advantage of his surprise and shoved him off her. She scrambled away and raced into the fray, hunting for Rome.

She found him. In the middle of the courtyard, trading punches with two attackers. She focused on the two in her mind and raised her hand, aiming a burst of clear energy at them. The surge leveled them, heaving them through the air several yards away.

She was nearly blinded by the relief in Rome's smile. Which quickly transformed into anger and then urgency.

"Duck!" he yelled. She crouched as he fired shots just beyond her, knocking down three of Jeff's men.

She and Rome were now back to back, watching the

oncoming wave of enemies heading their way from all sides.

"Harper," Rome shouted over his shoulder, "I have to tell you—"

"Not now," she barked back. She needed to focus.

"You need to know," he persisted even as the attackers closed in. "You're not—"

Gunshots filled her hearing. His voice was cut off. His body banged heavily against hers. She stumbled forward and twisted around in time to see bullets pummel Rome's chest, driving him to the ground with a heavy thud. Unmoving.

Suddenly, rough hands grabbed her arms, hauling her through the lashing rain, away from Rome's still body.

Pulled backward, she twisted, trying to break free to get back to him. More hands clamped around her legs, dragging her away from the fight. And Rome.

"Put her in!" Jeff ordered over the raucous sounds of combat. Harper craned her head to the side for a moment to meet his ruthless stare, realizing he meant to stick her in the wooden crate like a caged animal. She couldn't let that happen, knowing it would neutralize her psi powers. She had to get to Rome.

"No!" She madly struggled against the iron grips on her limbs.

Harper thrashed wildly to no avail, kicking out and jerking her body every which way. The burning pain in her shoulder mingled with the ache in her soul from seeing Rome on the ground. She couldn't seem to focus her thoughts to summon the energy she needed to escape.

She was airborne and then landed hard on the solid floor of the crate. On her back, she twisted to her knees and crawled to the opening, as the hatch began to shut.

She had a split second before the darkness overtook her. Enough time to see Rome's lifeless body lying on the wet grass.

Harper shuddered and froze. Then her world went black. The crate hatch was shut.

She was captured. Rome was dead.

It was over.

CHAPTER TWENTY-TWO

She was alone once again. In the dark.

Harper slammed her body against the wooden walls of the crate. She willed every ounce of power to her swirling mind, yet felt nothing but throbbing pain. Without even a crack of natural light, her psi powers were dormant. She could already feel the energy seep from her mind.

She had come here to die anyway, but Rome hadn't. He didn't deserve to die because of this. No one did.

Harper stilled her flailing and took a deep breath, stalling the raging anguish that assaulted her every fiber.

Rome was dead.

"It was supposed to be me," she whispered to no one, anguish filling her senses.

It wasn't supposed to end like this.

Bowing her head in solitude, she knew she had to do something, anything, to stop this. And make Rome's sacrifice worth it all.

He had said her inner strength was stronger than any artificial power. She had to believe he was right. She'd spent a lifetime forging her body into top physical form. She could do this.

Leaning back, she coiled her legs tight to her chest and then thrust them forward against the front of the crate.

A shot of pain streamed through her legs as the wood resisted.

No. She had to believe. She could do this.

Taking a deep, focusing breath, as she'd done before every race, Harper closed her eyes and pictured herself surging through the water with her powerful arms and legs, each movement bringing her closer to victory.

With that thought in her mind, she tried once more to break free. The pure strength of her swimmer's kick shattered the wood outward.

Shaking off her shock, Harper scrambled through the opening and crawled over the splinters out into the heavy downpour.

The moment the heavy rainfall hit her body, a swell of rejuvenation washed over her. Her shoulder ceased to sting and her mind cleared. The cloudy natural light sparked her energy as she raked her gaze over the continuing battle in the compound. There were bodies everywhere, some fighting, some motionless.

Out of the corner of her eye, she saw Jeff's stunned glare fix on her. But she had one focus: Rome. His still body was in the same spot.

Harper bowed her head and looked deep inside herself, knowing what she had to do. It was beyond what she'd come here for in the first place, even if she'd been blinded by revenge.

She had to stop this madness. Rome was gone. She was going to die anyway. Bobby's vision was the only thing left to lose.

Indeed, she knew deep down that what she was about to do would kill her. There was no way she could withstand the force she'd need. Even Bobby's notes had affirmed that. She'd burn up inside.

Yet her sacrifice would be for the greater good. It's what Rome had lived for. What better reason to use her psi powers but to surrender her life to honor the man she loved, and the work of the brother who loved her enough to bestow it upon her?

She could think of none. Decision made. She would call upon all the psi energy in her body to stop this.

Harper was tired of all the killing. And she knew that some of these people were here to help. Maybe she could give Rome's people time to get the upper hand by just stopping the chaos. So she would try to focus her power to immobilize everyone in the compound with a nonlethal pulse. Just as the sunlight rejuvenated her before, she'd try to harness the rainstorm's natural force. The amount of concentrated energy needed would no doubt kill her. How could her body physically handle it?

But she was dying anyway, right? It was a chance she was willing to take.

Closing her eyes, Harper allowed the raging thunderstorm to invigorate her body. She drew upon the lashing rain. The swirling wind. And the cleansing air. The organic elements gave her a boost beyond measure.

Her revitalized body began to tingle with shivers of lightning under her skin. Raw electricity throbbed through her mind. Her veins crackled as her blood raced.

All this energy. All this power. It would be the death of her. But she was okay with that. The last pure psionic power would live and die through her. And somewhere in between, she'd revere the brother she'd lost and honor the man she loved.

Snapping her eyes open, she spread her arms wide and watched the hazy shower of rain and the icy blustering wind snake and spiral around her as it intensified into a menacing tempest.

For the last time, Harper embraced the customary sensations as ice raced under her skin and heat flared inside her body for an instant before her psi power kicked in. The inferno burning in her veins was unbearable. The natural elements felt as if they were merging with the organic power radiating from her mind. Surrendering to her. And it also felt right.

With all that she was she concentrated, and then unleashed a massive surge of energy from her roiling body, shaking everything in its path with its overwhelming force.

The compound eclipsed around her. It was the last thing she saw.

CHAPTER TWENTY-THREE

A thunderous roar of wind and rain coiled inside the courtyard and surged across the compound, slicing through the sleet and crushing everything in its powerful wake. Heavy gusts of stinging rain pummeled him, forcing him to stay flattened against the slimy ground as consciousness slowly returned.

Face full of grass and muck, Rome stilled until the raging storm washed over him.

His chest ached at the pounding he'd taken from the bullets. The force had knocked the wind out of him and even caused him to black out for a few moments. It looked as if the storm was subsiding, though. Running his hand over the bulletproof vest, he loosened the straps and wheezed in some of the thick air. He was glad he'd had the extra protection, given the force of the blows.

Heavy mud sucked at his body as Rome peeled himself out of the glop and up on all fours. And fell back onto his rear with a sloppy thud as he surveyed the area in complete shock.

An eerie sight lay before him. The compound was shrouded in a dense gray curtain of relentless hammering rain and haze.

Other than the splattering hum of the rain drumming against the already saturated ground, he couldn't hear a thing. The air was still and deafeningly quiet.

And he couldn't see a damn thing. It was as though a fog had rolled in from the ocean and planted itself inside the confined space.

Wiping a grimy hand over his already smudged face, Rome hauled himself up to stand unsteadily on the slippery ground. The hard rain cut through the cloudy plume, but did not allow him to see what remained of the complex. And what was left of the courtyard where he'd last seen Harper being brutally yanked into a crate, just before he passed out.

No.

He would not, could not believe she was Jeff's captive. Again. He had to get to her somehow.

In his line of work, he'd witnessed explosions and disasters, but he'd never seen a natural storm contained like this. And never with the woman he loved sitting smack-dab in the middle of it.

It had to have been Harper. She'd escaped and was using her powers somehow. She had been learning to control it, and if she had focused hard enough, like he knew she could, she most likely was the source of this. But why? When he'd seen her release Jeff, he'd hoped she'd chosen justice over revenge. Righteousness over killing.

But the force of that staggering storm was so mortally strong. If Harper was the eye of the storm, how on earth could she endure it? Endure the raging force of the rain, wind, and lightning? Bobby's notes had said the subjects burned from the inside when they'd used their power to its fullest.

Then he remembered. Her brother's notes hadn't accounted for the fact that her powers were the real thing. The pure serum, not like the others. So, she'd have survived it. Right? Plus her powers were able to regenerate.

But Jeff had captured her. The bastard had thrown

her in a crate, in the dark, where her powers couldn't thrive.

He had to find her.

Skidding with every soggy step, he made his way as fast as he could past the dripping trees that stood within the compound. Rome recalled the map of the courtyard and tried to follow it in his mind. Though dangerously hard to orient himself through the incessant fog, he kept up his swift pace, desperate to find Harper.

Until he found himself flat on his face in the water-logged grass. Pushing up on his knees, he looked over his shoulder to see what he'd tripped on.

A body. Lying facedown, as he'd just been. Rome recognized the dark camouflaged fatigues from all the men who had surrounded Harper in the courtyard. Was he destined to find her unmoving body like this, stuck in the crate?

No, Harper was alive. He had to believe that.

Rome stood and looked around to regain his bearings. His gaze didn't cut very far through the mist and rain, but he began to walk in the direction he hoped he'd been heading. It was like walking through a perpetual fog machine.

Not ten feet later, he stumbled over another fatigue-clad body lying faceup on the grass. *Damn it all.*

Rome moved on at a slower pace, his impeded gaze darting from the thick haze ahead to the ground. Disorientation kept him from calling out to her. Who knew what he might run into? Though he imagined that anyone he found would want to kill her.

Pulling his gun from his shoulder holster, Rome readied it just in case.

A soggy squish broke through the eerily quiet murkiness. Someone was coming. Through the dense mist and rain, he couldn't see but could almost feel the air stirring as someone moved closer to his position. He stilled into a crouch and waited.

The stirring air swarmed into a brisk breeze. The breeze grew to a damp gust. The gust grew to a roar, deep and rumbling. Driven to his knees, Rome lifted his arm to shield his eyes as he struggled to see through the blustery onslaught.

Then it all ceased.

A ghostly silence befell the still, misty air that enveloped him. Rome wiped his eyes with his wet sleeve, trying desperately to see anything, gun raised and ready.

Steady rain continued to pour mutely, but the gray haze began to scatter like fireflies. A dark form materialized, forcing the mist to dissipate as it moved toward him.

Harper.

It was Harper. Seductive and powerful. Coming into clearer focus the closer she came. Her arms were slightly spread, palms out, radiating gentle translucent waves of energy, clearing the haze until it was simply gone, leaving only the rain behind.

Her unsteady movement seemed to grow stronger with every step. She came to stand directly in front of him. In the streaming rain. Mere inches away.

Rome's heart stopped and then pounded faster than the rainfall coming down. She held out a shaky dripping hand. He took it, squeezing gently, causing little mud bubbles to percolate where their palms joined. She gave his hand a slight tug and he rose slowly, just staring at her, an ethereal vision of wild beauty and untamed nature.

Her blonde hair was plastered to her head. Her sopping clothes were blotched with blood and mud, and she smelled like muck. Her endless green eyes were as clear as looking through dew on grass.

She was everything he would ever want. Ever need.

Taking a step forward, he reached for her other hand and leaned into her. Harper did the same, resting her wet forehead against his. He closed his eyes and savored this one perfect moment, wishing it could last forever.

CHAPTER TWENTY-FOUR

The spattering rain continued to trickle down around them. After a long, languid moment of simply being with Rome, Harper opened her eyes and gazed at the man she'd somehow grown to love. The blue in his eyes was an infinite stormy sky, churning and wild.

But he was alive. And so was she.

"I thought you were dead." Her husky voice sounded strained to her own ears as she just looked at him, reveling in his living warmth and the landslide of emotion that threatened to overtake her.

"I thought we had a plan." Rome's eyes narrowed, his voice hoarse as he tilted his head just a tad, his sharp gaze piercing hers. His tone was questioning, challenging.

"I got tired of waiting." She crooked her lips into a sheepish smile, injecting the hope in each word that he would somehow forgive her. That he would somehow love her in spite of everything.

Then she leaned forward and used her lips for something else. Harper kissed him fiercely, willing him to experience just how much she loved him.

In the pouring-down rain, with Rome's love surrounding her, Harper began to believe life would indeed go on. Even if it would go on without her. She could hardly believe she'd survived up to this point. She felt drained but oddly steady as her strength started to return with every breath of fresh air. That much power should've killed her.

His arms wrapped around her, crushing her hard against his chest as he deepened the kiss. She lost herself in the intoxicating moment.

Rome broke the intense connection with a gravelly chuckle against her lips and turned to glance around the courtyard area. "What a mess." He shook his head sadly.

Harper followed his gaze through the teeming rain, the blustery haze now all but gone. Bodies littered the squared area, some stirring, some not. She searched for Jeff and saw him still breathing.

She bowed her head in regret over all the lives she'd taken. Her need for revenge had stained her hands with blood she knew she'd never be able to wash away.

But then she raised her head, contentment overshadowing the remorse by the simple knowledge of the lives she'd saved by stopping Jeff and his faction. And by keeping Bobby's work safe, maybe the bloodstains could be honored with the good his formula could do.

As if reading her mind, Rome brought her hand up to his lips for a quick kiss, breaking through her heavy thoughts. He rested a hand on her wet shoulder and fished out a cell phone from his back pocket. It dripped as he pressed a button, making a call.

"Area secure," he said into the mouthpiece. "Proceed with caution. Lock down the facility and hold any survivors." She watched him end the call and tuck the phone away.

Barely a moment later, Rome's hidden backup team of black-clad men and women filed into the quad, splashing through the grass and mud, checking the prone bodies, securing the living members of the faction, passing by the others. Some saw to their stirring comrades while others filtered into the facility, guns ready.

"Harper, these are the good guys." Rome's somber tone drew her attention away from the surreal scene, something she'd seen only in action movies. "My guys."

Harper nodded her head sadly, her mind swirling with muddled emotions.

"I wish I'd gotten to Bobby's data sooner," he continued, grasping her hand, clearly wanting to tell her something. "Or at least known what he found out about—"

"Thank you," she interrupted quietly. She didn't want to hear the what-ifs. She sincerely doubted there was anything anyone could've done. Anything Rome could do now. What-ifs were useless. Jeff had clearly been in tight control of the operation. Her brother's death was probably the catalyst for taking that control away. A necessary sacrifice, just like her.

Now that this was over, grief threatened to pour into her. Though she'd won, her brother was still dead. And she'd be dead soon, too. It all seemed so senseless.

"Why?" Rome asked, now grasping both of her hands and holding them tightly against his chest. "Why did you go on your own?"

Searching his eyes, she knew she had to give him an answer. He deserved an answer. Even though she might lose him because of it. Well, she was going to lose him anyway, so what did it matter?

"All I could think of was revenge." She kept her gaze steady and locked with his. She needed to be honest and strong and to face whatever reaction it bred. She'd have to face it for only a limited time. "I thought revenge meant killing them all. Just as they'd done to Bobby. I was strong enough to do it, too. They couldn't stop me."

And they couldn't. The power she felt had been unequaled. As a matter of fact, she couldn't believe she was still standing there. The internal radiance of heat should've been more than the sun could withstand.

Harper looked deep into his blue eyes, searching the soul she loved so much, trying to find the understanding she hoped he had saved up for her.

"I thought it would be easy," she continued. "To take control and solve the problem once and for all. But you were right. The toughest choices are for the strong. And not acting on that vengeance is the hardest decision I've ever had to make. That's how I knew it was right."

She had become someone other than herself. Someone she didn't want to be. Regardless of her life span. And this man before her had helped her to see that.

Rome's powerful blue gaze remained glued to hers. He wasn't recoiling. That was good. Right?

"But you made me realize that my strength is bigger than that," she confessed as his grip tightened, warming her trembling hands. "I can't bring Bobby back. But I can bring them to justice. I can expose the wrongs the faction committed. And the good Bobby did."

Rome brought her clasped hands to his mouth, brushing her knuckles lightly with tender lips.

"You were right. I knew I'd lose myself if I went through with it," she whispered. "And I'd lose you." Her vision blurred as tears welled in her eyes, falling with the incessant rain trailing down her face. "I've lost Bobby. I couldn't lose you too, Rome."

"You could never lose me, Harper," Rome said quietly, his soft breath warming her chilled fingers. "Bobby's legacy will live through his work. Through you."

"What do you mean?" she asked, infinitely comforted by his words, though a little confused. She was ticking on a terminal clock. Had he forgotten? She certainly hadn't. It's one of the reasons she'd decided to go alone.

"I have some contacts," he said. "Good people. People we can trust. We can make sure that Bobby's work on the plants continues. We can pick out a research team."

Harper dropped to her knees, splashing onto the sodden mud and grass. Stunned to her core by the realization that her brother's revolutionary work could continue. It was everything she could ever hope or want. Well, not everything. Wait, Rome was still talking.

"Harper, I said I wished I'd gotten to Bobby's data sooner," Rome said. "After you'd gone, I found an unopened file."

"Holy cow, we missed one?" How was that possible? Well, they had been distracted. Warmth replaced the shock at remembering just what distractions Rome had applied on her. "What was in it?"

"Only the most important factor of all," he answered, a dazzling smile breaking across his gorgeous yet grimy face. "I tried to tell you before, in the fight. Harper, you're not going to die. Bobby had found that the plants Jeff stole from him continued to grow happy and healthy, while the ones they replicated kept dying." He looked at her with a happy look himself.

"We already knew that." Harper smirked at him, not quite sure what he was getting at. "Fake serum equals bad."

"Every plant that didn't have the original formula croaked," he continued, still smiling. "Every one that had it thrived." What exactly was he saying? "Harper, you have Bobby's original formula inside you. The serum you injected was pure. That means you won't die like those other guys that Jeff experimented with. The offshoots were terminal. The originals lived out their normal, healthy lives. Bobby found the proof."

The realization washed over her like a springtime waterfall. Cool and refreshing. She'd come here seeking revenge, believing it didn't matter what became of her. She thought she had no future to throw away. But now she could let relief settle inside her mind. The serum wasn't going to kill her. She wasn't going to die.

"And I'll be with you through it all." Rome knelt in the muck, facing her. There. That was everything she needed.

"You will?" she asked, wanting, needing to hear it again. "Holy cow."

"Damn right." Rome leaned in to slant his mouth over hers for a quick kiss. "We're going to be partners." Partners. She loved the sound of that. "If you want to go back to swimming, I'll understand. I just want to be with you." She watched him reach into his coat pocket and pull something out. "By the way, I think this is yours."

He opened his fist and revealed her gold medal. Her good-bye to him. She curled her fingers around his and closed his hand around the medal, wanting him to keep it. This time as a hello to a life together.

"And I want to start a new life," she stated honestly, overwhelmed, but insanely thrilled. Swimming was now part of her past. She knew she couldn't compete anymore now that the serum ran through her blood. And she could accept that, knowing that she could use the psi power for something worthwhile. Something that fed her soul even deeper than her life in the water.

Life with Rome. Righting wrongs. Fighting side by side. Just like Bobby would have wanted.

"Harper," Rome said, rolling her name as his fingers brushed her wet cheek. "I love you."

"I know you do," Harper said with a true smile. Heat surged from her mind, blazing a passionate trail to her heart.

Rome grinned, pressed his lips to hers, and stood. She watched him tread through the squishy grass toward two men who were holding up a bound and dazed Jeff. He grabbed Jeff roughly, and then walked alongside as they hauled him away.

Was it finally over? She glanced around the courtyard, watching the good guys take the bad guys away. Maybe it was.

And as Harper sat in the grass with the rain streaming around her, she wondered whether the heat from her psionic powers could hold a candle to the flame of their love.

She couldn't wait to find out.

So you like vampires? You're not alone.

Don't miss the part steampunk Victorian
historical, part futuristic thriller

Crimson & Steam
by
Liz Maverick
Coming January 2010

. . . He found her on a stretch of Santa Monica Boule-
vard, just inside an alcove. She stood frozen, silent, her
face obscured by shadow. He grabbed her by the shoulders and spun her toward some dull light oozing from a
nearby store's half-broken bulb.

"Coward," she spat. "Do I have to make it really easy
for you, so you can't refuse? Should I just rip my clothes
off and beg?" She pulled the tie holding together her
wrap blouse, and the fabric cascaded away. "Do it. Here
in this alley, Marius. Please."

"Jillian, don't!" Marius's blood raced. Exposed neck,
pale shoulders, pink-tipped breasts—all delicate flesh and
the black lace of her transparent bra. He'd never seen Jill
this way. He'd only dreamed of it.

"I will. I'll beg," she continued. "I'll do whatever you
need to make this okay. I'm not afraid of what we have.
Why the hell are you?"

She pulled the hem of her skirt up and leaned back
against the brick wall. Marius tried to wrench her skirt
down, but she was pulling out all the stops and rudely
pressed her palm against his groin. "Don't try to tell me

no," she murmured. "I know what you want. I know what I feel."

"Stop, Jillian. Stop!" Marius begged. He forced himself to ignore the pulsing of his erection in her hand and grabbed the ends of her shirt, tying them together as best he could. Without thought, he closed his eyes and pressed his mouth to the crown of her head. "Please," he whispered. "I never meant to hurt you, and—"

"'Hurt me . . . ,'" Jillian echoed.

She reached into her pocket and pulled out a switchblade. Flicking it expertly open she said, "Hayden gave this to me. Hayden, your worst enemy. At the time I thought it was a really shitty birthday present, but it always seems to come in handy." Transfixing Marius with her stare, she held the knife to her neck. "Could you resist me if I made myself bleed for you? I know what it's like when you smell blood. That means my blood will make you insane, if you feel half of what I think you do for me. You won't be able to stop yourself, and it won't be your fault." She swallowed hard. "I'm not afraid."

"Enough!" Marius roared, baring his fangs. The switchblade clattered to the pavement. "Enough." He took her face in his hands. "This isn't you. This is not who you are."

Jillian slowly pulled free and backed up, collecting her weapon.

"Do you think this helps?" Marius continued, unable to contain himself any longer. "Do you think I feel no pain? I watch you run around with Hayden Wilks, and you think it doesn't kill me? He gets to have you in every way that I cannot. It makes no difference that I understand why you're with him, that I know you don't love him. It doesn't matter, because . . . yes." His hands dug into Jill's shoulders as he struggled to stay in control. "I can feel you. Do you understand? I can sense you. I know

when he's with you, when he's touching you, when . . ."
He had to look away. "Knowing I could make you feel so
much more, that my feelings for you go so much deeper,
that you've given yourself to someone who doesn't deserve you because I'm not allowed to have the life I want
to live . . . It makes me feel like dying sometimes. You
must understand how much I care about you. But—"

"But not enough," she interrupted. Then, with a hitch
in her voice she added, "Soul mates aren't supposed to
end like this."

Marius dropped his hands. "I'm sorry."

CRIMSON & STEAM
by
LIZ MAVERICK